Foundation Enhancement

Books by C. R. Corwin

Morgue Mama: The Cross Kisses Back
Dig
The Unraveling of Violeta Bell

The Unraveling of Violeta Bell

A Morgue Mama Mystery

The Unraveling of Violeta Bell

A Morgue Mama Mystery

C. R. Corwin

Poisoned Pen Press

Poisoned Pen Press
6962 E. First Ave., Ste. 103
Scottsdale, AZ 85251
www.poisonedpenpress.com
info@poisonedpenpress.com

Printed in the United States of America

To Sandee LeMasters,
for that D in high school journalism,
and all the other help along the way.

I've never been one of those blame-the-victim types. If a woman gets flashed in the parking lot at the mall, it's not her fault because she has the audacity to have female parts. It's the flasher's fault for giving in to his creepiness. But I've got to agree with Ike on this one: Violeta Bell's own foolishness most definitely increased the odds she'd come to a bad end.

Dolly Madison Sprowls
Head Librarian
The Hannawa Herald-Union

1

I learned long ago not to give my story ideas to the editors. They grin at you like a constipated duck. They quack, "Ooooh, what a great idea!" Then they never assign anyone to write it. And if by some miracle they do, the reporter gets the story wrong. So I stay in the morgue and do my job, and hope the editors stay in the newsroom and try like the dickens to do theirs.

But there I was, scooting toward Nancy Peale's desk just as fast as my full mug of Darjeeling tea would let me go. But, good gravy, I couldn't help myself. The idea was just too good.

Nancy has been the features editor since the Jurassic Age, which means she's been at *The Hannawa Herald-Union* almost as long as me. So we've had our share of run-ins. "Sorry to bother you, Nancy," I said with as much cheeriness as I could muster on a Monday morning, "but I just had to pass along something I saw."

She looked up from her pecan roll. Gave me that duck look. "You know we're always looking for good stories, Maddy."

I bolstered myself with a long sip of tea and began. "Well—I was on my way to get some Milkbones for James, and a few groceries, and you know what Saturdays in June are like. More garage sales than dandelions. Anyway, I was on Pershing, just a couple blocks south of West Apple, and a taxi had pulled up in front of this house with a garage sale sign and a driveway full of junk. And these four old women were getting out, dressed in the most God-awful outfits, like circus clowns on their way to church." I took another sip, peeking over the top of my mug to make sure Nancy was still listening. "Anyway, it occurred to me that maybe they hired a cab every Saturday to drag them from one garage sale to another. And wouldn't that make a great story if they did."

Nancy's mouth was now full of pecan goo. "And do they?"

I was ready for her. "Every Saturday all summer. For the past four or five years. Garage sales and estate sales. I called the cab company. They always use the same driver, too."

Nancy gave me a rare smile. "The stories he could, tell, huh?"

"His name is Eddie French."

She scribbled it on her desk pad. "City Cab or Yellow?"

"Yellow."

"Well—it sounds like a great idea, Maddy. Thanks."

I went back to my desk figuring that would be the end of it. I got busy marking up the Saturday and Sunday papers.

That's my job. I've been the head librarian of *The Herald-Union* for the past thirty-four years. In the newspaper business we call the library the morgue. It's where we keep stories that have already run—the dead stories if you will—in case reporters need them for background on the new ones they're writing. In the old days, I'd clip the stories with my big, black-handled scissors, scribble a date on them, and cram them into those wonderful old battleship gray filing cabinets that used to grace the morgue. Now I go through the paper with a felt-tip pen deciding which electronic files to store them in. This new system cost the paper a bazillion dollars and took years to implement. And of course the stories are no easier to find in cyberspace than they were in those old A-Z filing cabinets. But you can't stop progress.

I do try, of course.

For one thing, I refuse to use my computer for anything more complicated than reading my email or ordering clothes from Chadwick's or Lands' End. I leave all the real computer work to my assistant, Eric Chen. Keyboard-wise he's a genius. Life-wise he's a Class A doofus.

Another thing I refuse to do is retire. I know I'm a royal pain in the ass around here, but there's no way in hell the morgue could function without me. And there's no way I could function without the morgue. So I stay on, one birthday cake shy of seventy, making everyone's life just as miserable as I can.

Anyway, I finished marking up the weekend papers and then walked down to Ike's Coffee Shop for lunch. I spent my usual two hours there, at my little table by the window, stuffing myself with tuna salad and potato chips, yakking with Ike about this and that. On my way back to the paper I stopped at the bank and renewed a couple of CDs, locking in that astronomical 2.3% interest rate for another eighteen months. I also picked up my Lipitor prescription at Walgreen's. By the time I got back to the morgue it was three o'clock. I made my afternoon tea and settled in at my desk to mark up the Monday edition. Before I could get the cap off my felt-tip, I saw Nancy Peale heading my way. Behind her was some snippet of a girl I didn't recognize.

"In the middle of something?" Nancy asked.

She'd been civil with me that morning, so I had no choice but to be civil with her. "Not yet."

"Good—I wanted you to meet Gabriella Nash. She just started today. I gave her that idea of yours."

I hadn't recognized her face—how could I without that awful spiked green hair she used to have—but her name sure rang a bell. Before I could force my frown into something that resembled a smile, she stuck out her hand. "Remember me, Mrs. Sprowls?"

I reached across my clutter and shook her soft, sweaty paw. "Of course I do, dear. Welcome to *The Herald-Union*."

Nancy seemed genuinely surprised that I knew her new reporter. "I thought maybe you could help Gabriella get started with her story."

"Of course I could."

Nancy wiggled her fingers good-bye and hurried back to the newsroom. Gabriella and I were left smiling at each other like a couple of brainless Raggedy Ann dolls.

Gabriella Nash was actually a very pretty girl without that green mess on her head. Her hair was straight now. Sensibly brunette. Her nose rings were gone, too. Instead of the ratty jeans and bare-midriff I remembered, she was wearing trim-fitting khakis and a striped blouse with white cuffs and collar, an outfit that even I'd wear if my dumpy, post-menopausal torso would permit it. For the record, I was wearing my usual baggy chinos, my Tweetie Bird T-shirt, white anklets and a pair of canvas earth shoes I've had since earth shoes were in fashion.

I guess we talked for a good twenty minutes. I told her everything I could remember about those four crazy women I saw crawl out of the cab. About the cabbie, Eddie French. I was just as helpful as I could be. After she thanked me and went back to her squeaky clean desk in the newsroom, I made a beeline for Alec Tinker's office.

Tinker has been the managing editor for two years now. He came to us from our sister paper in Baton Rouge with the impossible task of boosting *The Herald-Union's* sagging circulation. He's only thirty-four. One of those alpha-male types who shaves his head to cover up his bald spot. Anyway, I stormed right into his office, making sure the glass in the door rattled when I closed it behind me. I hissed at him like a forty-foot python. "What in the hell were you thinking?"

Tinker answered me without looking up from the avalanche on his desk. He had one stack of computer printouts in his left hand, another in his right, and a third clenched in his teeth. "About going into the newspaper business? Good question!"

This was the most frantic half-hour of Tinker's day—when he prepared for his afternoon budget meeting with the other editors to decide what was going in the next morning's paper and where. It was the perfect time for me to torture him. "Your decision to major in journalism is a good topic," I said, "but I was referring in particular about your hiring Gabriella Nash."

Tinker took the printouts out of his mouth. "She's a good hire."

"As good as Aubrey was?"

Tinker pushed himself as far away from me as the casters on his big, black managing editor's chair would take him. His decision to bring in Aubrey as police reporter nearly cost him his job. "Now come on, Maddy. Gabriella Nash is hardly another Aubrey McGinty."

I came around his desk. Propped my rear on the edge so his carefully stacked printouts slid into each other. I poured on the salt and pepper. "I'm not saying she is. I'm just saying your objectivity occasionally wanes."

"Are you accusing me of sexist hiring practices?"

"Of course not—you've hired plenty of ugly men."

Tinker enjoyed our verbal duels. But he had that budget meeting to get to. So he got right to the point. Or at least tried to. "I know you had a little problem with Miss Nash in the past—"

"Little problem? All that stuff she wrote about me? Without once calling to confirm it?"

Tinker conceded the point with a bobble of his shiny head. "But everything she wrote about you was true. It showed she's got a nose for news."

He was right enough about that. That day I went to see Gabriella at Hemphill College, quietly snooping into Professor Gordon Sweet's murder, she'd quickly put two and two together and came up with a very big scoop for the college paper. And she was only a junior then. God only knows how good she might be now. "But she didn't color inside the lines, Alec. Rule One of journalism is to let the subject of a story confirm or deny what you've got."

Tinker shooed me off his desk, scooted forward in his chair and gathered up his papers. "And if she had, Maddy? Would you have confirmed or denied?"

"No comment."

Tinker walked me to the door. "I had the same concerns you had. I talked to her about it. She was genuinely anguished."

I reached for the doorknob. "Was she now?"

He grabbed the knob before I could. "A lot more than a certain librarian when she was caught investigating another murder on company time."

"I did not investigate Gordon Sweet's murder on company time."

I headed for the morgue. Tinker headed toward his meeting. Both of us were laughing.

◇◇◇

My old Dodge Shadow likes June better than any month. It's neither too cold nor too hot for its delicate insides. I made it all the way home to my shoebox on Brambriar Court without a single warning light on the dash flashing at me. Which was a small but welcome victory given my foul mood.

Good gravy! Gabriella Nash? Of all the hungry kids with journalism degrees out there? If I didn't know Tinker better, I'd think he hired her just to get my goat. But he's a serious newspaperman. He wants *The Herald-Union* to have the best reporters possible. He wants the people of Hannawa, Ohio, to have the best coverage possible. So if Gabriella Nash hadn't had good grades, a good portfolio of clips from the college paper, and high praise from her professors, he wouldn't have hired her, no matter how much he wanted to punish me.

And I did deserve to be punished. I'd not only promised Detective Grant that I wouldn't interfere in his investigation of Gordon Sweet's murder, I'd refused to give the paper what I dug up.

So I was prepared to coexist with Gabriella Nash. As long as she had the good sense to tread lightly.

James was waiting for me in the kitchen. So were a puddle of spilled water, a chewed up potholder, and a big glob of poop. "Looks like your day was more fun than mine," I said, scratching his floppy ears.

James, I should explain, was not my husband. That worthless beast was long gone. James was my neighbor's American water spaniel. An enormous ball of brown knots. A drooling pink tongue the size of an Easter ham. Eyes that could melt the icecaps on Mars.

My neighbor, Jocelyn Coopersmith, left James with me when she went to California to take care of her daughter, who'd fallen apart after her husband was swept into the Pacific Ocean while collecting mussels for a paella. Jocelyn said she'd be out there for five months. That was fifteen months ago.

So after all those years of living alone, I had a dog.

And a man, too, believe it or not.

I cleaned up James' mess. And before I could stop myself I called that man. "Hi—you have your supper yet?"

"Good Lord, Maddy. It's only Monday."

"A bad Monday."

"I'll pick up a pizza."

"Thanks, Ike."

That's right. The new man in my life is a man who's been in my life for a good fifteen years. For a long time Ike Breeze and I were nothing more than coffee shop owner and cantankerous customer. Lunch hour by lunch hour we became buddies. Now all of a sudden we were, well, we were something a whole lot more complicated.

At my age, any man would be a complication. I'd been without one for decades. But Ike and I both came with a few high hurdles for the other to leap. Above and beyond the usual not-putting-the-cap-back-on-the-toothpaste crap. Ike, for example, was a man. And I, thank God, I was a woman. Ike was black. I was white. Ike, for some reason, was a Republican. I, like anybody with a thread of common sense, was a Democrat. Ike went to church. I went past them as fast as I could. Ike was a widower who'd loved his wife to pieces. I was a divorcee who had long ago picked up the pieces. Ike was even-tempered, understanding, excruciatingly tolerant of others, simply a beautiful human being to be around. I was, well, I tended to have trouble in those areas.

2

"Oatmeal, Maddy? On Sunday? What ever happened to bacon and eggs?"

I tilted back my head and looked straight up at Ike's unshaven frown. "My raging cholesterol."

He yawned his way to the Mr. Coffee on the counter. Joined me at the table. "So let me get this straight, Mrs. Sprowls—you've got high cholesterol and I've got to eat oats like a damn horse."

I went to the stove to get him some. "Can't sacrifice a little for a beautiful woman?"

He yawned again. This time like a hippopotamus. "I'm sacrificing plenty."

I knew what he was getting at. It was the one sore spot in our relationship. I spooned more oatmeal into his bowl just for spite. Banged the bowl down in front of him like a surly waitress. "I wait twenty-five years to get another man in my bed and he can't handle a little snoring?"

Ike scraped half of his oatmeal into my bowl. "It's not just the snoring. It's all that thrashing about you do. Kicking out the covers so my feet get cold."

"I like a man with cold feet."

Ike is a serious man. A retired high school math teacher who thinks the best way to spend his retirement is to work sixty hours a week running a coffee shop. "A sleep disorder is nothing to joke about, Maddy."

I sprinkled brown sugar over his oatmeal, a not-so-subtle hint he should shut up and eat. Our medical writer, Tabitha Geist, had done a four-part series on sleep disorders. Sleep centers were popping up like mushrooms. Significant others all over the country were begging their bed partners to get tested. But as far as I was concerned, sleep apnea was just the latest disease-of-the-week. Remember that scourge of the 1970s, hypoglycemia? When everybody was rushing to the doctor to get their blood sugar tested? Still, I could see that Ike was worried about me. And that wasn't such a bad thing—not that I was going to do anything about it. "I realize sleeping with me can't be easy," I said, "but people have been snoring for a million years."

"Dying before their time for a million years, too."

"Rub the sleep out of your eyes, Mr. Breeze. I've already jumped that hurdle."

Ike quietly ate his gruel. He'd apparently had enough of my stubbornness for one morning. I let James out the back door for his morning pee and then went to the front door to retrieve my Sunday paper off the four-foot rectangle of cement I call my front porch.

By the time I got back to the kitchen, Ike had not only finished his oatmeal, he'd finished mine. I handed him the business section. "You going to church today? You didn't bring your suit."

He went straight for the stock listings. "Of course I'm going to church. I just forgot to bring in my suit from the car."

I like Ike for a lot of reasons. One of them is that he never asks me to go to church with him. And it isn't because I'm white and he's black. At our age, Ike and I are quite comfortable in our respective wrinkled skins. We couldn't care less what other people think. Ike doesn't ask me about church because he knows I wouldn't go. I'm just not churchy. I guess I got my fill of it back in LaFargeville. I spent half of my childhood twisting in a church pew. Maybe I'd go to church if I could find one with a minister who gave five-minute sermons, or a choir that could resist singing all five verses of those awful, throat-burning hymns.

I scanned the front page. I read the first three paragraphs of every story in the metro section. I shook open the editorial pages to see what silly positions we were taking on the big issues of the day. I eyeballed the obituaries, looking for people I knew. I gathered my strength and pulled out the lifestyle section to read Gabriella Nash's feature on those four crazy garage sale ladies.

It was, as I expected, the top story. There was a huge color photo of the four women pretending to squeeze into Eddie French's taxi with armfuls of bargains. There was an intriguing headline:

'THE QUEENS OF NEVER DULL'

From garage sales to Caribbean cruises,
Life just gets better for these grande dames of Hannawa

There was Gabriella's first professional byline:

By Gabriella Nash
Hannawa-Union Staff Writer

And there was her first story:

Hannawa—Cab driver Eddie French pulls into the Carmichael House's curved drive at eight o'clock on the button.

Waiting for him under the condominium tower's portico are four seventy-something women. They are dressed to the nines in colorful microfiber pantsuits and wide-brimmed straw hats.

The women squeeze into the freshly washed yellow Chevrolet with their travel mugs of coffee and a big box of Danish. They also have the classifieds from that morning's paper. Every garage sale in the city and its near suburbs is circled in red.

"To the hunt!" commands one of the women from under her purple hat. "One-nineteen Plumbrook."

"One-nineteen, it is," French answers, tugging dutifully on the bill of his bright orange Hannawa Woolybears baseball cap. He swings his cab back onto Hardihood Avenue and heads for Greenlawn.

Ike was busy calculating the current value of his stock portfolio. But somehow my "Damn it!" penetrated his brain. "Something bad, Maddy?"

"I'll say. The girl can write."

Ike sadly shook his head. "I'll ask the reverend to say a special prayer."

"Thank you—unfortunately I don't think God will take her talent back."

"I was talking about a prayer for you."

"I don't think that one will get through either."

We laughed. Winked at each other. Went back to our respective sections of the paper.

French knows only too well what he's in for today. Every Saturday for the past five years—from early May to the end of October—he has been driving this spirited foursome on their search for treasure.

And when he's not driving them to garage sales, he's driving them to rummage sales and auctions. Or to charity luncheons and teas. Or to concerts or plays. Or to the airport.

"They've got to be the busiest ladies in Hannawa," says the bewhiskered, 61-year-old French. "I know I'm the busiest cab driver."

And just who are these four always-on-the-go golden girls?

Wouldn't you know it. Right when I got to the part of the story I wanted to read most, James let go with his *I'm-done-peeing-let me-in* howl. I looked at Ike for assistance. Ike pretended he didn't see me. So I let James in myself. And filled his bowl with his second breakfast of the day. And I poured myself a second cup of coffee.

"No fresh-up for me?" Ike complained.

"Sorry, I thought you were dead."

I took the empty mug out of his hand and filled it. Finally I sat down to what looked to be one of the best features I'd read in our paper in a long time. Apparently Alec Tinker was not the dunderhead I figured. And even though I was not about to forgive Gabriella for spilling the beans about my investigation into Gordon Sweet's murder, I had to admit our first week of colleaguedom had gone well enough. She'd waited patiently for the background stories she needed. She'd said nothing more long-winded than "Hi" when we bumped into each other in the cafeteria. Most importantly, she hadn't called me Morgue Mama to my face—a mistake most new reporters make and then forever regret.

Collectively they call themselves The Queens of Never Dull.

"It's a club without rules or dues," says Kay Hausenfelter, curled up on the pink loveseat in her sun-washed living room. "We started out as a bridge foursome in the clubroom here. I guess we just liked each other's company. Before you knew it we were bumming all over town together."

While all four of the Never Dulls call the upscale Carmichael House condominiums home, Hausenfelter has lived there the longest, a few months shy of ten years.

Hausenfelter moved into the pricey, ten-story tower after the death of her husband, Harold Hausenfelter. Before his retirement, he had served as president and CEO of Hausenfelter Bread Company, the city's largest bakery. They had been married for 41 years.

"Harold was the sweetest man on earth," she says, adding quickly that he was also one of the toughest. "He had to be tough to take on a project like me," she says.

Hausenfelter met her future husband in

1954, when she was appearing at the Orion
Theater on South Main Street.

"That's right," she laughs. "I was a
striptease artist. Twenty-four years old and
not so fresh out of Elk City, Oklahoma."

"Can you believe that!"

"Believe what, sweetie?"

Ike's question almost stopped my heart. He'd never called
me sweetie before. Either it was a term of endearment that I
wasn't ready for, or the mechanical response of a widower. I
peeked around the paper at him and decided it was the latter.
I read the quote to him. "'I was a striptease artist. Twenty-
four years old and not so fresh out of Elk City, Oklahoma.'"
Ike partially emerged from his trance. "I thought you were from
some little town in New York?"

"Not me *sweetie*—this old woman in the paper. I can't believe
the copy desk let a quote like that run. 'Not so fresh out of Hot
Springs.' Why didn't we just run a list of all the men she'd slept
with?"

He was listening now. Grinning at my fuddy-duddiness.
"Times they are a changing, Maddy. Anything goes."

It was my turn to grin. At his eclectic command of musical
clichés. "Bob Dylan and Cole Porter in the same sentence. Not
bad." I went back to Gabriella's story.

I finished reading about the former stripper and bread heiress,
and moved on to the next garage sale queen:

Ariel Wilburger-Gowdy pleads guilty to
"being something of an earth mother these
days." Her condo is filled with plants and
cats. Atop the stack of books on her coffee
table is her prized copy of Jane Goodall's
book, *Reason For Hope*.

She proudly shows the inscription to visitors. "Ariel," the famous scientist wrote,
"hear your heart."

"I've always had a noisy heart," Wilburger-Gowdy admits. "In the old days it
was preoccupied with men—most of whom I

married. Today it's animals, organic food
and recycling glass bottles."

And just how many times has she been married?

"Four and no more," she jokes.

Her first husband, former state sena-
tor Walter Wilburger, is the father of her
only child, a daughter who teaches business
ethics at Hemphill College.

The Gowdy part of her last name comes not
from a former husband, but from her late
father, roofing-shingle king Donald F. Gowdy.
For the past two decades she has headed the
philanthropic foundation he created, the
D.F. Gowdy Charitable Trust.

"I've been spending my father's money all
my life," she says.

I'd never met Ariel Wilburger-Gowdy, but I certainly knew
about her good works. The Donald F. Gowdy Foundation is
one of the bright spots in Hannawa's struggling economy. It
provides the seed money for inner-city businesses. It helps poor
kids go to college. It supports the arts, helps battered women,
teaches English to immigrants, spays and neuters cats and dogs,
plants flowers in the city's dreary parks. Oodles and oodles of
worthwhile things.

I moved on to Violeta Bell:

If the Queens of Never Dull have a leader,
it's Violeta Bell.

"I guess I'm the burr under everybody's
saddle," says Bell. "But the homestretch is
no time to slow down."

Bell is also the only member of the
foursome to admit her age. "I'll be 73 in
August."

This brings a disbelieving guffaw from
Kay Hausenfelter. "She also claims to be
Romanian royalty," she says.

The playful Bell pretends to be insulted.
"I will be 73 on my next birthday," she
insists again. "And if it hadn't been for

the damn Communists and their crazy ideas, you'd all be curtsying and calling me queen for real."

Whether she's a real queen or just one of the Queens of Never Dull, it is a fact that for nearly three decades the never-married Bell owned and operated Bellflower Antiques.

She's lived at the Carmichael House since her retirement eight years ago.

Bellflower Antiques was once the gemstone of Puritan Square, the snooty shopping *centre* on West Apple Street designed to look like a quaint English village. I was never inside the shop—its BY APPOINTMENT ONLY sign successfully kept riff-raff like me away—but I had driven by it a million times on my way to JCPennys. I read on:

Gloria McPhee is the only member of the Queens of Never Dull with a husband.

"It's strange that Phil and I ended up in this little cubbyhole," she says, referring to their spacious, glass-walled unit on the top floor of the Carmichael House. "Our whole life together was houses, houses, houses."

While McPhee worked as a real estate broker, her husband, Philip, ran a residential pest extermination business. Before they moved into the Carmichael, they lived in an eight-bedroom Tudor on Merman Avenue.

"Before you think me high and mighty, let me tell you about all the crummy little houses I lived in first," McPhee says.

I tried to finish reading Gabriella's story while Ike showered. But the rattling of the spray on the shower curtain made it impossible for me to concentrate. So I put the paper down for later and washed the breakfast dishes.

Ike put on his suit and went to church.

I put on the CELLO EVERYBODY! sweatshirt and took James for his walk.

The sweatshirt was a gift from Ike. The romantic old fool had given it to me for Valentine's Day. It came with the Yo-Yo Ma CD he got for pledging $120 to PBS.

3

Wednesday, July 5

Eric Chen pulled the Mountain Dew bottle off his lips and sniffed at my hair like a truffle-hunting hog. "You're not spontaneously combusting are you?" he asked.

We were clicking our way up the tile-walled stairway to the third floor. The building has an elevator, of course, but it's as slow as molasses. Anybody who has to get to a desk before noon takes the stairs. "I take it you didn't come downtown for the fireworks last night," I said, pulling my head out from under his.

"And you did?"

"As a matter of fact, I did."

It took the young genius half a flight of steps to put two and two together. "Ah—you went with Ike."

"He's a Republican. What can I say."

Eric opened the door for me. "So that's your smoldering love I smell."

We started across the empty newsroom toward the morgue. "No—that's the smoke and ash from $40,000 worth of fireworks you smell. There was a damn temperature inversion halfway through the big show. It was like Pompeii."

I couldn't blame Eric for being surprised. Or for teasing me. For years I've been poooh-poohing the city's schemes for luring suburbanites downtown. The annual Fourth of July "Star-Spangled Salute to the American Family" is its most atrocious effort. They cram Main Street with carnival rides and booths. The city surrenders the sidewalks to rock bands and hip-hoppers. They befoul the already tenuous air with barbecue sauce and overflowing Port-a-Potties. They finish off the four-day extravaganza with The Hannawa Symphony's stale tribute to John Philip Sousa and, of course, the damn fireworks, the stench of which I couldn't shampoo out of my hair.

Eric went to his desk to do whatever it is that he does. I went to mine to get my mug. The message light on my phone was blinking. It was Suzie Burns, the newsroom secretary. Her sugary southern Ohio twang almost always signals a hellish turn of events. *"Hiya, Maddy. It's Suzie. Mr. Tinker wants to see you in his office—right away please!"*

"Good gravy," I growled. "Doesn't anybody realize a woman my age needs to ease into her day slowly?"

I went to the cafeteria and made my tea. Then, with my mug in front of me like a Crusader's shield, I headed for Tinker's office.

Tinker was not alone. Police reporter Dale Marabout was there. Features editor Nancy Peale was there. And Gabriella Nash was there, bawling like a three-year-old who'd ridden her tricycle off the end of the porch.

Tinker smiled weakly at me. "I was hoping you could help Miss Nash through this."

My first thought was that they'd fired her. That she'd made up a lot of stuff in her story. My second thought was that this was no time for me to gloat. That there'd be plenty of time for that later. I kneeled by Gabriella's chair and patted her shoulder. "What's this all about, dear?"

Tinker answered for her. "One of the garage sale ladies was murdered."

That brought an anguished squeal from Gabriella and a fresh gush of tears. My knees were already beginning to hurt but I stayed put. I even offered the girl a sip of my tea—which she actually accepted. "That's just terrible," I said. "Which one?"

Dale provided the facts. "Violeta Bell. They found her on a mat in the fitness room. In her undies. Shot three times in the chest."

Nancy provided the context. "Gabriella is afraid her story had something to do with the murder."

"Oh, for Pete's sake," I snarled. I took my mug away from Gabriella. Struggled to my feet and headed for the door. "I've got work to do."

Nancy bristled at me. "It was her first story, Maddy."

I bristled right back. "Let's hope it's her last."

Tinker's hairless head turned into a giant salad tomato. He let me have it. "She admires you, Mrs. Sprowls. For some reason."

After hearing that you'd think I'd feel awful and apologize, wouldn't you? But I didn't feel awful and I sure didn't apologize. I just fumed while Tinker called me every name in the book. Gabriella, strangely enough, sniffed back her tears and came to my defense. "Leave Mrs. Sprowls alone. I wish I had her backbone."

Now I did feel awful. I reached out and gently scratched Gabriella behind her ear, the way I scratch James when he surprises me with respect. "What do you say you and I take a walk to the cafeteria," I said. "Get some fresh tea and maybe one of those big cookies in the vending machine."

And so we went to the cafeteria. I made the tea and Gabriella bought the cookie. We sat at the table by the plastic bamboo plant. I snapped the cookie in two and gave her the bigger half.

She took a chipmunk-size nibble. "I guess I've set the women's movement back a few years, huh?"

I wasn't in the mood for a cute back-and-forth. I just wanted to scare some maturity into the girl and get back to my desk. I took the biggest bite of cookie I dared. "That story you wrote wasn't about you, Gabriella. It was about those four crazy women and that scraggly cabbie who hauls them around."

"One of them was murdered."

"So what?"

"What if it was because of my story?"

"Again, so what?"

She slid down in her chair until she looked like a five-year-old sulking at the dinner table. "I guess I had a feeling about her."

"Good gravy, girl! You talk to some old woman for twenty minutes and you get emotionally involved? You sure this is the right profession for you?"

That got Gabriella's dander up a bit. Which, I must admit, I liked. "Not that kind of feeling," she said. "It was just—I don't know—like she was somebody other than who she said she was."

I laughed and, unfortunately, sprayed the table with cookie crumbs. "So you don't think she was really Romanian royalty?"

"I didn't believe that or anything else she said."

I liked that, too. "Your shit detector start beeping, did it?"

For the first time that morning she smiled. "Yes, it did. And it just wasn't the things she said. It was her—what's a good word for it?"

I'm an old woman. I gave her an old word. "Her countenance?"

"Yeah—her countenance."

I had no reason to doubt the reliability of Gabriella's shit detector. It had certainly worked that day I went to see her at the student newspaper office. She's seen right through my cock-and-bull story about wanting to rummage through the paper's old files to see what I could find about my own years at Hemphill College. She knew I was digging into Gordon Sweet's murder. "So why the tears when you heard that Violeta Bell had been murdered? If you had such a bad feeling about her?"

She corrected me. "I didn't say I had a bad feeling about her. She was a lot of fun. Just like the other three. But I had the sense she was hiding something. Or hiding from something."

I took a more modest bite of cookie and studied *her* countenance. Inside that snip of a girl lived a wise woman. "Why would she do the interview then?" I asked. "The pages of a newspaper aren't exactly the best place to hide. Although nobody reads newspapers any more."

Gabriella pulled her tea bag from her mug. Let it swing back and forth like a body dangling from a noose. "I think maybe she just wanted to be loved."

"Just wanted to be loved? For Pete's sake!"

"I know that sounds like a lot of mushy psychobabble, Mrs. Sprowls. But I think maybe that was it. On the outside she was confident and classy. Inside, totally a mess."

I couldn't stop myself. "Just the opposite of me, you're saying?"

She looked at me the way Aubrey McGinty used to look at me. With exasperation. "I'm saying that maybe she was one of those excruciatingly insecure people who need to be the center of attention no matter what."

"And so she did the interview knowing she probably shouldn't?"

"Yeah."

"And you did the interview knowing she probably shouldn't, too?"

"Yeah."

"Because it was your first story and you didn't want to blow it?"

"Yeah."

"And so when you heard she'd been murdered—"

"Yeah."

4

Thursday, July 13

I retrieved my morning paper from the azalea bushes. Which was nothing to grumble about. Too many mornings it's on the roof. On my way back to the kitchen I read the headlines. The news couldn't have been better:

Suspect Arrested In 'Never Dull' Murder

By Dale Marabout
Hannawa-Union Staff Writer

HANNAWA—Police Wednesday arrested a "person of interest" in their investigation into the murder of retired antique dealer Violeta Bell.

Bell, 72, was found dead July 5 in the fitness room of the Carmichael House condominiums where she lived. She had been shot three times at close range, police said.

The murder weapon, believed to be a .22 pistol, has not been found, police confirmed.

There was no Ike waiting for me at the breakfast table this morning—which was either a good thing or a bad thing depending which side of the independence versus companionship argument you come down on. I ate my oatmeal and read:

```
     Police identified the man they took into
custody as cabdriver Edward "Eddie" French.
He was arrested just before dawn at his
second-story apartment in the Meriwether
Square district on the city's near west
side, police said.
     Both French and Bell were featured in a
Herald-Union story earlier this month.
     That story explored the active social
lives of Bell and three other women living
at the Carmichael House. Calling themselves
"The Queens of Never Dull," the women hired
French to drive them to garage sales on
Saturdays.
     Police said that while they lacked evi-
dence to charge French with Bell's murder,
the 56-year-old Hannawa native had a number
of items in his possession that they believed
belonged to the slain woman.
     One source close to the case described
those items as "very pricey antiques."
     Court records show that French has had a
number of run-ins with local police depart-
ments over the years, including convictions
for burglary in 1981 and 1987.
```

"Good for you, Mr. Marabout," I whispered as I turned to the jump page. By that, of course, I meant good for me. Apparently the police had their man. That meant I'd no longer be responsible for Gabriella Nash's guilty conscience. Every morning for more than a week now she'd been checking in with me as if I were her parole officer.

I finished my oatmeal, took James for his walk, showered and trimmed my bangs—yes, I'm still wearing my hair in this silly 1950s Prince Valiant style—and searched my closet for something I hadn't worn to work in a while. Something that would express how good I felt. The best I could do was my lime green Liz Claiborne lawn shirt with yellow pinstripes and a pair of twill chinos from Lands' End in some sensible shade of white they call *Nantucket Clay.*

I got to the morgue right at nine. I made my tea, read the obituaries, zapped all the worthless emails in my inbox, and settled in to mark up that morning's paper.

And of course my phone rang. And of course it was Suzie. "Hiya, Maddy. It's Suzie. I've got Mr. Averill on the phone for you."

"Good gravy! What does he—"

"Morning, Maddy!"

"Bob! How are you?"

"Fine and dandy—so how long has it been since you and I had lunch?"

Bob Averill is *The Herald-Union's* editor-in-chief. An overstuffed teddy bear about to turn sixty. Unless you count spearing cheese squares at the newsroom Christmas party, he and I had never had lunch together. "It has been a while," I said.

"We should rectify that."

"I suppose we should."

"How about today?"

"Well—"

"Super. I'll have Suzie make reservations for us at Speckley's. Say twelve-thirty?"

I was too shocked to tell him that you don't need reservations at Speckley's. That as long as you comply with the NO SHIRT, NO SHOES, NO SERVICE sign on the door, they'll seat you. I told him twelve-thirty would be great. That I would meet him there.

"Meet me? Maddy Sprowls! What kind of men have you been eating with? I'll drive."

And so in three hours I was going to have lunch with Bob Averill. And it was no mystery why. He finally had the ammunition he needed to force me into retirement. Or as he once put it: "The common ground you and I need to find *vis-à-vis* your tenure at the paper."

I was not going without a fight. I grabbed a piece of scrap paper and drew a line down the middle. On the left I listed the various infractions he might bring up: my long lunches, personal long distance calls, my usually foul disposition. On the right

I listed explanations or denials. When I got to my snoopfests into the Buddy Wing and Gordon Sweet murders, I noted that while they had been unauthorized, on the sly, and initially troublesome for the paper, they both had resulted in some very good journalism.

Then, while I was pondering how I could good-naturedly threaten filing an age discrimination suit, Gabriella Nash appeared in front of my desk. She announced that she was "totally apoplectic."

"About what, dear?"

Like a bad actress in a bad movie, she flung that morning's front page on my desk. "That is my story, Mrs. Sprowls."

I knew what she meant of course. But with my hours at *The Herald-Union* down to a precious few, I was in no mood for foolishness. Especially hers. I pretended to study the story she was thumping with her finger. "According to the byline, it's Dale Marabout's story."

She curled her lips at my flippancy like a rabid raccoon. "This is serious business, Mrs. Sprowls!" She went on and on how the story shouldn't have been taken away from her just because it unexpectedly evolved from a "fluffy piece of shit" into a "hard news murder story." *The Washington Post*, she said, didn't take Redford and Bernstein off the Watergate story when it grew from a third-rate burglary into a constitutional showdown between President Nixon and Congress. She should be allowed to follow the Never Dull story wherever it lead, she said. Redford and Bernstein had been young reporters, too, she said.

I neatly folded the front page and handed it back to her. "In the first place, it was not *Redford* and Bernstein. It was *Woodward* and Bernstein. Robert Redford was the actor who played Woodward in the movie. But I suppose you deserve some credit for at least having heard about Watergate." Her eyes dropped. I hurriedly crumpled my list of job-saving excuses and slid it off my desk into the wastebasket. "And in the second place," I said, "you should be telling all this to Alec Tinker—not me."

She went from rabid raccoon to vulnerable bunny. "I was hoping maybe you'd go with me."

I showed her the most empathetic smile I could. Then I lowered the boom. "I just don't see that happening, Gabriella."

Bob Averill appeared in the newsroom at twenty past twelve. He gave me a big John Wayne thisaway wave. I grabbed my purse and followed him to the parking deck.

Bob is extremely well paid. And his wife comes from money. But he still likes to think of himself as the regular guy he was forty years ago. So he eschews his reserved parking space by the door and deposits his Mercedes wherever he can find a spot. It's not one of those big roomy Mercedes. It's one of those sporty, midlife crisis two-seaters. Yellow as a ripe banana. He wedged his 200 pounds behind the steering wheel with the help of a laborious "Augggghhhh."

We headed toward West Apple Street and Meriwether Square. "You think we can get there in five minutes?" he asked.

"If we don't get behind too many buses."

He chuckled like some old soldier fondly recalling the Battle of the Bulge. "I remember when I had to take the bus."

As we buzzed along, I pictured him that morning calling Suzie and asking, "Any idea where Maddy Sprowls likes to have lunch?" And when she answered Speckley's, him asking, "Where the hell is that?" And when she said Meriwether Square, him harrumphing, "That figures."

In case you haven't spent much time in Hannawa, Ohio, Meriwether Square is our city's version of Greenwich Village. It's a four-block strip of coffee shops, thrift shops, and hole-in-the-wall bars, each geared toward a particular sexual orientation. The strip is surrounded with wonderful art deco apartment buildings and once-grand turn-of-the-century houses. The brick streets are lined with shaggy oak trees and badly buckled sidewalks. Dale Marabout calls it Differentdrummerville. And he's pretty much on the mark. Meriwether Square is lousy with angst-riddled college students, old hippies, even older Beatniks, artists who never sell anything, writers who never get published. It's a real bouillabaisse of daydreamers, outcasts, and kooks. And I just love the place. And I just love Speckley's. I've been going to that wonderful old diner since my college days.

Bob found a parking space right in front. But he couldn't find any quarters in his pocket for the meter. "It's on me," I said.

Inside, he announced his name to the waitress. "Averill."

She squinted at him the way James squints at me when he's trying to decipher the strange sounds coming out of my mouth. Finally she figured it out—or at least thought she had. "I don't think we got any of them," she said. "But I've got some Tylenol if that would help."

It was Bob's turn to imitate James' squint. I came to the rescue. "He doesn't have a headache," I told the waitress. "He has a reservation."

"Oh, he's the one," she cackled. "We all thought that was a prank call." She grabbed a pair of menus from the counter. "Right this way, Mr. Averill. Your table's waiting." She gave us a booth by the eight-foot plastic bipedal cow statue drinking a chocolate milkshake.

I talked Bob into ordering the diner's legendary house special—meatloaf sandwich, au gratin potatoes on the side. I told the waitress I'd have hot tea. Bob pointed at the plastic cow and said, "I'll have what she's drinking."

Good gravy I was nervous. I decided to take the bull by the horns. "Bob," I said, "I know why we're here."

"You do?"

"Of course I do! Now shoot!"

He cringed. "Shoot? Don't you think that word is maybe a bit inappropriate under the circumstances?"

I attacked. "Come on, Bob. Give me your best shot. Then I'll give you mine. Then we'll enjoy the meatloaf."

He dug his elbows into the Formica. Propped his chin on his fist. Looked me straight in the eyes. "What in the hell are you talking about?"

"My retirement. What else would I be talking about?"

His face withered until it looked like one of those old cooking onions I keep on top of my refrigerator. "Oh no, Maddy Sprowls—you can't retire now. I need you."

It was my turn to look him straight in the eyes. "What in the hell are you talking about?"

"Eddie French."

"That cab driver they arrested? What does that have to do with me?"

The waitress brought our beverages. Bob pounded the wrapper off his straw. "Nothing to do with you—not yet, anyway—but unfortunately it does have something to do with me."

I zeroed in on the most pertinent part of his answer. "Not yet, anyway?"

He drilled his straw into his milkshake. Took a long suck. "I need your help with something, Maddy."

I finally knew where he was headed. "Absolutely not!"

He grabbed his temples. Grunted in pain. At first I thought he had an aneurysm in his brain that just popped. But when he started gasping like a beached fish, I realized he was just having a brain freeze from the milkshake. I laid into him without pity. "I'm not a detective, Bob. I'm a damn librarian."

The pain on his face slowly subsided. The self-confident, always-in-command Bob Averill I'd known for fifteen years was gone. "It seems that Eddie French is the worthless older brother of Tippy's sorority sister," he said.

Tippy was Bob's wife. Several years younger than him, trim and pretty. A real ballbuster. Bob would still be writing high school sports at that little weekly in Coshocton County if she hadn't rescued his dormant potential from the dustbin of happiness. "And this sorority sister knows her worthless brother couldn't possibly have murdered Violeta Bell?"

Bob took a much more modest sip from his shake. "She was on the phone half the night crying to Tippy about it. Which meant Tippy was crying to me the other half."

"And now you're crying to me?"

"You know how irascible Tippy can be."

I did know how irascible Tippy could be. I also knew it would be smart to stick to the facts. "According to Dale Marabout's story, the police found Bell's stuff in his apartment. And he's got quite a record, too."

"Yes they did, and yes he does," Bob admitted. "But sorority sisters are sisters for life and, well—"

I finished the sentence. "And I owe my shaky future at the paper to your good graces?"

The Bob Averill of old would have gone ballistic over a remark like that. The new one only got more docile. "I can't put Marabout or some other reporter on this. That would be unethical. This is a personal matter."

"But you can put me on it?"

"No putting. Begging."

The waitress arrived with our platters. The meatloaf was stacked high inside huge Kaiser rolls. The enormous globs of au gratin potatoes were steaming. "Frankly, it feels more like putting," I said.

Bob hadn't learned his lesson from the milkshake. He filled his mouth with potatoes, getting a dandy cheese burn on the roof of his mouth. "Look Maddy, I know this stinks. I've spent the last two years trying to stop you from snooping into murders and now I'm asking you to do exactly that. But for some reason you're good at it."

He was right about that. For some reason I *was* good at it. "What if I say no?"

Despite his weakened condition, he still had enough sense not to answer my question directly. "To tell you the truth, Maddy, I've never cared much for Jeannie. That's Tippy's sorority sister. Jeannie Salapardi. She's full of herself and full of ideas for making me a better husband."

I'm sure my eyebrows went up about a foot. "Salapardi? Of the Honda-Toyota-Mitsubishi dealership Salapardis?"

Bob grinned a bit. "That's right. She's married to Dave 'Drive You Crazy' Salapardi—"

Again I finished the sentence. "The paper's largest advertiser."

His grin wobbled into a frown. "I'm far more afraid of my wife than losing a million dollars a year in advertising."

"You're an honest man, Bob." I wasn't being sarcastic. He was an honest man. And almost as afraid of me as he was of his wife. I knew he wouldn't be asking for help unless he was in a real pickle. I summed things up. "So, you don't like Jeannie Salapardi, and you want me to prove that her brother didn't murder Violeta Bell?"

Bob's cheeks were stuffed full of meatloaf. He nodded as he chewed. "Actually, I'd consider it a personal victory if her brother were convicted. If he's guilty."

That surprised me. "If he's guilty?"

The tortured husband gave way to the truth-loving newspaperman. "When Eddie French was twelve years old he shot his best friend in the foot. With a pellet gun. Accidentally. Gangrene set in and the boy lost half his foot. The boy was the star of the junior high school basketball team. Destined to be a star in high school and college. Maybe even the pros. That's how good the kid was, apparently. Jeannie says that Eddie was so riddled with guilt that he smashed his pellet gun with a sledgehammer. He developed a physical aversion to guns of any sort. When he was drafted into the Army, during Vietnam, he refused to even touch a rifle. He spent the rest of his basic training shuffling between the psycho ward and the guardhouse. He was eventually given a dishonorable discharge."

I interrupted with the obvious. "But he's a convicted criminal."

Bob was really chewing and nodding now. "Yes, he is. Burglary. Auto theft. Fencing. Bad checks. Dealing the evil weed. But nothing that ever involved guns."

I did not want to be intrigued. Not for all the Darjeeling tea in India. But I was intrigued. "And Violeta Bell was found shot full of holes."

Bob didn't get me back to the paper until three o'clock. I immediately summoned Eric Chen. He dropped into the chair next to my desk and slid down until his neck was resting on the back. "Heaven's to Betsy," I barked, "this is a place of business. Show a little professionalism."

He crossed his legs and wiggled his dangling foot. He stuck out his pinky finger when he took a sip from his bottle of Mountain Dew. "That better?"

"Much better." I told him I'd just had lunch with Bob Averill. He told me that the entire newsroom was buzzing about it. That the boys in sports were offering odds on when my last day would be.

"I hope you put your money on When Hell Freezes Over."

He smiled at me like Buddha. "As a matter of fact I did."

Eric is the perfect assistant. Lazy and loyal. When Bob hired him fifteen years ago, it was not only to oversee the computerization of the morgue, it was to be my eventual replacement. But my refusal to retire hasn't bothered Eric in the least. He plays with the computers, reads his comic books, drinks his Mountain Dews, and collects a very good paycheck. I got down to the nitty gritty. "Bob's in something of a pickle."

"Which means you're in a pickle, too?"

"And you," I said. "And probably a whole lot of other people before we're through."

I handed him a copy of Gabriella's story with a lot of names underlined in red. "I need whatever you can find in our files on the four women. Kay Hausenfelter, Ariel Wilburger-Gowdy, Gloria McPhee, and Violeta Bell. There should be plenty on each."

Apparently Eric had been reading more than his comic books. "Violeta Bell? Didn't she just get murdered?"

"Yes she did. And the police think the cab driver, Eddie French, did it."

"But he didn't?"

"That's what Bob wants us to find out." I explained the predicament that Bob found himself in with his wife and her sorority sister.

Eric rolled his Chinese-American eyes. "Women."

I reminded him that I was a woman, too.

"Don't worry," he said. "I was including you."

"Good—I also think it's a good idea to see what we have on the sorority sister. Check Jeanette Salapardi."

"Salapardi? Of the Honda-Toyota-Mitsu—"

"That's the one. And when you're done checking the morgue files, see what you can find online."

"I'll Google the hell out of them."

I wagged my finger at him. "And you'll keep your lips zipped. Bob Averill doesn't want Tinker to know about this."

Eric finally showed a little enthusiasm. "Oh, baby! When the lid blows on this one there'll be smelly brown stuff dripping everywhere!"

I tried to remain sour-faced. But I'm sure at least one side of my mouth was curled into a smirk. "Yes, there will."

As soon as Eric went back to his desk, I swung around to my computer. I checked the metro desk's budget to see if Dale Marabout was writing a follow up on the murder. He was. Then I clicked over to the file where those stories are kept—the written basket—to see if he'd already filed it. He had.

He was reporting that police had found a single, bloody shoeprint on the landing outside French's apartment. They were having the blood checked to see if it matched Violeta Bell's. They'd also found French's fingerprints "just about everywhere" in Bell's condominium. There also was this:

> Police would neither confirm nor deny reports that they'd failed to find French's fingerprints in the basement fitness room where Bell's body was found.

This little, one-sentence paragraph was telling on a number of counts. It meant that police investigators almost certainly had not found French's fingerprints in the fitness room. And if not, why not? Would French have clumsily left his fingerprints in her condo after taking pains not to leave any at the murder scene? It also meant that Dale was digging into the story beyond what the police were officially giving him. He had already cultivated a source. The obvious candidate was Detective Scotty Grant.

Grant was always leaking little gems like that when it served his purposes. But it could be someone else. Someone close to the investigation in some other way. Someone who knew there was something more to this story than *Scraggly Cabbie Kills Rich Old Woman.*

I printed out copies of Gabriella's feature and the two police stories Dale had written so far. I put them in a fresh manila folder. I wrote NEVER DULL on the tab. Then I picked up the phone and punched Gabriella's extension. "I apologize for being snippy this morning," I said. "I had a lot on my mind."

She swiveled in her chair and waved at me across the newsroom. "It's my fault," she said. "I shouldn't have been such a noodge."

I took that proverbial deep breath. "What do you say we start fresh with breakfast Saturday morning?"

5

Saturday, July 15

I had breakfast with Ike at my house then drove to Waldo's Waffle House for breakfast with Gabriella. I ordered a multigrain blueberry waffle. Gabriella ordered the Big Waldo—scrambled eggs, bacon and sausage, hash browns, wheat toast and three buttermilk pancakes. When the waitress put all that food in front of her I was appalled. "You recently have a sumo wrestler's stomach implanted in you?"

Gabriella started smearing butter on her pancakes. "We Nashes are blessed with a high metabolism."

"Or tape worms," I said.

I watched her drench the pancakes with syrup. I didn't give a diddle how much the girl ate—and frankly I didn't have much room to talk inasmuch as I was about to put a waffle on top of the oatmeal I'd had an hour earlier—but prattling on about her gluttony did keep me from bringing up the touchy subject I'd lured her there to discuss. So I gave her another zinger. "You may not have anything to worry about now, dear," I said. "But twenty years from now you're going to wake up with Big Waldo clinging to your thighs."

She wiggled her perfect little eyebrows. "And all for just $5.95."

Yes, Gabriella Nash was a bit too emotional for my taste. Yes, like most young reporters, she was mesmerized by her brilliant future. And yes, I still had a bug up my behind about the things she'd written in the college newspaper about me. "Sprowls," she wrote, "is the desk-bound gnome who watches over the newspaper's morgue, where the stories real reporters write are filed away for future reference." But sitting there that morning, exchanging smart-ass comments, eating that sinfully good food, well, good gravy, what can I say? I liked the horrible girl. "There's a chance you may be right about Violeta Bell," I admitted.

"Are you trying to apologize?" she asked, slowly feeding a slice of bacon into her mouth.

"Let's not use the A-word, Gabriella. That only levels the playing field between us."

"Okay then—what word should we use?"

I speared a blueberry and dipped it in the mountain of fresh whipped cream atop my waffle. "The R-word. I've been re-evaluating what you said—about the possibility that your story had something to do with her murder."

She wasn't prepared to go there. Her tough-girl veneer began to crack like stale lipstick. "But the cops have the killer. And the motive."

I patted her hand. "They've got squat." I told her about Eddie French's aversion to guns. I did not, of course, tell her about Bob Averill's aversion to Eddie's sister.

She played with her hash browns, pulling away the crunchy ones on the outside to get to the soft ones inside. "Well, it's not my story any more, is it?"

"No, it isn't," I said. "But I don't think either of us want to see that wacky cab driver railroaded for something he didn't do."

"You want me to help you interfere with a police investigation?"

"Only if you want to."

Gabriella tightened her lips until they turned white. Either she was on the cusp of crying or squishing her last remaining pancake in my face. "This isn't fair, Mrs. Sprowls. You're trying to play on my guilt."

"Let's stay away from the G-word, too," I said. "You have no reason to feel responsible for anything. And neither do I. When I saw those women piling out of that cab at the garage sale, I knew it would make a good story. And you did a good job with it. A great job."

Gabriella, thank God, dug into that last pancake. "Now you're trying to butter me up."

I had no choice but to tell her more than I should. "I can't tell you who—but someone uncomfortably close to Mr. French's situation has asked me to sniff around a little. As a rather complicated favor. And in order to do that favor—well, I'm going to need a little favor from you."

She shook her forkful of dripping pancake at me. "I can see why they call you Morgue Mama."

I took the fork from her and devoured the piece of pancake like a snake swallowing a helpless tadpole. "It would be smart to stay away from those particular M-words, too, Gabriella."

"I will."

"You bet you will."

I let her eat in peace—for a minute—then took another bite out of her hide. "Your story on the Queens of Never Dull was really quite good. But there was one important thing you left out."

"I did?"

"Yes, you did." I wagged my fork at her. "Regarding Violeta Bell's claim that she was Romanian royalty. You failed to say whether she spoke with an accent or not."

It was as if she'd just had the Pulitzer Prize taken away from her. "You're right. That would have been a good touch."

I pretended to be incensed. In reality I was just playing with her. "A good touch? We're not discussing your prose here, Gabriella. We're talking about truth."

That rankled her. "The story was about four old ladies going to garage sales, Mrs. Sprowls. Not about whether one of them was the queen of Romania."

"Weren't you at least a little curious about her claim?"

"Well, sure. But the story—"

I let her off the hook. "All I'm saying is that you should have mentioned whether she spoke with an accent or not."

Gabriella was finally on to me. "This isn't about my story. This is about your investigation."

"Of course it's about my investigation. Whether Violeta Bell was Romanian royalty might be important."

"Why would that be important?"

"Anything unusual about a murder victim might be important," I said. "And claiming to be the queen of Romania is certainly unusual."

"That it is."

"Her quotes in your story suggest that the Communists ran her family out of Romania," I said. "I'm not sure when the Communists took over there. But it was shortly after World War II. That's when all those Eastern European countries fell to the Communists. Which means she would have been a teenager when she left. Which means she might have had an accent—a trace of one maybe—if she was telling the truth."

Gabriella folded her hands and leaned over the table as if I was her hard-of-hearing great-great-grandmother. "She did not speak with an accent."

"Did she sound like she was from Ohio?"

We left Waldo's in my car. It was nine-thirty already and both the eastbound and westbound lanes of Apple Street were clogging with people frantically trying to get to the supermarket before everybody else did. We turned onto Hardihood Avenue and drove north through the ever-bigger houses. We were heading, of course, to the Carmichael House, to see if we could make a surprise visit to one of the three surviving Queens of Never Dull. I wasn't exactly proud of myself for making Gabriella come along, but what was I to do? I needed her to get my foot in the door.

"You have a preference who we try first?" Gabriella asked as we wound through the landscapers' trucks parked on both sides of the street.

I rolled up my window to block out the roar of the mowers racing back and forth across the beautifully manicured lawns like morbidly obese bumblebees. "How about that stripper, Kay Hausenfelter? She sounds like the most fun."

"That's some criteria for investigating a murder."

"Nothing wrong with having a little fun," I said. "And besides she gave you the best quotes."

"She *was* talkative."

The real reason I wanted to see Kay Hausenfelter first was because she was the only member of the Never Dulls whom Eric had finished researching for me. What he found was now stuffed in my brain, at the ready, in case Kay said something that didn't jive with the facts.

Kay Hausenfelter was born on a farm in Oklahoma, 76 years ago, to Chester and Eleanor Pull. She was the last of seven children. The Pulls migrated to the fruit fields of California during the Dust Bowl years, to keep from starving. By the time she was seventeen, Kay was shedding her clothes in striptease establishments up and down the West Coast. She was billed as Klondike Kay, "Gorgeous Gold-Digger of the not-so-frigid North." She'd take the stage covered head-to-toe in an Eskimo parka and knee-high mukluks. By the time she wiggled off the stage, she was down to a furry g-string and papier-mâché pasties painted to look like gold nuggets. It was in Los Angeles that young Harold Hausenfelter caught her act, during the 33rd Annual Bakers & Confectioners Convention. Harold was the shy and impressionable scion of Hannawa bread-baking baron Gottfried Hausenfelter. Harold brought Kay home to Hannawa as his wife. What Gottfried must have thought of his son's bride is anybody's guess—albeit an easy guess.

Gabriella and I reached the Carmichael House. It was not a particularly handsome building. A ten-story cereal box with narrow, dangling balconies nobody in their right mind would go out on. Anyone over sixty could live there, if they could afford it, but from what I'd heard it was mostly filled with women whose husbands had done very well before they died. We parked in the visitors' spaces on the side and followed the pachysandra-lined walk to the front. Gabriella buzzed Kay Hausenfelter's unit.

Kay must have had her finger an inch off the intercom button. There was an instant "Halloooo!"

"This is Gabriella Nash, Mrs. Hausenfelter. From *The Herald-Union*. I was wondering how you're getting along. After everything that's happened."

Kay's Oklahoma twang wasn't helped by the tinny speaker box. "Well, aren't you a sweetheart. I'm just fine. You'll come up for something, won't you? A Diet Coca-Cola or something?"

"I've got a friend with me," Gabriella informed her. "If that's okay."

"Man friend or woman friend?"

"Woman friend."

"Oh, good. I won't have to put on a better robe—oh hell, I'll put on a better robe anyway."

And so the tower's impressive brass-covered door hummed and clicked and we went inside. We hadn't taken two steps toward the elevator when the phone in the lobby rang. Gabriella was content to let it ring. I was not. I hurried to the end table it was on, picked it up. It was Kay Hausenfelter. "That you, Gabriella?"

"This is her friend, Maddy Sprowls."

"Oh, good—I was hoping you girls could bring my mail up with you. The boxes are right there by the door."

I told her we'd be happy to.

"The boxes are locked," she said, "but there's a skeleton key under the bullfighter."

I scanned the lobby for the bullfighter. He turned out to be a foot-high ceramic statue on the table at the other end of the sofa. He was waving his red cape at a bowl of York peppermint patties. "I see him."

"Oh, good—I know it's not the safest thing, but with a building full of forgetful old farts, there's a skeleton key someplace for everything."

I got the key and opened her mailbox. Checked out the envelopes all the way to the fifth floor. Nothing but doctor bills and enticements for credit cards.

The hallway was a tribute to blandness: beige walls, even beiger carpeting, sleepy landscapes in ugly gold frames. The building's rulebook did, apparently, allow residents to express their individuality by decorating their identical beige doors. Most bore wreaths of fake flowers. A few had those atrociously cute wooden cutouts you find at church craft fairs—a bunny in overalls watering smiling carrots, a mama duck holding an umbrella over her babies, a WELCOME SIGN spelled out in tiny blue hearts. Kay Hausenfelter's door sported a cutout of a buxom woman in an itsy-bitsy-yellow-polka-dot bikini.

After loudly smooching our cheeks, Kay sat us in that bright red loveseat Gabriella mentioned in her story. "I guess the first order of business is to get something cold in our paws," Kay said, swaying her behind toward the kitchen. "What'll it be, ladies?"

Gabriella and I both chose those Diet Cokes she'd mentioned on the speaker. Kay's tumbler had something tan in it. She sat across from us in a white armchair. From the happy relief in her eyes as she studied me, I could tell she approved of my drabness. "That's a pretty robe," I said.

"Thanks. But I wasn't exactly going for pretty." Which was putting it mildly. It was as pink as the insulation in my attic. The fuzzy hem almost reached her knees and the loose, low-cut top showed more of her ampleness than anyone needed to see. What she was or wasn't wearing under that robe was anybody's guess. Her hair was much too long for a woman of her age and it was much too blond. And she should have spent more time touching up her roots and less time on her toenails. But having said all that, she was a naturally beautiful woman with good skin and bright green eyes.

Having read Gabriella's story, I was prepared for the red love-seat. I was not prepared for the art on the walls: black-and-white photographs of a much younger Kay Hausenfelter wearing almost nothing, publicity shots from her years in burlesque. Above the mantle hung a huge portrait of her, totally nude, hugging a bundle of baguettes, a very personal memento from her years as the wife of local bread mogul Harold Hausenfelter, I figured.

Kay pointed at the portrait. "I was a fine looking broad, wasn't I? The artist didn't have to exaggerate a damn thing."

I didn't know what to say. So I said the silliest thing I'd ever said to anyone. "I still buy Hausenfelter's bread."

Kay threw her arms open and sang like Ethel Merman. "If it ain't Hausenfelter's, it just ain't bread!"

Everybody in Hannawa of a certain age knows that line. It's the tagline from the Hausenfelter's Bread Song. When Kay married Harold, Hausenfelter's was the city's number three bread brand, behind Yodel's and Swann's Golden Crust. Soon after Kay wrote that jingle, and sang it in radio and television commercials, Hausenfelter's was no. 1, Yodel's a distant no. 2, and Swann's Golden Crust out of business. "Boy," I said, "didn't that little ditty ruffle a few feathers."

Kay's eyes sparkled. "It sure did, didn't it?"

The ruffled feathers, of course, belonged to the librarians and teachers who didn't appreciate a business using that evil non-word *ain't* in their jingle, not only once but twice. Old Gottfried, however, stuck by his daughter-in-law and her jingle. "We ain't changing it," he told *The Herald-Union*. And that was that. The company is still using it today.

I looked for a way to get the conversation back on track. "I can tell that you're a woman of few pretensions. And frankly so am I."

Kay was startled. "Don't tell me you got a naked picture, too?"

"Heaven's to Betsy, no," I said, "but I do prefer to get right to the skinny. And the truth is, I'm not tagging along with Gabriella today. She's tagging along with me. I'm here about Violeta Bell."

Kay shifted her eyes between Gabriella and me while she jiggled the ice cubes in her tumbler. "So you're doing another story on us old broads? One that won't be so fun?"

"No story," I assured her. "Not by us anyway." I'd just told her how open and truthful I liked to be, but already I found myself obfuscating like a congressman. "The idea for Gabriella's story came from me," I said. "And I guess I'm feeling a little responsible. A little guilty even."

"Unless you helped Eddie pull the trigger, I wouldn't worry about feeling either of those things," Kay said. Then she laughed. "You didn't, did you?"

Gabriella answered for me, with exactly what I was preparing to say. "The question is whether Eddie pulled the trigger."

"It looks like the cops think he did," Kay said.

I couldn't let her get away with a wishy-washy answer like that. "And that's okay with you?"

She took a quick, nervous sip from her tumbler. "I don't know if it is or not."

"I suppose you've read about his police record."

Her next sip was steadier. And longer. "I've always liked Eddie," she said. "And he was very open to us about his past. The same way I'm open about mine."

My crazy brain flashed a fanciful image of Eddie's apartment, the walls plastered with his various mug shots, the way hers were plastered with her old publicity photos. "So you had a sense that his life of crime was behind him?" I asked. "That's what you're saying?"

"Yes. I guess I am."

I was dying to know if she knew about Eddie French's aversion to guns. But I knew I had to be careful how I broached the subject. If Eddie didn't kill Violeta Bell, then somebody else did. And if somebody else did, then maybe that somebody was Kay Hausenfelter. And I sure didn't want to toss a bone like that to a possible suspect. Instead, I asked, "Do you know if Eddie owned a gun?"

Kay leaned forward until her elbows, not to mention other things, were resting on her knees. "That's the other thing," she said. "I think Eddie was afraid of guns."

I was smart enough to play dumb. "Afraid of guns? Why would you say that?"

She laughed into her tumbler. "Because when I showed him mine, he got so fidgety I thought he was going to piss his pants."

Gabriella was shocked. "You've got a gun?"

I was merely intrigued. "When was this?"

Kay headed for the kitchen with her empty tumbler. "Not recently—if that's what you're thinking." The refrigerator opened and closed, ice cubes rattled. She returned to her armchair with her filled-to-the-brim tumbler in one hand and a massive red leather purse in the other. The Diet Coke bottle was under her arm. She topped off our drinks. Took a healthy sip of hers. Then she reached into her purse and pulled out a shiny pistol.

"It was a couple of years ago," she said, "when Eddie was driving us downtown to the Amtrak station—you know how that damn train to New York doesn't come through until three in the morning—and when he asked if we were afraid to be going down there in the middle of the night, I pulled out my snubby nosed baby doll. And he just about—well, like I said, he nearly pissed himself."

I grew up on a farm in wild and woolly upstate New York. Somebody's always shooting something. So I had no concerns about my own bladder. I asked to see the gun.

Apparently Kay could see that I was squinting at the tiny numbers engraved on the barrel. "It's a Colt Commander XXE .45 semi-automatic," she said. "Violeta was killed with a .22."

I handed it back to her. "I wouldn't know one gun from another."

She slid her fingers over the wood insets on the handle. "That's real rosewood," she said. "Pretty, isn't it?" She put it back in her purse, raking her collection of makeup tubes over the top like dirt over a grave.

I asked her the one question I'd prepared in advance. "Let's say Eddie French did kill Violeta—during a robbery gone bad, presumably—why would he choose her? Why not you? Or Ariel? Or Gloria? You're all pretty well heeled. I'm sure all of your condos are full of stealable stuff."

Kay answered with a question of her own. "Why would he wait until now? He's been carting us around for years."

"Maybe the temptation got too much for him. Or maybe he needed more money than usual."

She brought her glass to her lips with both hands. She took a long, steady sip, with her eyes closed and both pinkies sticking out. Then she said this: "If it turns out Eddie did it—then I hope he really did—that's all I've got to say."

That strange sentence puzzled me at first. And so did the sudden bitterness in her voice. But after my brain was finished sorting through Eric's research, I could only agree with her. "Me, too."

What Kay was referring to, of course, was the very public squabble she'd gotten in over her husband's will.

Her brother-in-law, Gottfried Jr., had contested it. He claimed she didn't have either a legal or moral right to her late husband Harold's fifty-one percent of the Hausenfelter Bread Company. He claimed that Kay had bamboozled his brother into signing the new will while he lay dying of pancreatic cancer. He told the judge that Harold and Kay had been living apart for years. That Harold, fed up with her repeated infidelities, had wanted to divorce her. He brought up Kay's years as a stripper, her drinking and public ribaldry. Kay conceded that she sometimes drank too much, and occasionally did embarrassing things in public, and she conceded living apart from Harold, he there in Hannawa and she at their ocean-front house on Fripp Island, in South Carolina. Their estrangement was the result of his infuriating stubbornness, not her infidelities, she said. And the new will, she said, was Harold's idea. His older brother, he worried, had never showed a lick of interest in the bakery and would more than likely sell it the first chance he got. The probate court sided with her. The headline in *The Herald-Union* put it this way:

```
        Kay Gets the Bread,
    Gottfried Gets Out of Town
```

The conversation drifted to Kay's days in burlesque. She told us oodles of hilarious stories. Gabriella and I finished our Diet Cokes. She finished whatever she was drinking. At the door I asked her one last question. "Did you believe that stuff about Violeta being Romanian royalty?"

Kay Hausenfelter's mouth wobbled into an intoxicated smile. "She sure believed it."

I drove Gabriella back to her car at Waldo's Waffle House. Then I drove to Artie's supermarket for ground pork and a head of cabbage, for the pigs-in-a-blanket I promised to make for Ike on Sunday. When I got home I called Eric Chen. "How'd you like to give me a computer lesson?" I asked.

"Who is this really calling?"

I told him I was serious. That I felt bad about dumping so much research on him. That it was about time I learned a few of his research tricks. So he'd have more time to read his comic books on company time.

He can't resist me when I talk like that to him. "Not today I hope."

"Good gravy, no," I assured him. "It's Saturday. How about tomorrow?"

6

The minute Ike left for church, I left for the morgue. Not that I was anxious for my computer lesson. Egad and little fishes—I no more wanted to spend my Sunday morning being harangued by Eric than he wanted to spend his watching me hyperventilate. But I'd already given him a ton of research to do on Violeta Bell's murder, and if I dumped this new question on him, well, I might not get an answer for weeks. And I was far too curious to wait for weeks.

Eric, as I expected, was a half-hour late. He yawned his way to my desk. He had a bottle of Mountain Dew in one hand and a family sized bag of Peanut M&Ms in the other. I shook my head at his baggy shorts and flip-flops. He sarcastically shielded his eyes from my smiley face T-shirt. I summoned him to my desk.

He pulled up a chair with his foot. He immediately went into teacher mode. "Okay, I guess the first thing—"

I stopped him right there. "Let's say I wanted to find out if someone was royalty or not—how exactly would I do that?"

He glowered at me like a bulldog learning that his Beggin' Strips weren't real bacon. "This isn't me giving you a lesson. This is you bamboozling me into working on the Sabbath!"

"Everybody ought to work at least one day a week," I said. I put on my drugstore reading glasses and slid them down my nose until my computer screen came into focus. I readied my fingers on the keyboard. "Now tell me how."

He was smart enough to submit without a tussle. "You know what country?"

"Romania."

He pointed to the Google box on my toolbar. "Type in the person's name and then Romania. And then something like royalty or royal family."

I typed in *Violeta Bell, Romania, royal family*. "Now what?"

He sighed at my ignorance. "Click on the Google Search box."

I clicked. My computer screen blinked just once and told me it had found 14,600 websites for me to check out. I was amazed. And a little annoyed. Eric always made the research projects I gave him seem like a major chore requiring almost metaphysical skill. "That's it? I could have James do this for me!" Then I started scrolling down. Clicking on the websites. Reading. Finding absolutely nothing useful. "This could take all day," I grouched.

Eric forced a handful of M&Ms into his mouth. "Let's refine it a bit."

"How do I do that?"

"You need something more specific."

I stole a few M&Ms from his bag. Popped them in my mouth one by one while I thought out loud. "I doubt that Romania has had a king or queen for a long time. So if there are any living royals, they're hanging out there like forgotten socks on a clothesline. How about we try *pretenders to the throne?*"

He nodded his approval. I typed it in and clicked the Google Search box again. My computer screen presented me with a whole new collection of websites—430,000 of them in fact. But my dismay was short-lived. The very first site gave me exactly what I was looking for. It listed the modern-day pretenders to the throne for every country in the world. Including Romania.

The would-be king of Romania was, in fact, the former king of Romania, eighty-five-year-old Michael I.

The website also contained a ton of historical background on the Romanian monarchy. I was in seventh heaven. Eric was bored silly. He slid down in his chair and fished a bundle of comic books out of the enormous cargo pocket in his shorts. "Who are you—Captain Kangaroo?" I asked.

"Captain who?"

I keep forgetting how old I'm getting, that even someone in their early thirties like Eric would have no childhood memory of the avuncular Saturday morning television star pulling carrots out of his big pockets for Bunny Rabbit. "Never mind, Comic Book Boy," I hissed. "You just go ahead and fritter your life away with that crap while I make America safe for little old ladies."

"Sounds like a plan," he said. He buried his nose in an X-men adventure. I started mining the website for answers.

It was hard for me to believe, but Romania had only been an independent nation since the 1860s. That's when it pried itself loose from the old Ottoman Empire. In 1881, the Romanian parliament imported a German prince named Charles and crowned him as the nation's first constitutional king—Carol I.

Carol I had no living heirs. So when he died in 1914, his nephew, Ferdinand, became king.

King Ferdinand died in 1927. But his son, named Carol after his great uncle, was more interested in running around Europe with his mistress than running the country. So Carol's five-year old son, Michael, became king. That's right, he was five. Talk about dumping more on your children than they can handle. Anyway, little Michael's reign lasted just three years. In 1930, his playboy father had a change of heart. He booted the boy off the throne and had himself crowned Carol II.

European dictators were in vogue in those years, and so Carol II dissolved the parliament and ruled as an absolute monarch. Which was absolutely a mistake. He was forced to abdicate in 1940, and Michael, now nineteen, was put back on the throne.

Michael reigned until 1947, when the Communists forced him to abdicate. He settled down in England with his new wife, a French princess named Anne, and went to work as a commercial airline pilot.

Romania suffered under a succession of Communist rulers. The last one, Nicolae Ceausescu, was the worst of the lot. A popular uprising drove him from power in 1989. He and his equally hated wife, Elena, were arrested, tried in a makeshift courtroom, and executed just outside the door.

Today, Romania has an elected president and parliament. It also has a small gaggle of royalists who want to bring the monarchy back. They want a British-style king or queen who presumably would clank around in a turnip-shaped carriage and wave at the people. The website, however, reported that Michael I had little interest in getting his old job back.

My scroll bar had reached the bottom of the page. I slapped my computer on the side of the head. "Don't stop there you lazy son-of-a-bee!"

My screeching brought Eric back to the real world. And he wasn't happy about it. "What is your problem?"

"This damn website only lists one pretender," I said. "You'd think there'd be oodles."

"Well, Maddy, there are oodles of other websites."

"I can't spend all day playing with this thing, Eric. I have a cabbage waiting for me at home."

Eric dog-eared his comic book. "See all these underlined words in blue sprinkled throughout the text? Those are called links. When you click on a link, another site with more information on the topic comes up."

I clicked on *Michael I*. Another site appeared. "Well, look at that!"

He told me to "enjoy" and went back to his superheroes. I started scrolling and reading, and taking notes on the back of a corporate missive outlining the most recent changes in our medical coverage: Michael and his wife had four daughters. None of them were named Violeta. None of them were within twenty years of being old enough to be Violeta.

That website was a dud. But it did have a very useful link to the genealogy of the Romanian royal family. It listed every king, queen, prince, princess, count, and countess going back to the first Romanian king, Carol I. And among them was a Violeta!

My giddiness was short-lived. "Wouldn't you know it," I grumbled. "This Violeta was born in 1873. Which would make her fifty years too old to be our Violeta. And unless she was one of those vampires from Transylvania, much too dead to be our Violeta."

I took notes on her nonetheless: Her full name was Violeta Dragomir. She was the daughter of a Romanian cavalry officer of low nobility, and not from the principality of Transylvania, but Moldavia. When she was seventeen, she married Prince Anthony, the twenty-one-year-old son of King Carol I. Prince Anthony died when he was twenty-three and Princess Violeta slipped into oblivion.

I asked Eric how I could find out if Violeta was a common name in Romania. He looked at me like I was a Ph.D. candidate in English who'd forgotten how to spell cat. "Duh—Google female Romanian names."

I typed it in. Several websites agreed that Violeta was a rather common name in Romania. Next, I Googled her last name. Bell didn't sound very Romanian to me, but you never know. Again I got several websites with long lists of Romanian surnames. Bell wasn't on any of them. Neither was Bellescu, or Belleanu, or Bellici, or any other names that might be Americanized to Bell. "You do any of that research on Violeta yet?" I asked Eric, with a pretty good notion of what the answer would be.

"It's only been four days, Maddy."

"I was just wondering if she was ever married."

"Didn't Gabriella's story say?"

"Violeta told her no," I said. "But that doesn't mean anything. I tell people no sometimes, too."

I went back to the Romanian genealogy website. I scrolled up and down through the dozens of royals listed, both the living and the dead, in the hope of finding something to justify the late Sunday dinner Ike was going to get.

Then there it was. A very curious adjective. In the comments next to King Carol II. You remember him, don't you? The one who let his five-year-old son be king? So he could cavort with his mistress? Anyway, it said this: "When Carol renounced his right to be king, his recognized heir, Michael, was crowned instead." The curious adjective, of course, was the word *recognized*. Did that mean there was an *unrecognized* heir or two?

I started clicking links like a madwoman. And I found the website of a man who claimed to be the great-grandson of King Carol I, and therefore the rightful heir to the Romanian throne. "Well, would you look at this, Mr. Chen! Pretender number two!"

Eric didn't answer. And that's because he was no longer sitting next to me reading comic books. I scanned the newsroom. Some time during the last half hour or so he'd wandered off to play with the boys in the sports department. They were throwing one of those stupid Nerf footballs around. But I didn't bitch at him. A—it wouldn't do any good. B—it appeared I'd pretty much mastered the Googling arts, anyway.

The name of this second pretender was Prince Anton Alexandur Clopotar. There was a photo of him. He had a healthy thatch of white hair. A huge white mustache. He was wearing a polka dot bowtie and a double-breasted blazer with an emblem on the pocket. He was standing in front of a huge red, yellow, and blue flag. A long, straight-stemmed pipe was clenched in his teeth. I read what he had to say about himself:

He was seventy-five. Born in Bucharest. He'd fled to Canada with his parents and older brother at the end of World War II when it looked like the Soviet occupation of Romania was going to be permanent. Unlike his rival, Michael I, who had only daughters to give his country, he had three sons and seven grandsons. Best of all, he offered direct lineage to King Carol I, while Michael was only a distant nephew.

I was confused. I checked my notes. According to what I'd read earlier, Carol I had left no living heirs. That's why his nephew, Ferdinand, was given the throne. I read on:

Prince Anton's father, Dumitru Clopotar, was born in 1916. His grandfather, Constantin Clopotar, born in 1891, was the son of Prince Anthony and one Violeta Dragomir.

That's right, Princess Violeta. The cavalry officer's daughter who married Carol I's son. The young widow who slipped into oblivion. According to Prince Anton: "Perhaps we will never know whether my great-great-grandfather was aware that Princess Violeta was with child when he banished her. It is clear that he was distraught when his son and heir, Prince Anthony, was taken so unexpectedly. The royal biographies are not ambiguous on that point. Regrettably, there is also evidence in the king's diaries and letters that he did not approve of his son's betrothal to a native Moldavian of insufficient nobility."

Prince Anton went on to explain in his stuffy way that some months after giving birth to Constantin, the destitute Princess Violeta married a commoner named Gavril Clopotar, who gave the boy his name and raised him as his own. Wrote Prince Anton: "Inasmuch as my older brother, Prince Petru, is no longer living, it is clear that I am the rightful heir to the throne, should the hereditary monarchy be reinstated by the Romanian people. Let me state further, to those who may doubt my claim, that I am prepared to assist wholeheartedly in any and all scientific inquiries deemed necessary."

The prince also wrote glowingly about his sons and late wife, Agnes. About his satisfying career in the Canadian civil service. About his wonderful home and vegetable garden outside Kingston, Ontario. "Here on my beloved Wolfe Island I will await, with respect and patience, the judgment of my fellow Romanians."

Good gravy! I knew Wolfe Island. It was the largest of the famous Thousand Islands. It was on the western lip of Lake Ontario. Where the waters of the Great Lakes squeeze into the St. Lawrence River for their long trek to the Atlantic Ocean. I was born very close to there, in LaFargeville, on the New York side of the river. Oh yes, I knew Wolfe Island very well.

The attic doors in my brain swung open. Memories of my years in LaFargeville sprang out like so many mice, bats, and spiders. I herded them back inside. Kicked those attic doors shut. I focused on matters at hand.

I had two living pretenders but no evidence that the late Violeta Bell of Hannawa, Ohio, was related to either of them. Or any other member of the old royal line. And what did it matter, anyway? Romania no longer had a king or queen.

I typed in *Romania, restoration of monarchy*. The good folks at Google gave me 85,000 websites to read. I scanned through the first dozen or so. There was apparently quite a debate whether the throne should be restored or not. At least quite a debate on the Internet.

I did discover that Romania had a small royalist party. Something called the Constitutional Reform and Restoration Union. It had won thirteen seats in the most recent elections for parliament. That surprising showing was credited to public disillusionment with the country's current batch of leaders. It made me wonder how many votes Dr. Phil would get if he ran for president of the United States? Or how many Oprah would get if she ran for queen?

I clicked off my computer. I squinted at my watch. It was four o'clock. I squinted toward the sports department. Eric was gone. In metro, reporters and editors were straggling in to put out the Monday edition. I was pooped. I headed for the parking deck.

Had I found anything useful?

No, I hadn't learned if Violeta Bell was really Romanian royalty. But I had found a pair of bona fide pretenders. And I'd learned that there was a small, but apparently growing movement to restore the monarchy. Was someone in the royal family clearing the board in case the monarchy was restored some day? Had that someone somehow seen Gabriella's story on the Queens of Never Dull? Had Violeta Bell foolishly outed herself?

Or was Eddie French guilty as sin? Despite his aversion to guns? Or was somebody else guilty as sin? One of those other crazy old bags? Somebody else in the Carmichael House? Somebody else in Hannawa?

Or had I just wasted a beautiful day? A day I should have been at home making Ike those pigs in a blanket? "Dolly Madison Sprowls," I growled at myself, as my Dodge Shadow puttered down the exit ramp, "you are a damn fool—more than likely."

7

I spent the morning helping Margaret Newman scrounge through the morgue's files for old heat wave stories. Hannawa was in the midst of a doozy and Margaret, our environmental writer, wanted to find out if global warming was to blame. She hadn't written one word of her story yet, but I knew exactly what it would say. It would rehash the past. Speculate on the future. Quote a lot of experts. Come to the earth-shattering conclusion that maybe global warming was to blame, and maybe it wasn't. More than likely there would a sidebar packed with tips for surviving the current ninety-degree temperatures. Stay inside where it's cool. Drink plenty of water. Brilliant nonsense like that.

As soon as Margaret hustled back to her desk, I headed down Main Street to Ike's Coffee Shop. I walked in soaked with sweat. Ike had one little fan buzzing away on the counter and another on top of the cigarette machine. I sat at my usual table by the window. Ike brought me an iced tea—my one concession to the heat—and a tuna-stuffed bagel. After the lunch rush was over he joined me. He had a pamphlet in his hand. "I hope that isn't from your church," I said.

"From the doctor's office."

"Oh?"

"It's for you, Maddy. Not me."

"Oh?"

"I thought it might be helpful."

I snatched the pamphlet from him and read the fat, black type on the cover: IS SLEEP APNEA DANGEROUS? "For Pete's sake, Ike!"

"They've got a sleep test you can take."

I came to an instant boil. "I am not taking that test! Louise Lewendowski had one and said it was just awful. They glue wires all over your head. And everywhere else. They watch you all night like a laboratory rat."

Ike dug his fingers into the tabletop. To prevent himself from strangling me presumably. "Wouldn't it be worth it to see how serious a problem you might have?"

"I do not have a problem."

"Now Maddy, that snoring means you're not breathing right. And not breathing right could lead to a heart attack or something."

"I don't have a heart."

"Yes, you do. And so do I."

The sweet old bastard had me. I stuffed the pamphlet in my purse. "I'll read the damn thing. But I'm committing to nothing, Ike. Nothing."

He leaned over the table. Kissed me on the forehead. Right there in the front window. On Hannawa's busiest street. He retreated to his little kitchen behind the counter. Started loading dirty cups and plates into the dishwasher. Started singing that Johnny Mathis song, *Misty*: "Look at me, I'm as helpless as a kitten up a tree...."

I couldn't put up with that. I gathered up my dirty dishes and joined him. "Sorry I popped my cork."

He smiled at me in a way I sometimes wish he wouldn't. "I just want you to be around for a while."

We were getting precariously close to the L-word. I introduced a more manageable topic. "You see Dale Marabout's story this morning?"

Ike started the dishwasher. The old contraption was noisier than the Space Shuttle taking off. "You know I don't have time for the paper on weekdays," he shouted over for the banging and clanging. "I'm a working man."

I turned the dishwasher off. I wasn't about to compete with a machine. "Eddie French was arraigned today."

Ike turned it back on. "Finally have enough evidence, do they?"

"Not for the murder." I followed him out to the counter. "For the antiques they found in his apartment. They've charged him with burglary, grand theft, and receiving stolen property."

Ike took a Ghirardelli chocolate from the box by the cash register. He unwrapped it. Stuck it my mouth. "Aren't those sort of the same thing?"

The chocolate was warm and gooey. "According to Dale's story, the prosecutor's office wanted to make sure the judge set the bail too high for Eddie to get out."

Ike unwrapped a chocolate for himself. Led me back to my table. He let me have the chair that faced the fan on the cigarette machine. "I suppose the judge went along."

I nodded. "The prosecutor not only brought up Eddie's prior convictions, he also told the judge about Eddie's repeated failure to show up in traffic court."

Ike chuckled. "Has a few unpaid tickets, does he?"

"Dozens. The judge set his bail at $40,000."

"Looks like your Mr. French will be sitting tight for a while."

"Detective Grant must be convinced he's guilty," I said. "There's blood evidence coming back from the lab any day now. If that blood belongs to Violeta Bell, I don't think they'll waste a minute charging Eddie with murder."

I could see that Ike wasn't any more interested in discussing Eddie French than I was. He was staring at the empty storefronts across the street. "There's talk a Starbucks might be going in over there," he said.

"Oh pooh. There's always talk about this new business or that coming downtown."

"I've seen people over there measuring," he said. "Young, eager people with big dreams spilling out their ears."

"Your eyes are that good, are they?"

"I can compete with empty stores," he said. "But I can't compete with Starbucks."

"Of course you can," I assured him. "You'll just have to learn how to make cappuccino."

"I don't want to know how to make cappuccino."

◇◇◇

"You okay?" Gabriella asked me, as we sped around another stopped city bus.

"Just a little frazzled," I said. "It was a crazy day."

Actually I was a lot frazzled. In the first place, I don't handle the heat very well. And we were crammed into that silly yellow and black Mini Cooper her parents bought for her as a graduation gift, weaving in and out of the rush hour traffic like a pollen-drunk bumblebee. And I was worried about Ike losing his coffee shop. I wanted our lives to stay right where they were. God only knows what kind of crazy ideas he might get if he suddenly had nothing to do but make me happy.

Gabriella zipped onto Hardihood Avenue just as the yellow light turned red. We were going to visit with another member of the Never Dulls that evening, Ariel Wilburger-Gowdy. But when Gabriella pushed the intercom button at the Carmichael House, we heard a younger woman's voice. A cold, prickly voice. "Come up."

"That was certainly short and sweet," I muttered as the door clicked and we went inside.

"I think that was Ariel's daughter," Gabriella said. "I didn't meet her when I did the story but her mother told me what a horse's patoot she is."

"She said that about her own daughter?"

"Six or seven times. Those exact words."

We rode the elevator to the seventh floor. It was Ariel's daughter. She introduced herself at the door as "Professor Barbara Wilburger." She was fiftyish, middle-of-the-winter pale. Whatever color hair she was born with, it was very black now.

She apologized for her mother's absence. "She said she'd be back by now. But when mother's at the foundation—well I'm afraid the real world has to wait."

"Well, it was very gracious for your mother to invite us over," I said. "It isn't easy to talk about the murder of a close friend."

She tried to smile. "We can wait for her in the living room."

She led us down a hallway lined with Georgia O'Keeffe prints, into a room as big as my entire house. I absorbed as much of it as I could without appearing nosey. It was cluttered. A bit dusty. The furniture a bit old. Dozens of stained-glass hummingbirds were suction-cupped to the glass slider leading to the balcony.

Before inviting us to sit down, Barbara batted a trio of Persian cats off the sofa. "Sorry about the animals," she said, raking fur off the cushions with her fingers. "Mother lets them rule the roost."

Gabriella and I sat. Barbara didn't. She positioned herself behind one of the matching wingback chairs, resting her forearms on the doily, rolling the cat fur into a ball.

"You live here with your mother?" I asked.

"No way in hell," she said. Then she quacked a couple of "heh-heh-hehs" in an attempt to make a joke out of something that clearly wasn't.

I tried to remember what I could about Gabriella's story, grist for the uncomfortable small talk that was likely to last until her mother arrived. "I understand your mother has an autographed copy of Jane Goodall's new book."

"It wouldn't surprise me. She loves all those tree huggers."

I tried another topic. "Gabriella's story said you teach at the college."

"Business ethics."

"Oh my, that's got to be interesting."

"Not to my students," she said. She launched into a sour rant about how dumb and lazy today's kids are, all the time shaking that fur ball in her cupped hands like dice in a Monopoly game. "And they're so damn gullible," she screeched. "They accept anything as the truth except the truth."

"The truth is always a tough one," I said.

"I forgot I was talking to a couple of liberal arts majors," she said, adding a few more of those duck-like "heh-heh-hehs."

Her mother was right about her. She was a horse's patoot. I turned to Gabriella, hoping that she could read the Morse Code that my eyes were twitching at her: *Hurry up and say something before I throw a lamp at this insufferable woman!*

Gabriella thankfully got the message. "So professor, how well did you know Violeta Bell?"

"Well enough."

"And Eddie French?" I asked. "Were you okay with him? Driving your mother and her friends all over the place, I mean."

Her answer was equally cryptic. "With all the money those women have, you'd think they'd hire a limo."

I pretended to be on the same page. "A cab isn't very classy."

This time her response was as clear as Saran Wrap. "What kind of man drives a cab, for God's sake?"

To my delight, Gabriella proved she was born with that egging-on gene that all good reporters need. "In this case, a man with a long police record," she said.

"Exactly," the professor said. She was now grinding the fur ball between her thumb and finger like it was an effigy of Eddie French.

"And now Violeta Bell is dead," Gabriella said.

"On the other hand," I pointed out, "the police haven't been able to pin the murder on him."

Barbara checked her watch. It was a delicate watch. More than likely an antique. More than likely real gold. "I'm sorry my mother isn't here yet."

"We can wait a while longer," I said.

"I wish I could," she said. "I've got an appointment I simply cannot be late for."

Gabriella and I followed her to the door. I asked a final question. "One more thing about Eddie French—was it usual for him to come up to your mother's condo? The condos of the other women? Helping with the things they bought at garage sales? Or their luggage when they traveled?"

Barbara deposited the fur ball into the brass wastebasket under the foyer table. She eyeballed her hair and makeup in the mirror above it. "That was always my biggest worry," she said.

I poured on the empathy. "Well, thank goodness you won't have to worry anymore."

She tried her best to smile. Twisted her wrist to check her watch again.

"That's such a beautiful watch," I said.

This time her smile succeeded. But it was a strained, somewhat embarrassed smile. "It's a Rolex. A very early one."

"White gold, I suppose?"

Her smile faded. "The diamonds are real, too. If you're wondering."

"I was. I suppose it's a family heirloom."

"Just a gift from a friend," she said.

She opened the door for us. On the way out I stopped to admire the wastebasket. It was the shiniest thing I'd ever seen. Not a bit of tinge. Embossed on the side was a happy cat wearing a huge tam-o'-shanter. It was playing a bagpipe and dancing a jig. "Isn't that just darling," I said. "Is it an antique?"

Barbara rolled her eyes. "A gift from Violeta."

"Then I suppose it is—simply darling."

Gabriella and I retreated to the elevator. Gabriella pushed the button for the first floor. I cancelled her selection and pushed the B.

"The basement?" she asked.

"It's time we get to the bottom of this thing," I answered.

The elevator deposited us at the intersection of two dully lighted hallways. The cement block walls were painted a cheery peach. Every door was painted the same Bic-pen blue. One door was adorned from top to bottom with a huge yellow X made of crime-scene tape. "I'd say that's it," I said, locking my arm in Gabriella's.

"Which one of us gets to play the Cowardly Lion?" she asked as we padded down the stubbly gray carpet.

We reached our destination. Just in case I couldn't read, Gabriella read aloud the raised white letters on the door: "Fitness Center."

I squinted along the ceiling for security cameras. There weren't any. Which meant the police had no visual record of who used that door the night Violeta Bell was murdered inside.

It also meant I could try the doorknob. I took the hanky from my purse and draped it over my hand. Gabriella was horrified, reading for me the black letters on the crime tape: "Police Line Do Not Cross."

"Good gravy, girl," I growled, "I'm nervous enough without your narration."

I tried the knob. As I expected it was locked. I went to the fire extinguisher box on the opposite wall. Opened it. Picked up the key with my hanky hand and returned to the door. I slid the key into the slot on the knob and turned it until I heard the click. The door swung inward.

Gabriella was mystified. "And how did you know there was a key in there?"

I made a stuffy Sherlock Holmes face. Then I winked and explained my clairvoyance. "Remember the other day when Kay Hausenfelter asked us to bring up her mail? And said there was a skeleton key under the bullfighter? She also told me there were skeleton keys all over the place. 'With a building full of forgetful old farts there's a skeleton key someplace for everything,' she said."

I reached through the crack in the door and fumbled for the light. Clicked it on with the top of the nail on my thumb. "It's a good bet lots of people know where those keys are hidden."

I eased my head into the fitness room. It had the same peach walls as the hallways. There were no other doors. No windows. There were oodles of those shiny contraptions people would rather crucify themselves on than take a good walk. Exercise mats were scattered on the floor. The one closest to the door was splotched with blood.

According to Dale Marabout's reporting, the police figured that Violeta Bell had been murdered sometime in the early hours of July 5, more than likely between midnight and three. They based that estimate on the condition of the body when it was found later that morning when the yoga instructor unlocked the fitness room door just minutes before her nine o'clock class. Violeta's wide-open eyes were milky. Rigor mortis was reaching an advanced stage. The police had no way of knowing whether her assailant had forced her into the fitness room at gunpoint, or whether she had been ambushed there. There was also the possibility that Violeta had willingly accompanied her assailant, unaware that her final minutes were ticking down.

The police did know how Violeta Bell died. The assailant had forced her to take off her bathrobe. That bathrobe was then wrapped around the gun in the assailant's hand, to muffle the three pops that were coming. "We're pretty certain this was a planned killing," a police source told Dale Marabout. "If anyone in the building did hear the gunshots, they would figure it was just somebody shooting off the last of his Fourth of July firecrackers."

I turned off the fitness room light. Closed the door and made sure it was locked. Put the key back in the fire extinguisher box. We took the stairs up to the lobby instead of the elevator, to lower the risk of being seen. I pushed open the stairway door a couple of inches and peeked out. The lobby was empty. We hurried out the front door, into the gooey evening heat. We reached the visitors' parking lot just as a small black convertible popped out of the underground garage. It was Barbara Wilburger. We waved as she sped by. She lifted her fingers off the steering wheel and wiggled them.

Gabriella squawked with surprise. "Beemer Z4?"

"Interpretation please."

"That's pretty sporty for an anal retentive professor, isn't it?"

I thought about it. The car did seem like a strange fit for the woman we'd just met. I also thought about Bob Averill's yellow Mercedes. About Ike's modest Chevrolet and my old Dodge Shadow. About that clown car of Gabriella's that I was trying to pretzel myself into. "Our cars do give us away," I said.

We retreated down Hardihood. The rush hour was over. The landscaping crews had finished their work. I would have been content to think about which South Beach dinner in my freezer I was going to microwave for my supper. But Gabriella had other ideas. "We learn anything worthwhile today?" she asked.

"Good gravy—" I started to scold her but the drive-in movie screen in my cerebral cortex had already switched from cashew chicken with sugar snap peas to that sour-pussed woman rolling that cat fur into an ever-tighter ball. "Well, it was pretty clear our Miss Wilburger didn't much care for Violeta Bell."

Gabriella laughed. "Or Eddie French," Gabriella pointed out. "Or her students. Or her mother. Or us."

I laughed, too. "You're saying she may not be the most reliable judge of character?"

We reached West Apple. Puttered through the yellow arrow and headed toward downtown. "She obviously knows them a lot better than I do," Gabriella said. "I only spent a few hours with them doing my story. But I liked Eddie French. And I thought her mother was terrific."

"You did say you had an uneasy feeling about Violeta," I reminded her.

"Yeah—but I liked her."

I suppressed a yawn. "If I've learned anything the past two years, it's that likeable people murder other likeable people all the time."

"You're a regular Confucius."

"A confused Confucius," I said.

We stopped behind an unloading bus. A lot of dog-tired people got off. "So we learned bupkiss?"

"Unfortunately we learned plenty," I assured her. "We learned that Eddie French was very familiar with the building. And we learned that anybody familiar with the building could have easily slipped into the fitness room to ambush Violeta Bell."

"So maybe Eddie French is guilty after all?"

"Maybe he is."

Gabriella dropped me off in front of *The Herald-Union* and headed off to have dinner with friends. I went upstairs. Not to catch up on my work. To see if Eric had any more research on the Queens of Never Dull for me. He'd already found all he could on Kay Hausenfelter, Ariel Wilburger-Gowdy, and Gloria McPhee, but he still owed me big, fat folders full of interesting stuff on Eddie French and his sister, and of course Violeta Bell.

Eric wasn't at his desk. But Dale Marabout was at his. He was typing furiously with his two index fingers. Which meant he was writing an important story. When Dale has a routine cops story, he types with all ten fingers. But when it's a big story on deadline that requires every bit of gristle in his body and soul to get out fast, it's just those two fingers.

Dale Marabout is more than a good reporter. He is also my good friend. And if you don't know already, he and I once had a relationship that went well beyond having lunch. I was a skittish divorcée in my forties at the time. He was just-out-of-college, plump and frumpy, and woefully untrained in the manly arts. We fulfilled each other's modest expectations for several years. Then a young kindergarten teacher named Sharon moved into his apartment building and I was the odd woman out. But, like I said, we remain friends.

I waited at my desk until Dale clicked off his computer and headed for the elevator. Then I called up his story on my computer. Oh my:

```
Hannawa—Cab driver Edward French, whom
police had characterized as a "person of
interest" in their investigation into the
July 5 murder of retired antique dealer Vio-
leta Bell, has been released on bail.
    The 61-year-old French was arraigned
Tuesday on several charges relating to the
burglary of Bell's west side condominium.
    Court records show that bail was posted
late yesterday by local philanthropist Ariel
Wilburger-Gowdy.
```

That night, after I'd had my dinner, washed my dishes, watched *Antiques Roadshow*, and taken James out for his after-dark pee, I got up the nerve to read that pamphlet Ike gave me. He was right. Sleep apnea was dangerous. The pamphlet said people with it stop breathing hundreds of times during the night, up to thirty seconds at a time. It increases the risk of having a heart attack or a stroke, or a car accident the next day because you're so damn tired you fell asleep at the wheel. Even if it doesn't kill you, it can make you irritable, forgetful, even disinterested in sex. "No wonder Ike gave me this damn thing," I grumbled to James.

8

I never thought I'd hear the words come out of my mouth. "Eric," I said, "you'll have to mark up the paper this morning—I've got stuff to do."

And I did have stuff to do. Important stuff I didn't want to do but had to do.

The first thing I did was call Suzie and tell her I'd be taking the first week of August off. "You, a vacation?" she squeaked in disbelief. "For a whole week?"

"Don't worry," I snarled back. "I won't be having a very good time."

The next thing I did was hike down the sidewalk through the heat and haze to Ike's. I could see him inside filling a Styrofoam cup with coffee for his only customer. I opened the door just wide enough to stick my head inside and yell, "I'll take the damn sleep test!"

Then I huffed and puffed up Hill Street to police headquarters. I'd passed the monstrous building a million times but I'd never been inside. I sweated my way up the three tiers of steps, skirted the bronze statue of Roscoe Blough, Hannawa's legendary Roaring Twenties police chief, and pushed my way through one of the revolving doors. The lobby was cold enough to make ice cubes. Some people were actually wearing sweaters. I obediently put my purse on the conveyor belt and stepped through the

metal detector. I clopped across the marble tiles to the information desk. The crisply uniformed woman manning the desk was
blowing warm air into her hands. "Where can I find Detective
Grant?" I asked her.

She was clearly one of those people who didn't like their jobs.
"I suppose you don't have an appointment."

"Actually I don't."

"Name?"

"Maddy Sprowls."

It was as if that statue of Roscoe Blough had clanked in and
asked her for directions to the men's room. "Good Lord!" she
howled.

Her surprise didn't surprise me. In the past two years I'd inter-
fered in two major murder investigations. And made the police
look like a pack of doofuses both times. "I'm sure Detective
Grant will want to see me."

She pushed his extension button with more foreboding than if
she were launching a nuclear-tipped missile to start World War III.
"Maddy Sprowls is here for you, detective," she whispered. Then
she laughed. "No, she doesn't have a bomb—that I can see."

So I was told where to go. I took the elevator to the fourth
floor. It was just as cold up there as the lobby. An officer pointed
me toward Detective Grant's cubicle.

When Grant saw me coming, he stood up behind his desk
and put his fists on his hips Superman-style. He did not, however, suck in his belly, the way most middle-aged men do when
anybody remotely female appears. He loudly recited a Bible
verse: "Revelations 13:1: 'I saw a beast coming up out of the
sea, having ten horns and seven heads.'"

I like Scotty Grant. He's comfortable in his own skin. Which
is a good thing. He has plenty of it. What he doesn't have is a lot
of hair. Except for his eyebrows. They frame his puffy eyes like
the McDonald's arches. I plunked myself in the chair alongside
his desk. "Any way you could have the air conditioning turned
up?" I asked. "I can still feel one of my big toes."

He sat and took a noisy slurp from his mug. It had a picture of Daffy Duck on it. "I'm sure we don't have any of the crappy tea you drink, but I can get you an equally crappy cup of coffee."

I nodded gratefully. "One, real sugar."

He lumbered out, returning in a couple of minutes with a mug with Cinderella on the side. "We didn't have any real sugar—sorry."

"I trust you left it black," I said, taking a cautious sip. He had left it black. I thanked him with a smile and got down to business. "I need some information on Eddie French."

There was no more surprise on his face than if I'd told him that water was wet. "He a friend of yours?"

I wanted to make it sound like I was there in my official capacity as newspaper librarian. "I've been asked to do some research on him."

That made Grant grin. "For a second there I thought you were just sticking your shnozola into another police investigation. For no other reason than to make my life more miserable than it already is." He leaned back in his chair until both of his chins were resting on his chest. He pulled open his bottom desk drawer with his foot. Reached in and retrieved a folder. EDDIE FRENCH was scribbled on the tab. "Bob Averill told me he was going to twist your arm."

"Did he now?"

"We've become good friends because of you."

Grant loved to play gotcha with me. Even though he almost always lost. I looked the masochistic bastard straight in the eyes. "Then I guess he also told you about Eddie's aversion to guns."

"Indeed he did," said Grant. "So did Eddie's sister. And I personally tested him. Played with my service revolver in front of him during our interrogation. Sure enough, he started hyperventilating like a sonofabitch."

"You believe it?"

He opened the folder. Shuffled through the stack of official forms and scraps of paper covered with notes. "It looked real enough. Then again, my wife is deathly afraid of airplanes yet every April flies to Phoenix to visit her folks."

"So, Eddie could have overcome his fears long enough to murder Violeta Bell?"

"Yup."

"Or maybe he's not quite as allergic to guns as his sister thinks?"

"Yup. Yup."

"Or his sister is knowingly telling an untruth?"

"Yup. Yup. Yup."

I went for a fourth "Yup" while he was still so agreeable. "But it really doesn't matter since you don't have enough evidence to charge him with the murder anyway?"

He toasted me with his Daffy Duck mug. Then he set me straight. "When we had enough to charge him with burglary, etcetera, we charged him with burglary, etcetera. When we get enough to charge him with murder, we'll charge him with murder."

I toasted him with Cinderella. Then went straight for his jugular. "Unless I'm wrong, you've got no witnesses and no murder weapon. You've got no fingerprints or other proof of Eddie French ever being in the fitness room." The sour look on his face told me that either he'd just swallowed a bug, or I was right on the money.

I assumed it was the latter and went on. "Now, you do have evidence of him being in Violeta's condo. Then again, I'm sure you've got evidence of him being in the other ladies' condos, too. He drove them around for years. As for the antiques you found in his apartment—well, I don't know exactly what you found—but they could have been gifts, just like he said."

Grant handed me a sheet of paper from his folder. It listed the antiques they found in Eddie's apartment:

Victorian oak shaving stand	Stickley rocking chair
Louis XV Pompadour vanity	1926 leather club chairs (2)
1830s Biedermeier mirror	Cast iron Godin stove
Granite Art Deco fireplace	Art Nouveau fireplace
1850s rosewood cheval mirror	Grueby vases (4)

The list surprised me. "Fireplace mantles? Cast iron stoves? I was expecting watch fobs and pocketknives. Maybe a silver spittoon or two."

Grant grinned victoriously. "Not exactly gift material, is it."

"No, it isn't," I admitted. "And not exactly easy to steal from a seventh floor condominium without being seen."

"Not easy but not impossible," Grant countered. "The murder occurred at night and he would have had all night."

I recapped his hypothesis to make sure we were on the same page. "So you're saying he forced her to go with him to the basement fitness room—or otherwise finagled her into going—shot her dead and then went back up to her condo and took his good old time taking what he wanted."

"Yup."

I read the list again, picturing the wiry little cab driver frog-walking a two-hundred-pound marble mantle down the hallway. "And you're sure all of these things belonged to Violeta Bell?"

He snatched the list from me. "We didn't find an inventory list in her condo or anything, the kind people keep for insurance purposes," he said. "In fact we found no proof of her even having any homeowner's insurance. But all the items we found in Mr. French's rat hole do have her little sticker on the bottom somewhere." He fished another sheet of paper from the folder and held it up for me to read. It was an inky, out-of-focus blow-up from a copying machine badly in need of a service call:

Bellflower Antiques
119 West Apple St., Hannawa, Ohio USA
Violeta Bell, Proprietor

"This is your proof?" I huffed.

"Well—yes."

"No eyewitnesses? No jimmied locks?"

"Well—no."

"So they could have been gifts?"

Grant rallied. "And I might be invited to join the Olympic bobsled team."

I smiled. As disagreeably as I could. "According to the reporter who did the Queens of Never Dull story—Gabriella Nash—Violeta Bell's condo was stuffed to the ceiling with expensive antiques."

"That it was."

"And still is?"

He knew what I was getting at. "So why did Eddie take heavy fireplaces and furniture? When he could have stuffed his pockets with jewelry and other more wieldy thingamabobs?"

"It does seem strange," I said.

"It does. Until you have the stuff appraised. Find the right buyers and you've got a good fifty thou in cash." He enjoyed a long sip of his coffee. "And who knows what he might have fenced before we arrested him."

"Anything with Violeta's sticker show up yet?"

He shook his head no. "But we've got our eyes peeled."

The self-satisfied bastard had made some good points. Now it was my turn. "Speaking of things showing up—those blood results back yet?"

"Any century now."

"Funny about that blood, isn't it?" I said. "Eddie tracked it back to his apartment but not back to Violeta's condo."

"Ever think that maybe he took off his shoes?"

He had me again. I hadn't thought about that. "So he knew he had blood on his shoes and lugged all that stuff out of Violeta's condo in his stocking feet?"

"That's one theory."

"You find any matching stocking threads?"

I was suddenly Phyllis Diller. He laughed like a hyena on helium. "You, Mrs. Sprowls, have been watching way too much CSI!"

"How about his cab?" I growled. "Find any blood in there?"

"Do you really think all that stuff on the list would fit in a taxi cab?"

"I suppose not."

He answered my next two questions before I could ask them. "Yes, he has a truck. No, we didn't find any blood in it."

I didn't know beans about blood, of course, but I gave it my best shot. "Wouldn't the blood on his shoe have dried by the time he got back to his apartment?" I asked. "It would have been several hours later."

He was suddenly agitated. Uncharacteristically curt. "When the blood comes back we'll see what gives—okay?"

I let him have his victory. What choice did I have? "While we're on the subject of Violeta Bell's blood," I said, "anything to her claim that she's Romanian royalty?"

Grant's agitation vanished. He giggled like a kid who'd just won a year's supply of Chicken McNuggets. He fished another photocopy from his folder. Shook it at me. "I don't know about royalty," he said, "but her passport here lists her country of birth as Romania."

"No kidding?"

"Maybe yes, maybe no. The passport is a phony."

"No kidding?"

He shook other photocopies at me. "And so is her Ohio driver's license and Social Security card. Even her AARP card is a fake."

"Oh my." I took the copies from him. Sorted through them. "I don't see a birth certificate."

"There's no record of one," he said. "Nor could we find her naturalization papers, assuming she had any."

I sank into my chair. "Let me guess, no last will and testament."

"You wouldn't think so, would you?" he said, producing one from his folder. "But—"

I took it from him. "Is it real?"

"Yup. Prepared by J. Albert Ritchey himself."

Al Ritchey was one of Hannawa's most prominent attorneys. A million years ago he'd handled my divorce from Lawrence Sprowls. I gave the will a quick read. "She left everything to the Hannawa Art Museum?"

There was that giggle again. "Which, not counting her condo or the things in it, comes to a whopping thirty-five hundred bucks."

"That's it?"

"That's it. No insurance policies. No stocks or annuities. No CDs or savings accounts. Just a checking account dwindling toward zero."

"Dwindling? So she used to have more?"

Grant showed me a stack of printouts from the First Sovereignty Bank. It showed very few deposits but oodles of cash withdrawals. Over the past eight years she'd gone through $385,000. "Any tax records?" I asked.

"That's the fun part," he said. "She loyally paid her city taxes, but she never paid a penny in state or federal taxes. No sales taxes. No income taxes."

I went back to her will. In it she requested that her remains be cremated. She named one of her fellow Queens of Never Dull as her executor. "Why do you think she chose Gloria McPhee?" I asked.

Grant shrugged like the Italian he wasn't. "They were friends."

I scowled like the librarian I was. "Of course you're aware that Mrs. McPhee is on the art museum board of trustees."

He pretended to be surprised. "No kidding? We'll have to look into that!"

I was trying to see what else he might have in that folder. "Are those photographs of the murder scene?"

"Believe me, Maddy. You don't want to see these."

I impatiently wriggled my fingers at him.

He handed me the photos.

There were ten of them in all. They all showed Violeta sprawled out dead on the exercise mat. They were taken from different angles and different distances. I tried to be hard-boiled, the way cops on TV always are. "Tiny bullet holes," I said.

"Homicide-wise, a .22 isn't a very reliable weapon," Grant said. "Sort of a BB-gun on steroids. The assailant apparently understood that. Three quick shots at point-blank range right in the heart there. And only three."

I knew where he was going. "And the killer wrapped the gun with Violeta's bathrobe to muffle the sound."

"That's right," said Grant. "Small caliber gun. Middle of the night. Basement. Big, fluffy bathrobe wrapped around and around just to make sure. The assailant was very careful that nobody saw anything or heard anything."

"And nobody did?"

"Just the asswipe pulling the trigger."

I continued studying the photos. Violeta was flat on her back. Her arms and legs were spread-eagle, sort of, suggesting she just fell back dead without struggling or suffering. "You think she went pretty quick?"

"Died instantly, as they say."

Dale had correctly reported that Violeta was wearing only her underwear when her body was found. He had not, however, reported that it was a fancy red bra and matching panties. "She wasn't—"

Grant answered brusquely, "There's no evidence of this crime being sexual in any way."

"Well, that's something at least," I heard myself say. I handed the photographs back to him. I moved on to another subject. "So, what did you think when Ariel Wilburger-Gowdy bailed Eddie out? You couldn't have been overjoyed."

"Bad guys getting out on bail stopped bothering me long ago," he said. He put the folder back in his desk drawer. Closed the drawer with his foot. "Anything else the Hannawa Police Department can do for you today, Mrs. Sprowls?"

I was not disappointed that our chat was over. Between the black coffee and the damn air conditioning, I was fighting a losing battle with my bladder. I put the Cinderella mug on the corner of his desk. "I'm sure it has nothing to do with nothing, but are you looking into that queen of Romania nonsense?"

Grant knew me too well. "Which means you are."

"Not exactly looking," I said. "But it is interesting, isn't it? A few days after she publicly claims to be the queen she's dead."

It was clear from Grant's patronizing smirk that the Hannawa Police Department was not giving much credence to her claim. "I think this case has a lot more to do with good old, garden variety American greed than European history," he said. "But if you learn something interesting—"

"You'll be the first to know." I stood up to leave. He remained in his chair, swiveling back and forth. "It was good seeing you, Maddy."

"It was good seeing you." I was telling the truth and I think he was, too.

Grant stood up now. He stretched his arms until his shirt-tail popped out. He walked me to the elevator. "You're going to behave this time?"

"I always behave," I said. "Sometimes badly, but I behave."

"I don't want you getting yourself into trouble."

I knew he was getting at something. "And how might I do that?"

He pushed the down button for me. "Oh, I don't know—illegally entering a crime scene maybe."

"That's illegal now, is it?"

He smiled like a mischievous elf. "Don't let this go to your noodle, Maddy, but we didn't know about those skeleton keys."

I rode the elevator to the main floor. Used the ladies' room. Successfully spun myself through the revolving doors into a blast of hot wind. It felt as if The Almighty, for some reason, had decided to punish our sinful city with a giant hair dryer. I slipped past Roscoe Blough. Headed back to the paper.

Detective Grant is one of my favorite human beings. But between you and me, I'm always relieved when our jousts are over. He's just too good a match. He's just as willful as I am. Just as unpredictable. Just as exasperating. And that morning I knew he'd bested me in all three. He not only knew I was sticking my *shnozola* in another murder, as he put it, he didn't much care that I planned to stick it in even farther. Which meant he wanted me to stick it in farther. Which meant he had his own doubts about Eddie French's guilt. Good gravy! He didn't even care that I'd stuck my head inside the fitness room at the Carmichael House. Which meant he'd hidden a video camera somewhere. No doubt to catch the murderer returning to the scene of the crime. To retrieve or erase some little piece of evidence, maybe. He even volunteered that his department didn't know about the skeleton key in the fire extinguisher box. His way of admitting that he needed me, you think? And how about all that stuff he told me about Violeta Bell? No birth certificate. Fake Social Security number. All that. It sure confirmed Gabriella's suspicions. Not to mention mine.

I reached the paper. Pushed my face against the red-hot glass door so Al Tosi, our rickety security guard, could see me. He buzzed me in. Called after me as I drooped past him toward the elevator. "Scorcher today, no?"

9

I spent the afternoon redoing Eric's mark-up of Thursday's paper, making sure he heard my cussing. Actually, he hadn't done a bad job at all, but Morgue Mama does have a reputation to protect, doesn't she? Anyway, just when I was gathering up my stuff to get the hell out of there, Bob Averill appeared in front of my desk eating a Snickers bar. The wrapper was pulled back like a banana skin. "Everything hunky-dory, Maddy?"

"As hunky-dory as it was yesterday, Bob." It was the umpteenth time he'd pestered me about my progress that week. He always did so without mentioning Eddie French, or Violeta Bell, or anything else relating to the case. I suppose he figured just flapping around me like a bat was intimidation enough.

He tried again. "Doing anything interesting this weekend?"

"Hopefully not," I said. I headed for the stairs.

He fell in alongside me. He'd finished the candy bar. Now he was licking the chocolate off the wrapper. "Suzie told me you signed up for a week's vacation."

He was about ready to implode with frustration and I was loving it. "Actually, I'm thinking of changing it to two weeks."

"Two weeks?"

"I've got five coming."

The great man crumbled. He put his hand on my shoulder to stop me. He dug his chin onto his chest. "Maddy, please," he whimpered, "Jeannie Salapardi has been calling every night."

I patted his hand. Removed it from my shoulder. "That must be terribly annoying," I said. "Have a great weekend, Bob."

I fled into the stairwell. Hurried down to the parking deck. I got into my car and got the hell out of there. I didn't even take time to turn on the air conditioning.

My intention that afternoon was to go straight home to James, Alex Trebek, and the last fillet of that tilapia Ike had brought me in lieu of flowers or candy. Instead, I caught myself taking a left turn onto Hawthorne Avenue.

Hawthorne is very typical of the streets surrounding Meriwether Square. It's paved with bumpy bricks. It's lined with big oaks. There's not a house on it built later than 1925. I pulled to the curb just shy of the dilapidated monstrosity that Eddie French called home. My intention was simply to see where he lived and how he lived. Before I found the courage to actually knock on his door on some future date. It's a tactic I often employ. Years ago when I was pursuing the assistant librarian's job at *The Herald-Union,* I circled the building like a buzzard for two hours before going inside to apply.

According to the research Eric gave me, the house was divided into four apartments. Two down and two up. Eddie had rented 2A for the past nine years. Dale's story said the police found traces of blood on his porch. That meant Eddie's apartment was atop an outside stairway. Unfortunately, I could see no such stairway from my car. No doubt it was at the back of the house. I got out of my car and crept up the driveway. I'd never heard such noisy gravel in my life.

I reached the back of the house. I snuggled against the siding and peeked around the corner. Most of the backyard had been turned into parking spaces for the tenants. Eddie's cab was parked there. So was a rusty Hausenfelter bread truck. So was a shiny silver Volvo. It's not unusual to see Volvos in Meriwether

Square—there are oodles of them in fact—but it was a bit surprising to see one less than twenty years old.

"You need help?"

It was not exactly the voice of God. But it was a voice from above. From the small deck atop the wooden stairs that zigzagged up the side of the house. It belonged to Eddie French. I recognized his gray whiskers and his rumpled Woolybears ballcap. He was sitting sideways on the railing, flicking cigarette ashes into a coffee cup. I had no choice but to turn my scouting mission into a full-fledged visit. "Mr. French?"

His voice was sleepy. Nasal. "In the flesh, madam."

Gabriella in her ignorance had said he talked like an old hippie. Actually, it was more of a fifties' hipster voice, sculptured more by black coffee and nicotine than funny mushrooms and Pepsi-Cola. "I hope you don't mind me dropping by," I said, before realizing I hadn't introduced myself yet. "I'm Maddy Sprowls, by the way."

He'd heard of me. "Oh yes—the buttinsky responsible for my current conundrum."

I advanced to the bottom of the stairway. "I am somewhat responsible," I admitted.

He flicked a caterpillar of ashes into his cup. "And I am resoundedly irresponsible," he said.

It took me a few seconds to translate his particular brand of English. Even then I wasn't 100 percent sure of what he meant. I eased myself onto the first step. "For Violeta Bell's murder, you mean?"

"Is there somebody else I didn't kill?"

Had I actually planned on confronting Eddie that afternoon, I would have been prepared for his hostility. But I hadn't, and I wasn't. I found myself stammering like a little girl who'd just been caught drawing on the wall with her mother's bright red lipstick. I moved up another step. "No, no. Of course not, no. And there are people who don't think you killed Ms. Bell, either."

He flipped his spent cigarette in my direction. "Including the diminutive apparition sneaking up my backstairs?"

Before I could answer, the screen door to his apartment banged open. A woman came out. She was fiftyish. Impeccably and expensively dressed in white slacks, a melon crepe tee and designer flip-flops. She, too, was wearing a baseball cap, a bright pink one. A perky blond ponytail stuck out the back. She just had to be the owner of the silver Volvo. "Are you Jeannie?" I asked.

She pressed her palms on the railing and leaned out. Even from down there I could see her jaw muscles tighten. "I'm Mrs. Salapardi," she said. "Can I help you?"

Eddie filled her in before I could open my mouth. "That, sis, is Bob Averill's ace in the hole."

That changed everything. Suddenly Jeannie was smiling like Glinda the Good Witch, beckoning me to come up with both hands. "Maddy, I've been dying to meet you." She said when I reached the top. "Just dying."

"Bob told you about me, did he?"

Eddie remained perched on the railing. Jeannie warmly shook my hand with both of hers. "He sure did," she cooed.

I could tell by the twitches at the tips of her phony baloney smile that he hadn't mentioned how frumpily unimpressive I was. The only way to counter her correct impression of me—and hide the fact that after two weeks of snooping I hadn't learned a damn thing that would prove her brother's innocence—was to get right to business. "So Mr. French, is that old bread truck down there the vehicle you allegedly used to haul those antiques from Violeta Bell's condominium?"

Eddie splayed his hand across his heart. He pushed an opened pack of Newports to the top of his shirt pocket. He bowed his head low and pulled out a cigarette with his lips. A very cool move. "So say the gendarmes."

"You do own it, then?"

He struck a stick match on his fingernail and lit his cigarette. Filled his lungs with smoke. Suppressed a cough. "No one owns it that I know. It sort of belongs to the neighborhood. Anybody needs a short haul, there it is. Keys in the ashtray. Hopefully enough liquefied brontosaurus in the tank to get you there and back."

Knowing Meriwether Square as I did, I knew he could very well be telling the truth. "What about the license plates?"

Smoke rolled out of his nostrils. "That is the metaphysical part of the mystery. New stickers appear every April like tulips through the cold, cold earth."

I knew he could be telling the truth about that, too. "Exactly where did the police find that blood?"

Eddie pointed to a faint chalk circle on the floor of the deck, about a foot from the welcome mat. I kneeled next to it. Inside the circle was a dark brown blotch. When I got my nose close enough, I could see the faint zigzag of tennis shoe treads. I looked over at Eddie's feet. He was wearing a spotless pair of white Nikes.

Eddie clicked his toes together. "Brand f-ing new they are," he said, in an exaggerated British accent. "The bobbies in their 'aste confiscated all me bloody footwear, they did."

"And was there actually blood on one of your shoes?" I asked.

"I'm sure you can find all kinds of stuff on anybody's shoes," Eddie said. "Life being the untidy juggernaut it is."

"So, there was blood?"

"So sayeth the men in blue," said Eddie. "But I sternly cautioned them not to jump to conclusions. That if indeed it proved to be blood, then there was a high probability that said blood did not dribble from the veins or arteries of a bipedal primate."

I was pretty sure I was following him. "Not human?"

"Eddie's got a cat," Jeannie explained.

He corrected her. "It ain't my cat. Sort of a neighborhood cat. I put out a can of tuna every once in a while. And the grateful beast rewards me with a variety of headless beasts. Rats. Mice. Moles. Rabbits. Right here at my door."

I studied the stain again. "That's animal blood, then?"

"I'd be surprised otherwise," Eddie said.

"Why don't we go inside and talk," Jeannie said.

The living room in Eddie's apartment was exactly what you'd expect. Hot. Stuffy. Darkened by cheap, half-pulled shades. There was a plaid sofa decorated with an Indian blanket. A rocking chair stacked with newspapers. A bookcase crammed full of paperbacks. A sisal rug long overdue for the city's landfill.

Jeannie offered me the rocker. Eddie dutifully removed the newspapers. They sat on the sofa. He with his cigarette and coffee cup. She with her twitching smile. "Bob seems pretty confident you can find the murderer," Jeannie said.

"For all I know the murderer is sitting across from me, polluting my lungs with second-hand smoke," I said, rocking back and forth.

Jeannie was stunned. Her voice jumped two octaves. "I thought you were on board with Eddie's innocence?"

Eddie was merely amused. The result, I suppose, of being interrogated by the police a time or two. "Chill, darlin'," he said, patting his sister's knee. "She's good-cop-bad-copping me, that's all. Playing both parts with aplomb."

With no idea what I should say, or should not say, I blundered straight ahead. "Everybody knows about your gun phobia," I said. "So there's no need to get into that. And it's pretty clear your alibi for the night of the murder isn't worth a hill of beans. Otherwise you wouldn't have been arrested."

Jeannie immediately protested. "He was only arrested for the antiques."

"Antiques from the condo of a dead woman," I barked. "Your brother has got to take this thing seriously. We may be only a few days from a murder charge here."

The guilt of blowing smoke in my face finally got to Eddie, apparently. He smashed his cigarette into the cup. He told me what presumably he'd told the police. "Those antiques were gifts. She gave them to me approximately two weeks before her unfortunate demise. Perhaps the reason no one saw me load them into that truck I don't own is because it was late at night. The reason it was late at night is because the economic realities of my hardscrabble, law-abiding life force me to work from early morning to long after more affluent people are asleep. Hannawa ain't exactly New York cab-driving-wise." He sniffed the smoke wafting from his coffee cup. "The long and short of it is that I did not kill the lady and I did not steal her precious shit."

I told him that I'd seen the police department's list of the antiques they found in his apartment. "Why would she give you all those expensive things?"

"She knew how excruciatingly dire my financial situation was."

"So she knew you'd sell them."

"I imagine so."

I studied his body language. I couldn't tell if he was lying or having a nicotine fit. "Given your police record, it's easy to believe that you might know how to sell those fireplaces and things if they were stolen," I said. "But would you know who to sell them to if they weren't?"

Jeannie did not like the question. "I'm sure my brother knows how to use the Yellow Pages."

I apologized with an empathetic smile. Asked the big question. "So Eddie—if Violeta Bell knew you needed money, why didn't she just give you money?"

Eddie scratched his hairy chin. "A proposition I have pondered myself. Endlessly without a suitable revelation."

"Violeta Bell was a very successful antique dealer for many years," I said. "How much money would you say she had?"

"I wouldn't have the foggiest," Eddie said.

"Would you be surprised if I said a million?"

"A million ain't much in this hyper-inflationary time," he said. "So, yes, I guess I would be surprised if there was only a one at the left end of those six zeros, and not a number with more curves and curls."

My brain, thankfully, had adjusted to his convoluted hipster talk. I knew what he meant and went straight to the next question. "Would you be surprised if I told you she was almost broke?"

Eddie's eyes bugged. "Hell's bells! You shitting me?"

Jeannie's reaction was less expressive. "That would explain the antiques instead of money, wouldn't it?"

"Actually," I said, "it makes me wonder why she would give your brother so many of her valuable antiques if those were the only assets she had?"

Neither Eddie nor his sister had an answer to that. At least one they wanted to share with me. While they sat like bumps on a log, I laid out the theory bubbling in my brain. "Violeta Bell was a mystery woman. In fact, the Violeta Bell people knew really didn't exist. She created herself. For reasons that died with her. Apparently." I told them about her fake driver's license and passport and all her other fake or nonexistent papers. "She not only lived outside the law," I said, "she was a big believer in cash." I told them some of the things Eric Chen had found out about her. "She didn't own the building where she had her antique shop. She lived in a swanky apartment in Greenlawn. When she closed her shop, she bought her unit at the Carmichael House for cash. That still left her with a lot of money in the bank. Now that's all but gone."

If Eddie or his sister knew any of this, they weren't letting on. Eddie was gently drumming his fingernails on his smoldering cup. Clickety-click-click. Jeannie was studying her pedicure. I continued. "So for the last eight years, she had no money coming in and a lot going out. She also had a condo filled with valuable antiques. So unless she had a big Rubbermaid tub of cash hidden under her bed—and there's no evidence she did—she'd be forced to sell some of those antiques from time to time. For cash. She was not one to share her good fortune with the government. Which means she'd have to find an equally stingy buyer. Or an unsuspecting one."

Jeannie's eyes shifted, from her pretty toes to Eddie's anything but pretty face.

"Violeta's condo was big," I said. "But it wasn't the Smithsonian. She'd have to replenish her supply. I'm sure she found a few treasures at those garage sales. The tag sales. The estate auctions—"

"She was always buying stuff," Eddie offered. "More than the other three ladies put together. Tons of shit."

I went on. "But would that be enough? The other Queens of Never Dull lived pretty high on the hog? I've got to wonder if she didn't have another source or two."

"None that I know of," Eddie assured me.

I was coming to the heart of my theory. "We know that Violeta didn't own a car. Let alone a delivery truck. If she were still dealing in antiques, she'd have to have some help. Somebody to deliver things and maybe pick things up. Somebody she could trust."

Eddie started waving his cup like a white flag. "Mea culpa! Nolo contendere! Hang me high by my huevos grandes! Yes! Yes! I delivered a thing or two for the old bird—in that beautiful old bread box out there!"

Jeannie's twitching lips told me she wasn't happy hearing that. She defended her brother nonetheless. "Nothing illegal about driving a truck."

"Heaven's to Betsy, no," I said. "Not if Violeta truly owned the things she was selling."

"Or if the driver was oblivious to the pre-supposed illegality of the endeavor," Eddie added.

I pretended to absolve him. "Just a working man earning a little unreported cash on the side?"

"Nothing more convoluted than that," said Eddie.

Now I started closing the trap. "Where exactly did you deliver things for her?"

Not surprisingly, Eddie was suddenly opaque. "That, most unfortunately, is impossible for a professional driver like myself to reiterate. I've driven to so many places, I don't know exactly where I've been or haven't."

I rocked back and forth, drumming on the armrests, letting Eddie stew. Then I let him have it. "You know what I think Eddie? I think you and Violeta were in business together. Buying and selling stolen antiques. Those things the police found up here weren't gifts. They were a shipment for you to deliver. Maybe to a dealer in some other city or state who didn't know they were hot. Or didn't give a damn. You couldn't tell police that, of course. You'd go back to prison."

Jeannie's laugh was dripping with disbelief. Not to mention contempt. "And so he's risking a murder charge to hide his other crimes?"

I smiled at her like a senile aunt. Turned toward Eddie. He was slowly sinking into the sofa cushions. "That is what you're doing—isn't it Eddie? Betting the police won't find enough evidence to charge you with Violeta Bell's murder?"

That was the last straw for Jeannie. She jumped up and wrapped her arms around her waist like the sleeves on a straight-jacket. She started shouting at me. "My brother did not kill anybody! Bob said you believed that!"

Nobody shouts at Maddy Sprowls. Not without getting double the decibels in return. "Your brother is going to be twiddling his thumbs on death row if he doesn't start telling a more forthcoming version of the truth—that's all I'm saying!"

Jeannie stormed to the door. Threw it open for me. "I've never heard anybody talk so much bullshit in my life!"

I slowly rocked back and forth, staring into Eddie's gray eyes until they started to quiver. "Is your sister right, Mr. French? Am I talking bullshit?"

Jeannie suggested it would be better if I left. I agreed. I clomped down the steps as mad as a hornet. Not caring one whit if Eddie was innocent or guilty. If he spent the rest of his life in prison or Paris, France. When I reached the ground I headed straight for that bread truck. I was sure they were watching me. I didn't care one whit about that either. First I wrote down the license plate number for Eric Chen to check out. Then I checked the driver's side door to see if it was locked. It wasn't. I got in. I checked the ashtray for the key. It was there. I put it in the ignition and started the engine. I watched the gas gauge rise. The tank was almost half full. I checked the odometer. There was a string of zeros. When I looked closer I could see that a tiny smiley face had been painted inside each little white aught. Next I looked for that metal strip under the windshield that has the vehicle identification number. It was gone. I crawled out of the truck, got in my Shadow, and drove the hell home.

10

We were on our way to Oswosso Swamp Park, to dine on baked chips and turkey sandwiches from Subway, watch the herons stand perfectly still in the stagnant water, and try not to get trampled by the joggers. Ike's idea of a perfect Sunday afternoon.

"I think I may need professional help," I said, as we zipped along West Apple Street.

He slipped his right hand off the steering wheel—the reckless old buzzard always drives with both hands like some kid in driver's ed—and lovingly scratched the top of my head. "Come on now, Maddy. I know Bob Averill's got your brain in a twist, but it's not something that requires psychoanalysis, is it?"

"Not that kind of professional help," I growled. "Somebody who knows something about the antique business."

He put his hand back on the wheel. Chuckled with relief. "I know Joseph Lambright, if that'll do you any good."

"It might if I knew who Joseph Lambright was."

He squeaked with disbelief. "What? You've lived in Hannawa all these years and you don't know who Joseph Lambright is?"

"No, I don't know who Joseph Lambrigh is."

"I can't believe you don't know who Joseph Lambright is."

Now my brain was in a twist. "Jesus Christ, Ike! Who is Joseph Lambright?"

Ike's fingers tightened around the steering wheel. "Somebody who doesn't use language like that on a Sunday, far as I know."

Ike had just come from church. Changed into walking shorts and that khaki shirt of his with the epaulets. Bought those chips and submarine sandwiches for us. I bit my tongue and started over. "This Mr. Lambright knows the antique business, does he?"

"I can't believe you don't know who Joseph Lambright is!"

We were sitting at a red light now—but I would have done the same thing even if we were speeding along at eighty miles an hour. I grabbed his chin and twisted his face toward me. I purred like a saber-tooth tiger. "Unless you want a 12-inch turkey sub sticking out your ear, you will kindly accept my ignorance and tell me who Joseph Lambright is."

Ike pried my fingers off his chin. Kissed the back of my hand. "He owns that shop on German Hill."

"You mean Joey Junk?"

"I guess some people call him that."

"Even he calls himself that. Heaven's to Besty, Ike, sometime you make me mad enough to scream."

"Please don't do that."

"Then take me there—now!"

And so, we delayed our happy afternoon at the park and drove straight to Joey Junk's Treasure Trove. It was located right there on West Apple, just three blocks east of Meriwether Square, on Herders' Hill. The area was named after the Scotch-Irish farmers who grazed their sheep on the slope back in the 1800s. Those picturesque days are long gone, of course. Today it's a sad strip of low-rent apartment buildings, empty storefronts, gas stations that sell more beer and lottery tickets than gas, and one ramshackle motel that rents rooms by the hour. Because of that motel, snooty suburbanites call it Herpes Hill.

Joey Junk's Treasure Trove is one of Hannawa's most familiar landmarks. You can't help but twist your neck when you drive by. The worthless crap stuffed inside pours right out the front door. It fills the sidewalk and half of the parking lot on the side. Old claw-foot bathtubs and bathroom sinks, chairs missing a

leg or two, yellowed wedding dresses on chipped plaster man-
nequins, rusty iron beds, and gaudy living room lamps that
should never have been made. I'm sure you've got a place like
that in your town.

Ike pulled into the parking lot. Parked alongside a twisted
pile of old bicycles. We went inside. It was bric-a-brac heaven in
there. The musty air immediately made my eyes itch. Joey spotted us. He stepped across a box of old magazines and waddled
toward us. "Maddy Sprowls and Ike Breeze! Don't tell me you
two know each other!"

"For too long," I said.

I'd known Joey for a long time, too. He was about my age.
Overweight and sloppy. Happy as a clam. He'd had his shop
there since the sixties. Every once in a while I drop in to see if
there's anything I don't need but can't live without.

Joey wanted to pursue my relationship with Ike. I cut that
touchy subject off at the pass and got right to business. "Ike
thought maybe you could help me learn something about the
antique business."

Joey froze. Like a bull walrus caught in the headlights. "You're
not thinking of opening a shop are you? It's not as lucrative as
it looks."

"Don't worry," I said. "You've got Herders' Hill all to yourself.
I'm looking into Violeta Bell's murder and thought maybe you
could give me some idea how she did business."

Joey dug his hands into the pockets of the shiny pair of suit
pants he was wearing. "She was one tough woman to deal with."
He rubbed his neck again. "Like you without the compassion."

Ike liked that—too much. I shushed him. "Deal with, Joey?
You did business with her?"

"She came in all the time," Joey said. "Twice a month maybe.
And she bought a lot of stuff. I knew she'd probably turn right
around and sell it for a lot more than what she paid."

"That bother you?" I asked.

Joey smashed his lips together. Shook his head no. "She had
a lot more knowledge about the value of things than I did. And

a lot more connections. And I always got a buck or two more for the things I sold her than what I paid. That's all the matters to me."

Ike wandered off to look at Joey's collection of political memorabilia. I charged ahead. "She had a pretty exclusive shop. Who exactly were her customers?"

"Hannawa's la-de-das mostly."

"Mostly?"

"Junk dealers like yours truly sell anything we can get our hands on. But real antique dealers tend to specialize. They buy from other dealers."

"Where's the money in that?" Ike asked from across the shop. He had his nose in a box of old campaign buttons.

"There's plenty of money in that," Joey explained. "Say I'm a dealer in Ohio and I get my hands on some fancy old French chair that maybe Napoleon himself sat in. But I specialize in 18th century coo-coo clocks. Which means my customers aren't going to pay top dollar for a chair, no matter whose ass once graced it. But I know so-and-so in Timbuktu who could sell that chair for a ton of money. So I give it to him for a pretty good price and he turns around and sells it for an even prettier price."

"How about Violeta Bell?" I asked. "Did she specialize?"

Joey smashed his lips together again. This time he nodded. "Big pieces mostly. Furniture and the like. Some European but mostly American. Nineteenth century. Early twentieth. Art Nouveau. Biedermeier. Arts & Crafts. She absolutely went schizoid over Art Deco."

I was impressed. I remembered some of those names from Detective Grant's list. "For a mere junk dealer you know your stuff."

Ike loudly reprimanded me. "His shop's full of junk, not his brain."

I smiled apologetically. Joey smiled back, somewhat grimly. "I gather she was big into old fireplaces and stoves."

"They do bring a pretty penny," he said.

"You ever sell her any?"

"I come by a few now and then—so I suppose I might have."

Maybe it was imagination, but Joey seemed to be getting a little nervous. "Where do dealers get their antiques, other than junk shop owners and other dealers?" I asked.

"A good fisherman fishes many ponds," he said. "Antique malls, auctions, estate sales, classified ads, garage sales, tree lawns on garbage day."

I knew I was going to make him really nervous now. "And where would a dealer who isn't exactly on the up and up get her stuff?"

Joey got less nervous instead of more. Downright steely in fact. "You're saying Violeta Bell dealt in fakes?"

Ike appeared at my side wearing a big "I Like Ike" button on his khaki shirt. "She's not saying that, Joseph. She's just trying to figure out why somebody might have popped her."

I asked my next question before the conversation shifted to the Eisenhower button. "You think it's possible she could have been selling fakes?"

"There isn't a dealer alive who hasn't sold a fake or three," Joey answered. "The antique business is lousy with reproductions being passed off as authentic pieces. Sometimes it's almost impossible for dealers to tell. Even if they're an expert in that particular area."

"I guess I'm taking about knowingly selling fakes."

"There are a few unscrupulous dealers who do that."

I asked a final question. "Do you think that Violeta Bell could have been one of those few?"

"I never had any reason to suspect it."

Ike paid Joey two dollars for the "I Like Ike" button. On the way to the car, Ike pinned it on my tee shirt. I immediately took it off. "You're forgetting I'm a Democrat."

He flashed me that damn don't-you-love-me smile of his. "Lots of Democrats voted for Ike."

"Not this one!"

We drove to Oswosso Swamp Park. We followed the trail around the rim of the marsh until we found an empty bench.

We sat next to each other, our shoulders just barely touching. We didn't say a word. We nibbled our sandwiches and chips. We slurped the sun tea I'd brewed that morning. We watched the long-legged heron do their impressions of lawn ornaments. We watched the ducks paddle by. We watched the turtles stick their snoots through the algae. We watched the human beings dumb enough to jog during what Margaret Newman in her story had called "the nation's most blistering hot spell since rough-tough Teddy Roosevelt roasted in the Oval Office." I didn't know what Ike was thinking, but I was thinking about how much fun I was going to have telling Margaret that, while I enjoyed her alliteration, the Oval Office wasn't built until the presidency of William Howard Taft.

It was Ike who finally broke the oath of silence he'd imposed before we got out of the car. "You can't possibly think Joseph Lambright killed that old woman," he said.

"When did I ever say that?"

"I know you were asking your questions carefully. But I also know how that wicked little brain of yours works."

I snapped one of those tasteless baked chips between my teeth. The heron closest to us took off like the space shuttle. "I'm still at the early stages of my research. I have to suspect everybody."

Ike shifted his attention to another heron. "What possible reason would Joseph have?"

"Maybe she snookered him."

"Found out she sold some piece of junk from his shop for a ton of money?"

"That's exactly right," I said. "And when he confronted her, wanting his fair share, she refused."

"And so he snuck into her building in the middle of the night? Took her to the basement and killed her?"

"Uh-huh."

"That's not the Joseph Lambright I know."

"Nor is it the Joey Junk I know. But who knows what evil lurks in the hearts of men?"

I dug another potato chip from the bag. Ike took it away before I could scare the bejeebers out of another big dumb bird. "Or women," he said.

11

I waited until five-thirty, then I dialed Detective Grant's direct line. I crossed my fingers that he wouldn't be there. I hadn't had one mug of tea all day and my head was pounding. The last thing I needed was to get laughed at, or lectured, or both, by Scotty Grant. The finger-crossing worked: "*This is Detective Grant. Please leave a message. If your call is urgent, press extension 119.*"

My call was important but not exactly urgent. I waited for the beep and left a message: "This is Maddy Sprowls. I suppose you've left for the day—I'm leaving myself in a couple of minutes—but I did want to pass along a tip. Well, I guess it's not so much a tip as an unnecessary suggestion. Most likely. Anyway, if I were you I'd check the authenticity of those antiques you took from Eddie French's apartment. And the ones still in Violeta Bell's condo. It wouldn't surprise me if they're fakes. I'm not saying they are. But they might be. Bye-bye." I grabbed my purse and headed for the elevator.

◇◇◇

I reached my bungalow on Brambriar Court, Ike's car was already in the driveway. He'd had my house key for three months but this was the first time he'd used it. When I hit the button on my garage-door opener, James started barking up a storm inside. It's good to be wanted.

Ike greeted me at the kitchen door. "Baked tilapia, wild rice, and asparagus with hollandaise sauce!"

I ducked under his arm. "I hope you used my fake eggs."

He kissed my throbbing forehead way too hard. "Begrudgingly."

I scratched James' ears and headed for the bathroom. When I got back, dinner was on the table. So were a pair of candles, wine glasses, and a big bottle of Caffeine-Free Diet Coke. "How romantic!"

Ike knew enough to let me eat in silence. And then watch *Wheel of Fortune* and *Jeopardy* in silence. At eight o'clock I made him a deal: he could watch *The O'Reilly Factor* if he turned the volume down. I went into my bedroom to pack. At nine o'clock we loaded James into Ike's car—it was a lot like Sisyphus trying to roll that rock up the mountain—and headed out into the night. Ike knew enough not to hum along with the songs on the radio.

That's the problem with Ike, by the way. He's known me long enough to know what not to do.

It took us twenty minutes to get there. The huge, double-story building was dark except for a few windows at the rear. We drove toward them across the empty parking lot. Ike pulled up to the curb. He already had his instructions, but he knew enough to show a smidgeon of empathy anyway. "You sure you don't want me to come in with you?"

"James would just throw a fit."

He leaned across my overnight bag and kissed my lips. "You behave in there, okay?"

I got out of the car. Bent down and gave him the evil eye. "Not a minute after six!"

"I'll be here."

I forced myself up the walk to the door. The gold letters on the glass looked three feet high: HANNAWA SLEEP CENTER.

Behind the candy bowl on the counter sat a big woman wearing a white smock covered with happy blue bunnies. She was lost in a romance novel. "I'm here for my sleep test," I said. "Sprowls."

Without looking up she handed me a questionnaire snapped to a clipboard. "After you fill it out I'll take you to your room." Her voice was soft and breathy, no doubt very much like the voice of the beautiful heiress in her book at that very moment surrendering to the passions broiling within her for so very long.

I answered the questions as truthfully as I could. When I went back to the counter, she dog-eared her page, stuck the book in the pocket of her smock and led me down the hallway to my room. It was not the sterile hospital room I expected. It was as homey as anything you'd find at a Best Western. Double bed with a real wooden headboard. Paintings bolted to the flowery wallpaper. Fuzzy rug. TV on the dresser. I put my overnight bag on the bed. "How many are being tested tonight?"

"All five rooms are filled."

"Men and women?"

"Men one night and women the next," she said. "We don't need anything interesting happening, do we?"

I was relieved. I'd been worrying about some grisly old sleepwalker trying to nuzzle up to me in the night. "You're going to glue lots of wires to me, I gather."

She headed for the door. Her hand was already retrieving the book from her smock. "Get into your PJs. Patti will be in shortly to prepare you."

Patti turned out to be Patti Kapustova, a sawed-off girl with impressive hips that would serve her well once she was old enough to bear children. "You look too young to be a nurse," I said.

She took it as a compliment. "I'm thirty-three—but thanks." She looked tired and a bit agitated. She was having a devil of a time trying to untangle the wad of wires she'd brought in with her. "And I'm not a nurse," she said. "I'm a polysomnographic technologist."

She went into a lengthy explanation of the test, how those electrodes in her hand would be attached to my scalp, face, chest, legs, and fingers. How she would monitor my sleep from an adjoining room. How if nature called during the night I could call her and she'd help me waddle to the bathroom. "You have any questions, Mrs. Sprowls?"

I did have a question. "Kapustova—that wouldn't be Romanian, would it?"

She softened a little. "It's Slovak. My ex-husband's name. I'm actually French Canadian and Welsh. Barbou and Jones and I end up with Kapustova."

"I'm saddled with my ex's name, too."

She glued an electrode to the top of my head. "I recognized your name on the test order. You're that newspaper woman who solves murders."

Unfortunately, *The Herald-Union* had glowingly reported my role in solving the Buddy Wing and Gordon Sweet murders. "Just my luck," I cracked. "A polysomnographic technologist with a newspaper subscription."

Patti pushed up my pajama legs and glued an electrode to my calf, to record, she said, how much kicking and squirming I did in my sleep. "That's got to be exciting. Solving murders, and all."

"It's a pain in the ass."

She held up the last of her electrodes. Devilishly swayed it back and forth.

"Oh no you don't!"

She glued it on my other calf. "Why did you ask if I was Romanian?"

It was time to obfuscate. "Names intrigue me."

She hooked a small plastic tube under my nose, to monitor my breathing. "I thought maybe you we looking into the death of that woman who claimed to be a queen or whatever."

Now it was time to lie. "Heaven's to Betsy, no."

"One of my uncles is married to a Romanian."

I pretended not to be interested. "I had an uncle who married a Lithuanian. They're both dead now, of course."

"My uncle and his wife are still alive. In Youngstown."

"That's only half alive, dear."

Patti was finally finished with me. "Comfy?"

"With all these wires I feel like a fly caught in a spider's web."

She smiled at me—just like a spider—and headed for the door. "You'll be surprised how well you sleep."

I hadn't been very nice to her and I was struggling with an emotion that rarely bubbles up in me. Guilt. I called out to her. "Kapustova is a very pretty name!"

This time she smiled at me like a puppy. "You know what Kapustova means in Slovak, Mrs. Sprowls? Cabbage! Patti the Cabbage! Nighty night!" She pulled the door shut behind her. I clicked off my lamp and closed my eyes. I twisted this way and that until I was comfortable.

You'd think I would have used that opportunity to wrestle with the few facts I had about Violeta Bell's murder, wouldn't you? The skeleton keys. The lack of blood everywhere but on Eddie's porch. Eddie's aversion to guns. Kay Hausenfelter's pretty pistol. Violeta's fake Social Security card and surprising poverty. But all I could think about was Ike and why I was taking that damn sleep test for him. I didn't like what my inner voice was telling me. Not one iota.

◇◇◇

Saturday, July 29

Patti the Cabbage woke me up at 5:30. The poor girl had been worn to a frazzle the night before, but now, after eight hours of watching a gaggle of other women sleep, she was wide awake. And way too perky. She started prying the electrodes off me, humming through her nose like a Hawaiian guitar.

"How'd I do?" I asked her.

"You snored."

I was afraid that was going to be the answer. "How bad?"

"Like a herd of wild pigs."

"Sorry."

"For what? I get $18.50 an hour to listen to people snore."

The night before I'd had to struggle with guilt. Now it was envy. The young twit made fifty cents more an hour than I did! Then again, to be fair, all I did all day was test the upper limits of people's blood pressure. "I didn't stop breathing, did I?"

She pried off the last electrode. The one on the top of my head. "Your doctor will give you the bad news."

I got dressed and headed for the parking lot. Ike and James were waiting for me. They both wanted to kiss me. But I wanted no part of that. I just wanted to go home and shower. I had little blotches of itchy glue all over me. "This might improve your mood," Ike said, handing me a folded copy of *The Herald-Union* as we zipped across the empty parking lot. He proudly used the newspaper lingo he'd learned from me. "B-1, below the fold."

I pulled out the Metro section. I immediately spotted the story Ike wanted me to read. It was a small story:

Blood On Cabbie's Porch
Not Violeta Bell's

HANNAWA—The blood found on the second-story porch of cab driver Edward French was not that of slain antique dealer Violeta Bell, police said.

In fact, Police Department Public Information Officer Sgt. Michael Giannone said that laboratory tests determined that the blood was not human at all, but from a rabbit.

Giannone refused to say if French remains a suspect in the 72-year-old woman's murder.

The rest of the story offered nothing new—just a rehash of Eddie's arrest and bail. I tore the story out of the paper and stuck it in my overnight bag.

"Looks like Mr. French was telling the truth," Ike said.

"About the cat at least."

12

Monday, July 31

I backed out of my driveway at six on the dot. It was going to be a long day. And a long week. I was driving home to LaFargeville, New York. Not because I wanted to. Or had to. I was going to LaFargeville because it was right next door to another place I was going. To Wolfe Island. To pay a surprise visit to Prince Anton Alexandur Clopotar, vegetable grower extraordinaire, pretender to the Romanian throne. I knew if I drove all that way to see the prince without making a perfunctory pilgrimage to my own hometown, well, I'd be pounding myself on the head in regret for the rest of my life. The way those idiots in the commercials pound themselves for having a plate of Krispy Kremes for breakfast instead of a V8.

I drove out West Apple to Hemphill College then took the Indian Creek Parkway north to I-77. It was still dark but already the traffic was picking up. Sleepy, coffee-slurping suburbanites on their way to their jobs in Cleveland.

I'd asked Ike to close his coffee shop for a week and come with me. But as I expected, he said no. "You know I can't be taking off willy-nilly like that," he said, as we stood side by side in front of my bathroom mirror brushing our teeth. "My regulars rely on me."

Being the proud old bird I was, I could hardly tell him that I was afraid of facing my childhood alone. All I could do was shrug, spit my Tartar-Control Sensodyne into the sink and say, "Okay, but you're going to miss out on one of the worst experiences of your life."

Ike did show some concern about my going alone. "I hope you're not thinking of driving that cranky old Dodge of yours," he said. "You won't get to the Pennsylvania line before something under the hood goes kerflooey."

And that's why I was floating up I-77 in his big, sensible Chevrolet. Thermos of Darjeeling tea on the empty seat next to me. James in the back seat licking himself. Bush-Cheney '04 sticker on the bumper.

I must confess that Ike was not my first choice as a travel companion. My first choice, believe it or not, would have been Eric Chen. He'd already taken a couple of road trips with me on past investigations. He was surprisingly easy to handle—as long as I kept him well supplied with junk food and Mountain Dews. Gabriella Nash might have made another good travel buddy. She was afraid of me. She was already up to her eyeballs in my secret effort to learn the truth about Violeta Bell. Unfortunately she'd only been at the paper for six weeks. She could hardly take a week's vacation. Another possibility was Effie Fredmansky, my old college pal and owner of Last Gasp Books. The previous summer we'd driven to Harper's Ferry, West Virginia together. We had a damn good time even though I suspected her of murder. But Effie, like Ike, had a business to run. And so James got the nod.

Thanks to the heavy traffic, and my decision to pour myself a cup of tea at the worst possible time, I missed the bypass and had to drive straight into downtown Cleveland. I made it around that hellish bend the locals call Deadman's Curve—not something everybody does successfully apparently—and headed east on I-90, along the southern shore of Lake Erie. The water was just as pretty as it could be.

For a long while I drove past abandoned factories and empty railroad yards. Then little by little I eased into Ohio's grape country. It isn't the Napa Valley, but it is still quite impressive. One vineyard after another, for I don't know how many miles, taking advantage of the warm lake air. I reached Erie, Pennsylvania at nine. Buffalo, New York at 10:30. Buffalo is a big Hannawa. Which doesn't say much about either city.

I got on the turnpike and headed into the bumpy bowels of upstate New York. At a service plaza outside Rochester I stopped for gas. I bought a rubbery chicken sandwich for my lunch. I found a nice plot of grass for James to irrigate.

I reached Syracuse at two o'clock. I took I-81 north. Ninety minutes later I was in Watertown, population 27,705. What London is to the English and Paris to the French, Watertown is to the people of Jefferson County, New York. The big city they outwardly loathe while secretly lusting to visit.

LaFargeville was just 15 miles up the road. But I'd been driving, and thinking, for ten hours. I was pooped. Physically and psychologically. I got off the interstate and drove downtown. I checked into the Best Western. It was right there on Washington Street. Right about where fifty years before I'd caught the Greyhound Bus to Hannawa and Hemphill College. It was a pet-friendly hotel, meaning that James could stay in my room for an extra ten dollars. I didn't take him with me into the lobby. I figured they'd take one look at the big bear and charge me an extra hundred.

◇◇◇

Tuesday, August 1

I walked James around the hotel grounds until he found just the right spot on the dew-soaked grass to pee. Then we headed up Route 12 toward LaFargeville. Outside Watertown we were immediately surrounded by cow pastures and cornfields. As far as I knew, those were the very same cows and the very same stalks of corn that drove me out of LaFargeville in the fifties.

This narrow plain between Lake Ontario to the west and the Adirondack Mountains to the east is low and scruffy. Which makes it hot and buggy in the summer and absolutely uninhabitable in the winter. The lake winds drive the temperatures low and pile the snow high. There's not much for people to do up there but make babies and cheese. And they make a lot of both. And both leave as soon as they're properly aged. I turned onto Route 180 and headed toward LaFargeville.

My first stop was Grove Cemetery. I followed the looping drive around to where we Madisons have been burying each other for 150 years.

Grove Cemetery is well named. The graves are forever in the shadows of the great oaks towering above them. The older stones are covered with moss. I let James run free and walked across the slippery grass to my parents' headstone. I hadn't been there in sixteen years. Since my mother's funeral. And I'd never seen the date of her death chiseled on the stone. It threw me for a loop.

My mother had survived my father by twelve years. Those twelve years weren't very happy ones for her. But neither were the forty-two years she'd been married to my father. She loved my father, I think. And she loved us kids, I'm sure. But she wasn't so keen on herself. She never kept herself fixed up as well as she might. "What's the use with all the work I've got to do?" she'd say. And she never allowed herself to have a good time. "How can I enjoy myself with all the work I've got waiting at home?" she'd say. Today your family would force you to see somebody. You'd be diagnosed with clinical depression and given some pills. But back then when my mother was struggling to stay afloat, depression was seen as a moral weakness. And a stigma on the entire family. All my father could do was warn my brother and me that, "Mama's a little down in the dumps today."

My father, on the other hand, was the happiest man on the planet. He loved being a dairy farmer. He loved his cows. He loved going out to the barn and sticking those milking machine nozzles on their teats. He loved taking his filled cans of milk to the dairy. He loved handing the money over to my mother when he got back. "Not much for all the work, is it?" she'd say.

My brother, George Jr., is buried next to my mother and father. He died when I was sixteen. In Korea. When he was nineteen. My parents bought a plot next to his for themselves. They bought one for me, too. One big enough for a future husband and for any future children that might, like George Jr., die before their time.

I can't blame my parents for thinking that I'd stay in LaFargeville, or at least settle down nearby in Depauville or Clayton. Even when I went off to Hemphill College to study library science, I'm sure they figured I wouldn't end up any farther away than Alexandria Bay, or, since I was proving to be a headstrong girl with gumption, Watertown. Little did they know that my sights were set on Syracuse. When I was ten, my Aunt Dorothy took me to the main library in downtown Syracuse. I was staying with her that summer, helping her with her housework while she was recovering from her "women's problem" surgery. Anyway, I took one look at that big castle full of books and knew I wanted to spend the rest of my life in there, bathed in all that respectful silence, sniffing in all that slowly decaying ink and paper, far away from the smell and moo of my father's cows.

Instead, I met and married Lawrence Sprowls, who after a few fairly happy years of marriage metamorphosed into a skirt-chasing skunk. But that marriage did keep me far away from LaFargeville. And it did land me the best-possible job in the world: head librarian of *The Hannawa Herald-Union.* I remember what I wrote my aunt a few months after getting the job: *It's better than a castle, auntie. It's a newsroom.*

I sat on the ground in front of my parent's stone. I clapped my hands for James. He came running. He plopped next to me. Begged me to scratch his floppy ears. "There's nothing wrong with spending your life in LaFargeville," I told him, "being a dairy farmer or a dairy farmer's wife. But I sure knew it wasn't for me. I knew from the get-go I'd have to go somewhere else and be somebody else. I would have exploded like an over-baked potato if I'd stayed here. And maybe that's what Violeta Bell did, James. Maybe she was from some boring little place like this. She knew it was either escape or explode. She gave herself a new name and a new history. More than likely she's no more Romanian than you are." I took him by the ears and stared into his eyes. "You're not, are you?"

James waited for me to struggle to my feet then followed me to the car. "Maybe she had an aunt who took her to an antique store once," I said. "Maybe she fell in love with all the fancy old stuff and knew that was just the life for her. Not that we want to paint her too sympathetically, of course. She was very likely a crook. Very likely she changed her identity to stay out of jail. We're not talking about Mother Teresa here, James. But criminality aside, you've got to admire someone who knows what it takes to be happy inside their own skin."

We drove into LaFargeville. It was as humble as it was when I was a girl. A hundred modest houses. A bank. A school and three churches. No real downtown.

LaFargeville is—how should I put it—very white. Everybody is either German or English. Everybody is either a practicing Catholic or a well-practiced Protestant. Everybody is either a Republican who votes Republican all of the time or a Democrat who votes Republican most of the time. Everybody is either married or wishes they were.

I drove past the house on Maple Street where my niece, Joyce, grew up. After my mother died, Joyce was my only living relative in LaFargeville. Now she was gone, too. For thirty odd years she'd militantly extolled the virtues of remaining single. Then five years ago she met a widower at a stamp collector's show in St. Louis and married him. She now lives in Wahoo, Nebraska. She keeps begging me to visit.

I drove by the house on Mill Street where my girlfriend Edna Schwed used to live. It used to be painted white, like most of the houses in LaFargeville. Now it was painted pink. Which made me suspect that Edna still might live there. Pink was always her favorite color. I thought about stopping. But good gravy, what if Edna did still live there? What on earth would we talk about? Other than what her neighbors thought about her pink house?

I drove down Ford Street to see if the house where Chuck Crouse lived still had that fancy slate roof. It did. All through high school I daydreamed about Chuck Crouse. What it was going to be like being married to him. What the s.e.x. would be like. What the four children we'd have would look like. Would the two girls favor me and the two boys favor him? Or, heaven forbid, would it be visa versa? Don't get me wrong. Chuck and I never dated. Chuck was too shy to ask any girl out. And I was too below average-looking for him to overcome that shyness. As I drove by, I wondered what had happened to Chuck. I'd Googled his name before leaving Hannawa. There were several Chuck Crouses but none of them were my Chuck Crouse.

I pulled into at Waggoner's Grocery, the only real business in town. There was a single Sunoco pump in front. There was a big blinking New York State Lottery sign in the window. It was getting hot already. I left the windows down a crack so James could get whatever breeze there was. I went inside. The store hadn't changed much since I was a girl. Pop and candy. Milk and bread. Cigarettes and beer. Lunchmeat and cheese. Tubs of ice cream for making cones. "You a Waggoner?" I asked the girl behind the counter.

"I think them's all dead," she said. "I'm a Gertz."

The name didn't ring a bell. I asked her to make me a double chocolate cone. I bought a Slim Jim for James. We ate our treats in the car and then drove north past Colby's Dairy. When I was a girl just about everybody who wasn't a farmer worked at Colby's. I suspect it's still that way.

Before leaving Hannawa I envisioned spending a day or two in LaFargeville, visiting all of our family's old friends. The Siewertsons. The Griffens. The Wildenheims. I envisioned visiting the old Central School and the Methodist Church where I spent so much of my first eighteen years. I envisioned driving out to my parent's farm on East Line Road. Getting a tour from the alpaca breeder who owns it now. Getting a peek inside my old bedroom maybe. Seeing if that big crack in the ceiling was still there. If the closet door still stuck. But now that I was in LaFargeville, well, I felt silly and lonely and a total stranger.

So I kept on driving, all the way to Philadelphia. Not the one in Pennsylvania. The one ten miles down the road. The one that's about the same size as LaFargeville. The one that's the home of Martin's Pretzel Bakery. Their hand-twisted German-style pretzels are sold in fancy-schmancy stores all over the country. I bought a three-pound bag for Ike. For $14.50. I made James promise that he wouldn't tell the old penny-pinching fool how much I paid.

I drove back to Watertown and checked out of my room at the Best Western. Then I drove up to Cape Vincent and pulled into line for the noon ferry to Wolfe Island. I was a day early for the cabin I'd reserved over there, but I was prepared to take my chances. James and I could spend a night in the car if we had to.

The attendant motioned me forward onto the little ferry. I stayed with James in the car. James is an American water spaniel. I was afraid if I took him up to the deck, he'd cannon-ball into the river and paddle back to shore. I didn't need a scene like that.

Wolfe Island is the biggest of the famous Thousand Islands that choke the St. Lawrence River. While its southern shoreline tickles the American border, every inch of the island sits in Canada. It is 24 miles long with lots of pretty bays and points. Our family made two, one-day trips to Wolfe Island every summer. In June we'd go to one of those pick-it-yourself farms for strawberries. In August we'd pick wild blackberries. A couple of times in high school I went there with girlfriends to bicycle and picnic. It's a lot more touristy now.

The ferry pulled out. I rolled down my window and stretched my neck to see. The water was flat and blue. In just fifteen minutes we were in Port Alexandria, pulling up to the Canadian customs booth.

I was ready for the girl with the Dudley Dooright hat. I handed her my birth certificate and driver's license. As she looked them over it occurred to me how many times during her life Violeta Bell must have held her breath while her phony-baloney papers were given a perfunctory once-over.

The girl handed my papers back to me. "You aren't bringing in any perishable vegetables, meats, or dairy products, are you?"

"Nope. No live minnows, firewood, or automatic weapons either."

"Any dog food?"

"Only what's already in him."

She smiled. "You've done your homework."

I handed her James' records from the veterinarian, proving he'd had a rabies shot. "You wouldn't know Prince Anton, would you?"

She didn't. But she did know where I could buy food for James. At the grocery in Marysville. What the Canadians have against American dog food, I do not know.

Using the directions Eric printed out for me from Mapquest, I found my way around Button Bay to Clemens Road. At the end of that bumpy gravel path I found McWiggens' Cottages. Four tiny white bungalows lined up along the rocky beach like bars of ivory soap.

On the porch of one cottage I found Alana McWiggens. She was a tall, bony woman with a face full of wrinkles. She had a thick thatch of gray, permanently windblown hair. She had a big ball of sheets and pillowcases in her arms. "I'm afraid I'm a day early," I said after introducing myself. "My plans down in LaFargeville fell through unfortunately."

"No problem," she said. "I just now finished putting on clean bedding for you."

She helped me with my suitcases. She made a fuss over James. She confided in me that she made enough money over the summer renting her cottages to spend her winters in Sarasota. "I'm one of those Canadian snowbirds you hear *aboot*," she said. "Six months here, six months in the U.S." She asked me if I'd come for the mystery writers' festival.

I told her I hadn't. That I didn't even know there was a mystery writers' festival. That I wasn't a writer.

"You do look the type," she said, quickly explaining by that she meant I was clearly well educated, sharp as a tack, and maybe a little on the eccentric side, in the most admirable way of course.

I was not about to tell her why I was really there—to solve a real murder rather than write about a made-up one. "I'm afraid I'm just a harried old librarian looking for a little peace and quiet."

"You should go anyway," she said. "They've been holding it for several years now. A real big deal. Scene of the Crime they call it. It lasts all day Saturday and afterward there's a jim-dandy supper at the United Church. Barbecued pork and all kinds of pie."

I remembered the pies my mother used to make with Wolfe Island berries. "It does sound fun. And speaking of mysteries—what do you know about that man who claims to be the king of Romania?"

She sat on the bed and let James put his chin on her knee. She scratched his ears. "Alex, you mean?"

"Alexandur Clopotar, yes."

"He stays on the island all year from what I hear. A very nice man. Why do you ask about him?"

I sat on the other side of James and scratched his back while Alana continued to work on his ears. "I just happened to see something about him on my computer. You think he's really royalty?"

"Oh, sure. Like I say, a very nice man. His wife's gone though. So that's sad."

"He's lived here a long time, has he?"

"I guess he retired here *aboot* twenty years ago. He was in the government up in Ottawa. Not a bigwig or anything."

I had a lot more questions. But I also had a lot more days to ask them. "I am going to need some groceries," I said.

She gave me directions to Marysville, the only real town on the island. I bought enough food to last James and me the five days we'd be there.

13

You'd think a pretender to a throne would live in a big old castle, wouldn't you? At least a pretend castle. There are more than a few of each sprinkled throughout the Thousand Islands. But Prince Anton Alexandur Clopotar lived in a bungalow only slightly less modest than my own shoebox back in Hannawa. It was located on the western end of Wolfe Island, on the southern shoreline of Reed's Bay. On Easy Lane, if you can believe it.

It was ten in the morning. A reasonable time, I figured, to show up uninvited at the prince's door. I'd left James at the cottage. Not everybody likes dogs. Especially dogs that bump into things and shed like a Christmas tree. I parked on the lane, played with my hair in the rearview mirror until my adrenaline was pumping, and then followed the winding brick walk to the front porch. The bricks were slippery with moss.

Prince Anton came to the door on my fifth knock. I was expecting a Romanian accent—whatever that sounds like—but his voice was as sterile as any other Canadian's. "Hope you didn't have to knock too many times," he said.

I was also expecting him to be dressed like he was in that picture on his website. That double-breasted blazer with the emblem on the pocket. That polka dot bow tie sticking out on each side of his many-layered chin. That big pipe clenched in his teeth. Instead he was wearing a baggy pair of shorts, old canvas shoes, and a pink oxford shirt with the tails hanging out and the sleeves rolled up above his droopy elbows. I extended my hand. "My name is Maddy Sprowls. I'm renting a cottage from Alana McWiggens. I wanted to meet you."

He didn't exactly kiss the back of my hand. He just shook it once and let go. "I hope you're not one of those mystery writers."

"Heaven's to Betsy, no. I'm a librarian."

He was not the least bit relieved. "It's a busy morning for me."

He wasn't going to close the door in my face that easily. "I wanted to meet you for a purpose. Regarding your claim to the Romanian throne."

You would have thought I'd showed up with a bundle of balloons and a huge check from Publishers Clearing House. "I am boiling water for tea—if you've got time to join me."

"All the time in the world."

He stood aside. In I went.

I'd already been surprised by his small house, casual dress, and accent-free voice. Now it was time to be surprised by his interior decorating skills. There were no dingy tapestries on the walls, no suits of armor, no stag's head over a be-gargoyled fireplace. Instead his living room was decorated, if that's the word for it, with the same lifetime of good buys you'd find in anybody's house. The only sign of his purported royalty was a big blue, yellow, and red flag dangled from the ceiling on a pair of cheap plant hangers. "Is that the Romanian flag?" I asked, already knowing the answer. More than likely it was the same one he's posed with on his website.

He hurried to the flag. He smoothed out the furls, like a sales girl in the drapery department. "This is the old royal flag," he said. "The new one is a little simpler. No eagle, no tongue-wagging lions, no crown. Just the three stripes." Then he rolled his eyes. "It is a little big for the room, isn't it?"

I smiled graciously. "It's a very cozy cottage. Right out of a magazine."

"It's been in the family forever," he said. "Well, since we came to Canada. We had a more substantial house in Toronto, of course. But most summer weekends we were here."

"I heard you live here year round now."

"Oh, yes. Agnes and I retired here after my stint with the government. She just loved it. And so do I, of course." His eyes danced about the room. No doubt he was savoring some special memory. "Anyway, I'm happy that you like it."

I nodded that I did. "And the mansion in Toronto—your family still owns that?"

He laughed. "Mansion? I only said it was more substantial than this little box. My mother sold it and bought a condo on the lakefront after my father died." He motioned me toward the kitchen. "We can have our tea by the water if you like."

He poured a boiling saucepan of water into a beautiful bone china teapot. He placed it on a silver tray, along with a pair of matching cups and saucers, a sugar bowl and creamer. He emptied a canister of teabags on the counter. "I'm a Darjeeling man myself," he said, picking through the bags. "But I've got at least one of everything."

"I'm a Darjeeling man, too," I said.

He lowered two teabags into the china pot. He picked up the tray and headed for the back door. "Too good a day to hide inside, wouldn't you agree?"

He held the door open for me with his rump. We headed down his backyard toward the bay. There were plots of vegetables everywhere, surrounded with low chicken wire fences to keep out the rabbits or raccoons or whatever other short-legged beasts lived on the island. On a knoll just above his boat landing he had a small garden table and chairs. He poured my tea for me. It was so European. So aristocratic. No way was I going to tell him I grew up just over the border in LaFargeville. No way in the world.

"So Miss Sprowls—it is miss isn't it?"

"Miss and Mrs. I've been widowed for some time." Just as I wasn't going to tell him that I was from LaFargeville, I wasn't going to tell him that my husband had died long after I'd divorced his womanizing behind. I wanted him to relate to me. So he might just tell me things he'd never told anyone before.

He stirred a small mountain of sugar into his tea and then licked the spoon. "I'm a widower, too."

"I saw your website."

He brightened. "Did you, really? I don't get anywhere the hits I thought I would." He laughed. "Nobody gives a damn about grouchy old men who think they should be king these days."

I took a sip of my tea. The sailboats and gulls made it taste that much better. "It's a cruel world, isn't it?"

"Actually, it's a beautiful world." He toasted me. Took a sip of his own. "If you read my website, then you know I'm quite content if the people of my homeland don't want to restore the monarchy. But if they ever do vote to restore it, they ought to do it right."

"Recognize the Clopotars."

"The throne is rightfully ours."

He was right, assuming that everything I read on the Internet about the Romanian royal bloodlines was true, of course. Prince Anton was the great-great-grandson of King Carol I. His great-grandfather, Prince Anthony, to the king's dismay, had married the daughter of a cavalry officer. When Anthony died unexpectedly, his bride—baby in her belly—was banished from the royal household. That baby was Prince Anton's grandfather.

It was time to steer the conversation to my investigation. "As I recall, your great-grandmother, Princess Violeta, married a commoner after she was banished from the royal family."

The prince became a bit defensive. "Gavril Clopotar. A very fine man."

"He raised Prince Anthony's son as his own," I agreed.

"Yes, he did. A fine thing for him to do."

I let him know I'd done my homework. "And Prince Anthony's son—your grandfather, Constantin—should have followed Carol I as king. Instead, the throne went to a nephew of the king. And the living heir of that nephew is King Michael

I. Who was kicked off the throne when the Communists took control in the forties. And if the monarchy were restored, Michael would get the throne back. Unless the parliament did the proper thing and recognized you."

He toasted me again. "You are a diligent student."

I was ready to let the cat out of the bag. "The truth is, I'm working on a murder investigation for my newspaper—the Hannawa, Ohio, *Herald-Union*. In a roundabout way it may have something to do with you."

He reacted to this startling news by warming up my tea. "Such an American thing, murder."

"We're very good at it, no doubt about that."

"And just who was murdered, Miss Sprowls?"

"Another Violeta."

His eyeballs were floating, a sign that a lot was going on inside his head. "Violeta is a common Romanian name."

"This one claimed to be the queen of Romania."

"Claimed?"

I got his point. "She never offered any proof. And she proved to be a fraud in other ways. But she did make the claim publicly in our newspaper. And a few days later she was found dead."

"How old was she, this Violeta?"

"She claimed to be seventy-two."

"And her last name? What did she claim that was?"

"Bell."

"Bell?"

"Doesn't ring one?"

An expression that could be interpreted as relief calmed his wrinkles. "That's not a Romanian name. Of course it could be a married name, I suppose."

"She was never married," I said. "As far as anybody knows."

I kept my mouth shut now. Let his mind work. We sipped our tea and watched the sailboats and gulls. Let the sun and the quiet soak in. "Is the fact that she claimed to be the queen of Romania your only hypothesis for her demise?" he finally asked.

"The police think her murder is connected to the theft of antiques from her condominium," I said.

His ears perked up, the way James' do when my microwave beeps. "Antiques? None of them had anything to do with Romanian history, did they?"

Knowing what was found in Eddie French's apartment I had to laugh. "A bejeweled crown, you mean?"

He did not appreciate my little joke. "All of the crowns are accounted for, Miss Sprowls. But there are plenty of important family heirlooms floating about."

I told him that Violeta Bell had been an antique dealer. I showed him a list of the antiques found in Eddie's apartment. I told him that I had a suspicion they were fakes. "More than likely her murder had nothing to do with her claim to be royalty," I said. "It's just one of the improbabilities I need to put to rest before tackling more fruitful possibilities."

A sad smile turned up the ends of his mustache. "Forgive my irritation, Miss Sprowls. I've spent much of my adult life trying to find a set of lead soldiers that had been given to my great-grandfather when he was a boy. By Prince Albert of England. One hundred tiny Romanian Hussars in all their glory. Cavalrymen. Romania, you see, won its independence for helping Russia drive the Turks out of the Balkans. And the British, who had sided with the Turks, wanted to repair relations with the new Romanian nation. So they were more than toy soldiers. They were diplomatic chess pieces."

My next question was obvious. "You wouldn't kill for them, would you?"

He laughed. "Not literally, I wouldn't. But it is quite a coincidence that my great-grandfather would grow up to marry the daughter of a cavalry officer, isn't it? Who knows, I may owe my very existence to the romantic roilings fostered by those lead soldiers." His manner suddenly changed. He became passionless. Analytical. "Let's get back to why you came to see me. You're wondering if I had something to do with this woman's murder. In the event her claims were true, I might want her out of the way in case the monarchy is restored. Yes, there is a small royalist party in Romania today. And a few of its members actually support my cause. But there is no room in the new constitution for a monarch. Not even a toothless figurehead."

He was right. I'd Googled the new Romanian constitution. It didn't say boo about a king or queen, except, somewhat cryptically, that no one could *exercise sovereignty in one's own name.* "Couldn't the constitution be amended?"

"Yes, but it would take quite a groundswell of public support," he said. "And that's not very likely. Certainly not in my lifetime. Or old King Michael's."

That, too, jived with what I'd read. "What about the next generation of heirs? You have three sons. King Michael has five daughters."

He poured more tea for us. "Surely you don't expect me to opine on the possibility of my own sons thinning the royal herd."

"Of course not. I'm sorry."

He winked at me. "If they were so inclined, I think they would start with me."

I toasted him. He was a funny man. An attractive man. "You had an older brother. Petru. Did he leave any heirs?"

Prince Anton shook his head no. Pointed across the bay. "He drowned himself right out there. A half-mile off that point. Fifty-two years ago. When he was twenty-six."

"Drowned himself? Suicide?"

"The authorities ruled it an accident. How do you accidentally get an anchor rope tied around your feet?" His eyes were cloudy with tears. "A passing boater found our boat. The motor was still running. The propeller turned sharply to the right. The boat going round and round like the hands of a clock. X marks the spot. Intentionally it seemed to me. "

My eyes were clouding up, too. "I lost my brother when he was nineteen. In Korea. His death was an accident. If you can call anyone getting killed in a war an accident. He was accidentally shot in the leg by one of his buddies while crossing the Han

River. He tumbled off the pontoon bridge and drowned before they could pull him out."

The prince pulled a handkerchief from his pocket and handed it to me. While I dabbed my eyes with it, he pulled the tears from his with his pinky fingers, studying each tear before he wiped it off. "Both drowned," he said softly. "Horrible."

"I always felt sorry for the boy whose gun went off," I said. "His name was Andy Brown. He was from Connecticut. Over the years he must have written me a dozen letters apologizing."

The prince was still working on his eyes. "Horrible."

"When he died they sent me a letter he'd attached to his will apologizing one last time."

"Horrible."

I changed the subject before we both fell apart. "The only thing I need to know, I suppose, is whether Violeta Bell was telling the truth about her royalty."

He stood up. Stretched until I could see his belly. "I am something of an expert on the Romanian royals, as you can well imagine. There are no living Violetas. And certainly no Bells. Like I said, Bell is not a Romanian name."

"Well—I'm sure there's nothing to it."

We walked back to his bungalow. Along the way he showed me his vegetable gardens. Like every other backyard gardener in North America, he had enough zucchini to feed an army. Back inside, he led me into his tiny den. There was nothing on his desk but a gooseneck lamp and a long rack of smelly pipes. He rummaged through a bottom drawer, pulling out a folder filled with shiny photos of himself. He took one out, careful not to get his fingerprints on it. It was the same pose that appeared on his website, the one with the big Romanian flag, the silly little bow tie and big manly pipe. He rustled through the top drawer until he found the fancy gold ballpoint he wanted. When he was finished scribbling, he read the inscription to me: "To Maddy. Thank you for your company on such a beautiful summer morning. Anton."

It was so informal. So unassuming. Then again, printed across the bottom of the photo, in raised gold letters, was a less humble assertion:

His Royal Majesty
Anton Alexandur Clopotar

He slipped the photo into a white envelope. The prospect of him giving me an easy DNA sample nearly buckled me at the knees. But just as he was about to lick the envelope, he seemed to think better of it. He tucked in the flap and handed it to me.

Before leaving I gave him copies of the various stories we'd run, including Gabriella Nash's original feature on the Queens of Never Dull. I gave him my business card. "If anything comes to mind, you'll let me know?"

"I will." He took my hand and kissed it. I almost dropped my car keys.

I spent the afternoon at my cottage. I tried to nap in the most uncomfortable Adirondack chair ever built. Which is saying something. I walked along the rocky beach until my feet ached. I tried to coax James into fetching a piece of driftwood. I made six pancakes for my supper and ate every damn one of them. I went to bed at nine and, for all I know, snored up a storm.

In the morning I wrestled James into the backseat of Ike's car and drove straight back to Hannawa.

14

Eric Chen stood in front of my desk, sucking on his morning bottle of Mountain Dew while shaking his head in pity, an impressive display of his multi-tasking skills. "I knew you couldn't take an entire week off," he said.

"Some people have a work ethic," I growled back.

"And some people don't have a life."

"My life is more than adequate," I assured him. "I accomplished everything I wanted to accomplish. Including getting away from you for a few days. I'm rested and restored. The sweet, lovable Maddy Sprowls of old. Now get to work before I fire your ass."

Eric sauntered off to BS with the boys in sports. I started deleting four days of worthless voice mail. There was one call I actually had to listen to: *"Hello, Mrs. Sprowls. This is Dr. Menke's office. The doctor wanted you to know that your results are back from the sleep center and that you should make an appointment as soon as you can to discuss them."*

I deleted the message from my phone. But I couldn't delete it from my brain. I called the doctor's office. There was an opening at 4:20 that afternoon. I hemmed and hawed for a minute then took it. I went on deleting messages like it was an Olympic sport.

Just as I was nearing the finishing line, Bob Averill pressed his huge palms into my desktop like a couple of toilet plungers. "I heard you were back!"

"Yes, Bob, I'm back. And I'm no closer to solving your little problem than when I left."

"I was just hoping we could pick up the speed now," he said. "Bear down a bit."

"I'm one little woman, Bob. I can pick up speed or bear down. But I can't do both."

He left in frustration. And despite my snippiness, I got busy doing both. First I motioned Eric back to my desk. I used my best sign language to have him bring along his clipboard and a pen. "I've got a shitload of stuff for you to research," I said, patting the seat of the chair he'd just pulled up with his foot.

He was not happy. "We? What about that lesson I gave you?"

"One lesson and I'm Bill Gates?" I motioned for him to put pen to paper. "Find out everything you can about the death of Petru Clopotar. Prince Anton's brother. He drowned in the St. Lawrence River. Fifty-two years ago. In Reed's Bay."

Eric scribbled away. "Any idea how Canadian law enforcement works? Who would handle something like this?"

"Just find out everything you can from whoever you can," I said. "The prince says it was suicide, but apparently some authority or the other ruled it an accident. Let's see if we can find out which was most likely."

"And that's important because?"

"Petru was the prince's older brother," I explained. "Which would have made him king some day—if the monarchy were restored and the Clopotar family recognized as the rightful heirs."

"You're saying that maybe Petru's death wasn't an accident or a suicide? That maybe the prince off'd his own brother?"

I gave him a rare smile of affection. "If Prince Anton wanted the throne so bad that he'd kill his own brother—and that kind of thing does happen in royal families—then maybe he'd kill Violeta Bell now."

"Why would the prince care if the official cause was accident or suicide?" Eric wondered. "Just as long as he was dead?"

It was a good point. "Maybe your investigation will answer that," I said. I moved on. "I also want to know when Prince Anton's father died. His name was Dumitru. Dumitru Clopotar. Maybe he died suspiciously, too. Also, find what you can on Prince Anton's three sons. Where they live. What they do for a living. Their views on the monarchy. Whatever you can. I guess that's it."

Eric angrily tapped the bridge of his nose with his pen. Tap-tap-tap-tap. Transferred aggression, I suppose. "Well, this shouldn't take more than a couple of minutes."

I matched his sarcasm. "Take all weekend."

"And what will the well-rested Maddy Sprowls be doing while I'm frying my eyeballs?"

I shooed him away from my desk. "Don't worry, Mr. Chen. I'll be frying my eyeballs, too. I need to find out what was so urgent fifty-two years ago that Prince Anton might have killed his brother. And what is so urgent now that he'd kill Violeta Bell. Or more likely, have both of them killed." I motioned him back. "Any idea how we can we find out if Prince Anton left Wolfe Island shortly before the murder?"

Eric played dumb. "I wouldn't have the foggiest."

"Me neither. Start with the ferry operators."

I got busy marking up that morning's paper. I made it all the way to the bottom of page one before Gabriella Nash smiley-faced her way to my desk. "You're back!" she sang out.

Good gravy! How many times was I going to have to hear that? "And I see you're still working here."

"Yes, I am—you know about the funeral, right?"

"Not Violeta Bell's?"

"Uh-huh. This morning."

I went immediately to the metro section and the death notices. It was that morning. In just ninety minutes. At the Umplebee & Meyers Funeral Home. "We'll have to go," I said.

She scrunched her face apologetically. "I can't."

"Don't be silly. You can drive."

"I can't. I'm on deadline."

I'd been in the newspaper business for fifty years. I'd heard reporters use that *I'm on deadline* excuse a million times. Then watched them play at their desks most of the day like it was kindergarten. "Whatever story you've got to crank out—you can crank it out when we get back."

"I really can't. Nancy needs my story for Sunday."

I picked up my phone and dialed Nancy Peale's extension. "Hi, Nancy—it's Maddy."

"I heard you were back."

I bit my tongue. "I just saw in the death notices that Violeta Bell's funeral was this morning. Would you mind if I went along with Gabriella? I feel a part of the story. Sort of. And there'll be lots of important people to oogle."

I waited patiently while my words worked their way through Nancy's synapses. "I'm sure it would be okay," she finally said.

I put my phone back in the cradle and smiled at Gabriella. "You'd better scamper back to your desk, dear. You've got an assignment coming."

So, at ten-thirty, Gabriella and I headed for Umplebee & Meyers. In Gabriella's Mini Cooper. Chuck Weideman, the paper's best photographer, and a real believer in three square meals a day, was crammed into the backseat like a semester's worth of college laundry.

Gabriella's assignment, of course, had nothing to do with the questions roiling around Violeta's murder. That was my assignment. No, Gabriella's assignment was to write a respectful story on the funeral of a woman much loved by the city's la-de-das. Weedy's assignment was to get a nice respectful photo of a tear running down the cheek of somebody important.

Umplebee & Meyers is one of Hannawa's better funeral homes. It sits right on the city's shared border with Greenlawn. White brick. Hunter green window shutters. Oodles of grandiose columns. It fits right in with all the neighborhood's fancy beauty parlors and real estate offices. We parked. Weedy stayed outside with his cameras and Snickers bars. Gabriella and I hurried inside.

We followed the spongy rose-colored carpet down the central hallway to the chapel. I'd been to several funerals there over the years, so the fancy touches didn't surprise me. They did surprise Gabriella. "A real live harp player, wow."

The chapel was half full. Fifty people, maybe. I spotted the mayor's wife and a number of retired judges. There were lots of older women in new outfits. We sat in the back, even thought there were several rows of empty chairs in front of us. I nodded at Joey Junk, who was also sitting in the back, and like us, not appropriately attired for such a fancy funeral. And what was Joey Junk doing there? One professional paying respect to another? One partner in crime to another? A murderer too curious to stay away?

Gabriella took out her reporter's notebook and started jotting down her impressions of the gathering—the little bits of color that can make a so-so story sing. As for my impressions, well, I recorded them directly into my noodle.

There was a wall of flowers across the front of the chapel. Centered in front, on a beautiful marble-topped stand, rested a bright, violet-colored urn. To the right of the urn stood a blue, yellow, and red flag. I poked Gabriella. "Looks like somebody believed her."

She responded with a "Huh?" Which was not a bad response given that there was no way in hell she could know what I was mumbling about.

"That's the old Romanian flag," I explained. "It has the royal coat of arms on it. Either Violeta left detailed instructions for her funeral, or somebody knows for sure what we don't know for sure."

There were several big sofa chairs in the front row. The family chairs. In one sat bread heiress Kay Hausenfelter in a flowery summer dress that showed too much back and probably too much front. In another sat Ariel Wilburger-Gowdy. Next to her sat her antsy, hot-tempered daughter, Professor Barbara

Wilburger. Both were dressed in black. Both wore wide-brimmed black hats. Next to the professor sat Gloria McPhee, wearing a somber gray and brown plaid suit. Next to her was husband, Phil, sweltering in tweed. Just as the minister stepped behind his portable pulpit and tapped the microphone to make sure it was on, I recognized someone else. His arms were folded across his chest, pulling his suit coat tight across his ample back. It was Detective Scotty Grant. What in the hell was he doing there?

The harpist stopped plinking and folded her hands in her lap. The service began. The minister read a slew of Bible verses, including that one I like from Ecclesiastes, about there being a time for everything. He didn't say much about Violeta herself, except that, "I'm told she loved life" and "From the looks of things here today, she had many devoted friends." Clearly this minister wouldn't have known that woman in that purple jar from Adam.

The minister read a final verse of optimistic scripture then stood aside. Kay Hausenfelter swiveled her way to the pulpit. Good, I thought. The other Queens of Never Dull were going to regale us with their favorite memories of the dearly departed. There was a chance I was going to learn something interesting.

Said Kay Hausenfelter, "As you know, I was an exotic dancer during my youth. Only back then we ladies of the burleycue called ourselves *striptease artists*. Anyway, Violeta never once looked down her nose at me. Unlike so many others in this town. She loved people for who they were." Kay raked the tears out of her eyes with her thumb and said this: "Violeta Bell never said much about her life before coming to Hannawa. But I always figured it must have been a little like mine. Memorable but worth forgetting. Anyway, we had so much fun together." She blew a kiss at Violeta's urn. "You were a hoot and a half, sweet woman. I will miss you to pieces."

Kay went back to her chair. Ariel Wilburger-Gowdy went to the pulpit. Said Ariel, "My friend Violeta Bell loved antiques. And I'm not talking about Kay Hausenfelter or Gloria McPhee! And I'm sure not talking about me!" Everyone laughed. People love to laugh at funerals. It's permission to spit death in the eye. I looked to see if Gabriella was writing it down. She was.

Unfortunately it proved to be the last interesting thing Ariel Wilburger-Gowdy said. For the next ten minutes she talked about homelessness, global warming, eradicating adult illiteracy, and the need to spay and neuter our pets. I could see why she drove her daughter up the wall. Finally, she got around to Violeta Bell. "Each of us is born with a gift, which God expects us to pay forward during the time She has allotted us here on Mother Earth." I reached over and stopped Gabriella from writing that down. No way in hell was I going to let anything icky get into *The Herald-Union.*

"My gift was spending my father's money," Ariel continued. "Violeta's gift was spreading joy. The minute you met her, you just knew she loved who she was. Inside and out. And she expected you to love yourself inside and out, too. As Three Dog Night once sang, 'Joy to the fishes in the deep blue sea. Joy to you and me.'" Again I stopped Gabriella's pen.

Ariel now turned and spoke to Violeta's ashes, just as Kay Hausenfelter had. "In some ways I never really lived until I met you, my beloved friend. And I promise you, I am going to keep on living just as long as I can."

That I let Gabriella write down.

Now Gloria McPhee came to the pulpit. She didn't speak from the heart like Kay, or from an over-active social conscience like Ariel Wilburger-Goudy. She read off a sheet of pink stationary. And for my money, she'd labored over it far too long. "Perhaps we will never know why Violeta had to die the way she did," she began. "Perhaps we will never know the secrets she kept inside her while she lived and lived and lived. But we do know of her generosity. Day by day she gave us everything she had. And since her passing, we've learned that she left all she had to the Hannawa Art Museum."

Well, that sure made my antennae spin. I knew from my talk with Detective Grant that Gloria was the executrix of Violeta's will. Which meant she knew Violeta died pretty much penniless.

Gloria, for better or worse, had more to read. "Violeta Bell claimed to be the queen of Romania. That's right, the queen of Romania. She told us a million times. In that whimsical way of hers that said, 'I don't care if you believe me or not.'"

Detective Grant took that opportunity to look over his shoulder and wink at me.

Gloria finished reading. "If Violeta was not the queen of Romania, she should have been." Before sitting down, Gloria curtsied to the urn. I didn't know whether to cry or throw a shoe.

The minister led a final prayer. The harpist starting plinking. Row by row, people shuffled past the urn. Some brushed their fingers across it. Some bent and kissed it. Many said a silent prayer. I went straight to Gloria McPhee. I introduced myself. I told her that I'd worked with Gabriella Nash on her story about the Queens of Never Dull. "Putting that Romanian flag by her remains was a very nice touch," I said.

Gloria smiled weakly. "She just loved that flag."

"That particular flag?"

"She said she'd had it since she was a girl."

"And her leaving everything to the art museum," I said. "Isn't that something."

Her eyes got as cold as those little round ice cubes they put in highballs. She knew I was laying it on thick, or, as Ike likes to say, giving her the old schmaltzaroo. "Kay told us you came to see her," she said. "That you were feeling guilty about the story your paper did on us."

I bobbled my head contritely.

"And do you know what I told Kay, Mrs. Sprowls?"

"I can't imagine."

Gloria moved in close, to make sure I could hear her whisper over the harpist. "I told her you were that librarian who sticks her nose into murders."

I'd been outed again. And I was glad. It made my nose-sticking easier. "I went to see Ariel, too. But all I got was her daughter's two cents on the matter."

Gloria pulled back. Her eyebrows shot up. She gave one of the best Lauren Bacalls I've ever seen. "I'd bite down hard on those two pennies if I were you," she said. "To see if they're made of real copper."

"I'll put it on my to-do list."

She mellowed. "I suppose you'd like to talk to me, too."

"I'd like that."

"Expect a call," she said.

I looked for Detective Grant. He was at the front of the chapel, reading all the little cards on the flower baskets. I snuck up beside him. "Any surprises?"

He flinched. As if a scorpion had just crawled up his pantleg. He took a couple of deep breaths. "No."

And there weren't any surprises. No flowers from dukes or duchesses. No flowers from anybody named Bell. No flowers from outside Hannawa.

We followed the other people outside. A black limousine was waiting under the portico. Weedy was circling the crowd like a wolf, clicking away. After a few minutes the four Queens of Never Dull came out. Kay and Ariel had their arms around each other. Gloria had her arms around Violeta's urn. Weedy got the picture.

"Any objections if I ride out to the cemetery with you?" Grant asked.

"Not a one." A few minutes later we were in the funeral procession, buzzing up West Apple in Gabriella's little bumblebee car, me up front, Weedy and Grant scowling from the back like a pair of adjoined hippopotami.

It took the procession a good half hour to reach the cemetery. It was out in Bloomfield Township. It was one of those new corporately owned jobbies that don't allow gravestones—just those flat, bronzed plaques to make the mowing easier. It was called Riverbend Moor. As if there actually was a river nearby, bent or otherwise. As if anybody in America knew what a moor was. And according to the big, flagstone-encased sign in front, it was not a cemetery at all. It was a "family memory garden."

There was an 800 number on the sign, so you could call and make your reservations on their nickel.

The procession snaked through the gates and parked along the drive. People got out of their cars, stretching and twisting until their undergarments were back in place. It was a big cemetery. Big and sterile. The grass was short and brown. There was a sprinkling of small trees still tethered to their stakes. There was a chalky-white angel statue surrounded by a ring of red geraniums. At the top of the hill sat the columbarium, the modern glass and brown-brick monstrosity where Violeta's ashes would spend eternity.

"I've never been in a columbarium before," I confessed to Detective Grant as we followed the walkway toward a pair of tall, copper-covered doors. "But I'd hear they're quite the thing these days."

"You're in for a real treat," he said.

I can't say it was a treat. But it was interesting. The building had a high, vaulted ceiling. All glass, so that rays of sunlight were shooting down at every angle, and in every color, like rainbows almost. The marble walls were lined with niches for the urns. Each niche was maybe a foot-and-a-half square. They were lined up eight across and eight high. They looked like giant trophy cases.

Anyway, each individual niche had a glass door and a lock. And what made it all so interesting is the way the niches were decorated. Next to the urns were favorite family photos and keepsakes. Baseballs. Teacups. A favorite pair of shoes or fishing lure. Military medals. Big-eyed Precious Moments figurines. Bibles opened to special passages. One niche contained a half-smoked cigar resting in one of those horrible topless-woman ashtrays. But most were in good taste and quite touching. I'd always envisioned myself being lowered into the ground in a casket. But the place did make me think.

Violeta Bell's niche had a very nice view of the pond and sitting garden outside. It was in the third row, too, so you didn't have to stoop too low or stretch too high to see inside. Gloria put the urn into the niche. Kay placed a ceramic bell next to it. It was covered with hand-painted violets. Ariel put a folded classifieds section from *The Herald-Union* inside. A half-dozen garage sales were circled. Gloria took a small wooden box out of her purse and put that inside. The box was about the size of a harmonica, maybe five inches long and a couple of inches wide. A fancy little box.

Gloria closed the glass door. The click of the lock echoed across the columbarium. The minister conducted a brief service. There was a little sniffling and a lot of silence. People headed for their cars.

Detective Grant locked his arm in mine and eased me off the walkway, away from Gabriella and Weedy. We walked along a row of those bronzed plaques, twenty or thirty of them, until we were well out of eavesdropping range. "So, Maddy," he asked, grinning like a Buddha statue. "How's your investigation going?"

"Badly. And yours?"

"It's taken an interesting twist. One I figured you'd want to know about before the brown stuff hits the fan."

"Before Dale Marabout's story comes out tomorrow, you mean?"

"Pretty much the same thing—no?"

Maybe I was only the paper's librarian, but I was a newspaper-woman. And I was a good friend of Dale Marabout's. I had my loyalties. I took the offensive. "Given that it took you so long to release the body for cremation, I gather this interesting twist of yours has something to do with the autopsy."

He was still grinning but he suddenly looked a lot more like Beelzebub than Buddha. "It seems that when the coroner did his thing—how can I put this—a few things were missing inside."

The sun was suddenly very hot. "Things missing?"

"Everything you'd expect to find on the outside was there—but inside."

"Scotty—what are you saying?"

He knew me well enough to get to the skinny. "It seems that once upon a time Violeta Bell had been a man."

The sun was now sitting directly on top of my head. "Are we talking sex change here?"

"Yes, we are," he said. "Yes, we are."

"Heaven's to Betsy! First she's the queen of Romania and now she's a man?"

Grant took my arm and started us toward the car. "We live in interesting times, don't we?"

I slipped my arm out of his. "I hate to go liberal on you, but does the whole world have to know? She was who she wanted to be. And apparently didn't want anyone to know."

"I'm a very open-minded guy," he said. "I've got a transgendered officer in my department. I'd be happy to let Violeta Bell's secret stay right up the hill there in that jar."

"But it's public record?"

"And it could be pertinent to the case," he added. "Transgenders get murdered all the time. Boyfriends who aren't too happy with the news."

"Boyfriend? She was seventy-two!" I laughed at my own stupidity. "What am I saying—I'm sixty-nine with a boyfriend."

Grant helped me over the droopy chain that ran along the edge of the drive. "I've got a press conference at four to spill the beans. You want to come?"

"Unfortunately, I've got a doctor's appointment."

◇◇◇

Dr. Menke finished his examination. He scooted back on his stool. "I figured they might be the culprits," he said.

It was not what I wanted to hear. "They're that big?"

"A couple of beauts. You should have them removed."

"Absolutely not."

"It's a relatively simple procedure."

"Absolutely not."

He stood up. Deposited the tongue depressor in the wastebasket. "Like I said, your test results show that you have obstructive sleep apnea. Which is often caused by enlarged tonsils. And like I said—"

"A couple of beauts?"

"More than likely your swollen tonsils are the result of an allergic response to something," he explained. "Your body has ordered immune cells to take up residence in your tonsils to fight off the infection. That's what puffs them up."

I slid off the examination table. "I thought allergies made you sneeze."

"They can cause all sorts of interesting reactions," he said. "And given that your snoring is a relatively new problem—or so you say—then I'd say you were only recently exposed to this allergen."

I rewound my memory tapes and played them fast forward. "Can you be allergic to a man?"

He chuckled. Let me know that my time was just about up by grabbing the doorknob. "Have you recently exposed yourself to one, Mrs. Sprowls?"

I sure wasn't going to answer that. "How about a dog?"

"A much more likely culprit," he said.

15

Ike was not happy. Not with the Cream of Wheat I'd made for our breakfast. Not with my refusal to have my tonsils out. "I'm not mad at you," he assured me as we sat in the breakfast nook watching a pair of squirrels plunder the birdfeeder outside. "I'm just pointing out the inconsistency of your stubbornness."

"The inconsistency of my stubbornness?"

"That's right," he said, wagging his spoon at me. "We're choking down this tasteless gruel because of your *bad* cholesterol—"

"The male species comes with good and bad cholesterol, too, you know."

"—But you don't care one iota how many times a night you stop breathing!"

"If I make you eggs will you shut up about my tonsils?"

"Good try."

"I'm just trying to be consistent, Ike."

"And I'm just trying to keep you from falling over dead."

"Good! We've met each other half way. Now eat your gruel so I can read the paper." I snapped the paper open and read the headline across the top of page one:

```
            Stunned Police Say
        Slain Woman Born A Man.
```

I'd already read the story twice that morning—once on the trunk of Ike's car, where the paperboy had graciously thrown it, and once sitting on my front step—but how can you not read a story like that over and over?

By Dale Marabout
Hannawa-Union Staff Writer

HANNAWA—The autopsy of 72-year-old antique dealer Violeta Bell revealed that she had undergone a sex change operation earlier in life, Police Detective Scotty Grant said.

"We debated long and loud whether to release such a personal detail about the deceased," Grant told a hastily called press conference yesterday. "But given that Miss Bell's murderer is still at-large, we decided that public disclosure might facilitate our investigation."

While Grant refused to discuss what he called the "more intimate details" of the coroner's examination, he did say that the autopsy report "shows unequivocally that Bell had been born male."

"Makes you wonder if the other Never Dullers knew," I said.

Ike scraped the last lump of Cream of Wheat from his bowl. He spooned it into his mouth and pretended to enjoy it. "How could they not know? Every time I see a person of that variety I know it."

"And how do you know that?"

He laughed at his foolishness. "I guess I wouldn't, would I?"

"Still, you've got to wonder if the killer knew."

"Yes—you do have to wonder that."

The phone rang. It was Bob Averill. He was in a tizzy. "You've seen the paper, I assume?"

"That, I have, Bob."

"Did you know?"

"I learned the same time Dale Marabout did. Give or take a couple of hours."

He hesitated just long enough to take a drink of something with ice cubes in it. "Well, I just want you to understand that this doesn't diminish my interest in the case."

"Mine either, Bob."

Ten seconds after I hung up, the phone rang again. This time it was Gloria McPhee. After inquiring about my well being, apologizing for bothering me so early, and then rattling my eardrum with one of the most agonizing sighs I'd ever heard, she got to the matter at hand. "Well, I guess you know what was in the paper this morning."

"Quite a surprise. But I suppose you already knew."

"Actually, I didn't know," she said. "The possibility never dawned on me. She was as much a woman as you or me. I'm absolutely flabbergasted."

Her bewilderment sounded genuine. Which meant it was either real or beautifully played. "I imagine it came as a surprise to Kay and Ariel, too."

"It was. Which reminds me why I called. How would you like to go garage-saling with us today?"

That, I wasn't expecting. "Well—"

"I could have Eddie swing by and get you in a hour."

"Eddie?"

"It's no fun without Eddie."

A day with those three could be very profitable. It could also be deadly. I twisted the receiver toward Ike, so Gloria could hear my every word: "Ike, dear? Do we have any plans for today?"

And so she could hear Ike's very manly voice: "For crying out loud, Maddy! You know I'm working today!"

Having established that it would be a bad idea to drive me out to the middle of nowhere and knock me in the head, I accepted the invitation. Fifty-seven minutes later Eddie French pulled into my driveway. Ike had already left for the coffee shop but when I came out, I yelled, "See you later, honey!" anyway.

Eddie invited me to sit up front with him but I sat in the back. Harder for him to strangle me while he drove.

I was acting like a paranoid fool. I knew it. Oh yes, garage-saling with Eddie and the surviving Queens of Never Dull was a dangerous thing for me to do. But not physically dangerous. The danger was that I'd be seduced out of my objectivity.

Eddie didn't make a peep until we were on West Apple. Then he sang like a cage full of canaries. "I am truly remorseful for my attitude the other day," he said, flicking his cigarette ashes out his open window. "But law enforcement matters always seem to aggravate my stressfulness."

"No need to apologize."

"Nevertheless I truly appreciate your graciousness in assisting my problematic cause."

"I'm not being gracious," I said. "I'm just trying to prove you didn't murder Violeta Bell."

"*Comprendo.*"

"You are still insisting that you're innocent, aren't you?"

He took a long draw on his cigarette. "That part of my story remains unflinchingly consistent."

"But other parts don't?"

"Let's just say that you came very close to hitting the nail on the head the other day."

"About you transporting stolen antiques for her?"

"Let's just say we're on the same page."

It was a good time for me to unveil my suspicion. "Any chance that they weren't stolen, Eddie? That they were fakes?"

He swung onto Hardihood Avenue, using nothing but the heel of his hand. "You do have a way of making the less-than-innocent squirm," he said.

"It's one of my specialties," I said. "So, were they?"

"Given the precariousness of my position, I would prefer to use the word reproductions."

"Okay, reproductions then."

"*Merci beaucoup.*"

I could see the top of the Carmichael House in the distance. I had to hurry. "And were they reproductions?"

He ground his cigarette into the ashtray. He popped his glove compartment open. He pulled out a can of Glade and started spraying. A sickening vanilla smell filled the cab. "Ariel is a fierce foe of the tobacco industry," he said.

I took my voice up a notch. "Eddie—were you transporting reproductions for Violeta Bell?"

He shook several Tic-Tacs into his mouth. "Neither the making nor selling of reproductions is illegal, Mrs. Sprowls. Nor is the *transportating*."

I could see where he was going with this. "As long as everybody knows they're reproductions?"

"Bingo."

"But given your record, it might be hard to convince the police that everyone knew?"

"The lady wins a toaster!"

We were one traffic light away from the Carmichael House. "Speaking of the lady—did you know Violeta had once been a man?"

Eddie went right through the red light. "*Mama mia!* I simply could not believe what I was reading!"

I pressed him. "You're a very street-smart man, Eddie. You had no clue at all?"

"May I expire on the spot, I hadn't the foggiest." He pulled into the Carmichael House. "I always took her as just another old bird whose time had come and gone—lookwise."

Gloria McPhee, Kay Hausenfelter, and Ariel Wilburger-Gowdy were waiting on the walk outside the entrance. Gloria, trim as an asparagus spear, was fashionably dressed in a pink three-quarter-sleeve polo shirt and stone-washed capris. Ariel, more on the rutabaga side, was wearing baggy khakis and an oversized tee shirt sporting a cute but dire message about global warming: Penguins On Thin Ice. Kay was wearing red Bermuda shorts and a sleeveless pink western shirt with sparkly, ace-of-spades buttons.

Gloria and Kay squeezed into the back next to me. Ariel sat up front with Eddie. While we'd eyeballed each other at the funeral, we hadn't formally met. We shook hands across the seat. "I just love penguins," I said.

"If we can't save them how are we going to save ourselves?" Ariel answered.

Gloria, apparently, was in charge of our itinerary. She was clutching a folded classifieds section. The garage sales were not circled. "Okay, Mr. French," she said. "Seventeen-eighty-three South Grabenstetter."

That address excited Kay. "There's always good buys in Tudorville," she said.

Eddie headed back south on Hardihood. We crossed West Apple and wound our way into the dark and hilly Hannawa Heights neighborhood. Not all of the houses were Tudors, but most were. And they were all big. Eddie parked along the curb. He stayed in the cab while we ladies made a beeline for the great clutter of treasure that covered the grand old house's blacktop driveway.

Gloria headed straight for a table covered with jewelry and other artsy trinkets. Kay went for a box of old LPs. I followed Ariel into the garage, to a table stacked with moldy old books. "I'm always looking for first editions," she whispered to me. "I found a signed *Sound and the Fury* once."

"I remember trying to read Faulkner in college," I said. "I could never get past the first chapter."

Ariel laughed. "That's farther than most people get." She got busy checking publication dates.

"What kind of things did Violeta look for?" I asked her.

"Anything made in Romania, of course."

"Of course."

"She never found much of course."

"Of course not."

"But she mainly bought furniture. Old crap that had been antiqued or painted and left in somebody's basement for forty years."

I picked up an old Lassie novel. *The Mystery of Bristlecone Pine*. My niece, Joyce, collected them. "And she'd turn around and sell it for a bundle?"

Ariel stuck a tattered book under her arm and continued down the table. "That's what you'd expect, wouldn't you? But she was very honest about it. She'd tell the homeowner what it was worth and then bargain down from there."

Ariel drifted off to look at a card table sagging with kitchen gadgets. I was left to reconcile the two Violeta Bells. One trafficked in fake antiques. The other was as honest as Abraham Lincoln.

I bought the Lassie book. Ariel bought two old books for herself and an almost-new dehumidifier for the Harvest Hill Homeless Shelter. Kay bought a fifties' Peggy Lee album, *I Like Men*. Gloria didn't buy a thing.

We drove off to 119 Buffington. When we saw all of the plastic toys and tables stacked with children's clothes, we kept on driving. "Violeta always told us not to waste our time on garage sales with piles of kids stuff," Kay said. "'The homeowners are too young to have inherited anything,' she'd say, 'and too poor to have accumulated anything worth a damn on their own.'"

We drove on to house number three. Three hundred and six Chancellor Circle. The house was a behemoth. Built in the twenties probably. We hurried up the uneven brick driveway. The woman holding the sale sat in an aluminum lawn chair. She was yakking away on her cell phone. She was surrounded by several perfectly groomed toy poodles. I followed Ariel again. There wasn't a book table, but there were enough holiday crafts to decorate a landfill. "You and Gloria were good to invite me today," I said, "and I don't intend to spend the day peppering you with questions, but—"

Ariel put a finger to her lips to hush me. "You're wondering if I knew about Violeta's—what should we call it—previous life?"

"Well, yes," I admitted, "but not as much about that as why you paid Eddie's bail."

She smiled. "You're more interested in what's important than what's sensational. I like that, Maddy."

I smiled back. I liked her. "You and Gloria obviously trust him. But given what happened and what everybody's learned about his past—well, good gravy, most people would have dropped him like a hot potato."

She picked up one of those glass pickles the Germans like to hang on their Christmas trees. She dangled it in front of her eyes, to see if it was an old one or a new one, I suppose. "Violeta knew Eddie long before she moved to the Carmichael House and the four of us started bumming around together. And we knew he did more for her than drive a cab." I must have squinted or something because she quickly explained herself. "We knew he made deliveries for her."

I found myself playing with a Thanksgiving turkey candle. It was nearly big enough to stuff and roast. "Did it surprise you that he was arrested?"

"Not at all," she said. "Considering his police record, he was prime for the plucking."

"You knew about his record then?"

"Not until I saw it in your paper."

Ariel put the pickle down. I hung onto the turkey. I figured Ike could use it to spiff up the coffee shop that coming fall. "You're confident he didn't kill her?"

She sorted through a stack of Easter baskets. "Obviously. I made his bail."

"And you don't think he stole those antiques from her either?"

"I'm willing to give him the benefit of the doubt," she said.

I didn't tell her about Eddie's confession to me that morning about his role in Violeta's fake antique business. She and the other Never Dullers would have to learn that from someone else. I wanted my day with them to be as friendly as possible.

We moved away from the crafts, to a table covered with ceramic flowerpots and old board games. There were also several Slinkys. "You'd think one would be enough," I said.

I not only bought the turkey candle for Ike, I bought a Slinky for Eric. Gloria bought a Ziploc bag of assorted safety pins. Kay brought a set of imitation jade chopsticks. Ariel went away empty handed.

We drove on to the next house. It was a big fifties' ranch on Plumbrook. White with gray shutters. There was a charming stone wishing well in the front yard. The shrubs and hedges were immaculately trimmed. My target this time was Kay Hausenfelter. I followed her to a cardboard box filled with picture frames. Kay bent over the box so the back end of her red Bermudas was sticking out like a huge ripe tomato. "I have so many pictures of myself that deserve a proper hanging," she joked.

She seemed in the right mood for the questions I had in mind. "I've been dying all morning to ask you about Violeta's sex change. Were you surprised?"

"Nothing surprises me," she said. She held a backless silver frame over her face and puckered her lips like Marilyn Monroe. "What do you think?"

"Very nice. You had to be a little surprised."

"She always looked like a real woman to me." She slid the frame up her arm like it was a bracelet. It was a keeper, apparently. "And as far as I'm concerned she was a real woman. Who you are is how you live. Not how you were born."

"I couldn't agree more."

She studied my eyes to see if I really believed that. She smiled. Then she frowned. "I just hope it wasn't the reason she died."

I eased into my next question. "There are so many little things about Violeta's death, aren't there? Interesting things that more than likely have nothing to do with anything. The sex change thing. All that silly queen of Romania stuff. Eddie's ongoing relationship with her."

Kay ran another frame up her arm. "Ongoing relationship? What on earth are you suggesting?"

I'd gotten the reaction I wanted. "Not that," I said. "If Violeta was having that kind of relationship with anybody I'm sure it wasn't with Eddie French." I gave her one of those pregnant pauses you see in the movies. "Actually, I was referring to Eddie delivering antiques for her."

Kay seemed relieved. "Oh. We all knew about that. He'd been doing that for years. When she still had her shop I guess."

I laid my little Morgue Mama trap. "Ironic."

As I expected, she misunderstood my meaning. "That he worked for her all those years then ended up driving for us? Nothing ironic about that at all. She's the one who got him driving us around."

"No, dear. I was referring to the bread truck."

She was never going to land a major role with the Hannawa Little Theater. "The bread truck?"

"The bread truck," I explained. "He delivered her antiques in an old Hausenfelter bread truck and you're the widow of Harold Hausenfelter."

Her acting improved a bit. "That's just a coincidence. That's what that is."

"I'm not saying otherwise."

I left Kay and the box of picture frames and wandered off to look at an exercise bicycle. Not that I was ever going to buy an exercise bicycle. It was just time for me to wander off. It was pretty clear that Kay Hausenfelter knew more about Violeta Bell's very complicated life than she was letting on. Which meant she might also know something about her very complicated death.

All-in-all, Kay bought four picture frames and a bright pink bud vase. Ariel bought three vegetarian cookbooks. Gloria bought an ant farm as a gag gift for her ex-exterminator husband. I bought nothing.

Before calling it a day we stopped at another six houses. In addition to my prying, there was a lot of laughing and good-natured ribbing. I could see why these women enjoyed each other's company. Each was a hoot in her own way. But despite all the fun, I had not been seduced out of my suspicions. They all knew more than they were letting on.

"Lunch time!" Gloria McPhee sang out as Eddie pulled away from the last house.

Eddie wound through the city's hilly northern neighborhoods. I figured we were heading for a restaurant. But before I knew it we were on Hardihood Avenue heading back to the Carmichael House.

Eddie pulled up to the entrance. Gloria handed Eddie an envelope. "You can pick Maddy up in an hour," she said.

"It will be my unconstrained pleasure," he said, playfully tugging on the bill of his Woolybears ballcap.

We piled out of the cab with our treasures. Eddie drove off.

It seemed odd that Eddie was dismissed in such a business-like way. He'd been so much a part of the Queens of Never Dull for so many years. You'd think they would have invited him up for lunch, wouldn't you? Then again, Eddie had appeared quite content to take the envelope and motor off. Clearly, Eddie French had been a lot closer to Violeta Bell than the other three. Nothing more than a hired gun, if you will. Unless that efficient little scene I'd just witnessed had been prearranged for my benefit, of course.

We crowded into the elevator. Gloria punched the button for the sixth floor.

Gloria's condo was really something. Artsy. Modern. Walls had been knocked out between the kitchen, dining room, and living rooms. The hardwood floors looked brand new. The furniture clearly was. Everything was either black or gray, or creamy white. Two black and white Shih Tzus were running around like a couple of nuts.

Gloria's husband waved at us from the kitchen. "I hope everybody likes cat and rabbit," he called out. He was wearing one of those stupid mushroom-shaped chef hats.

Gloria must have caught my wince. "Cat food and rabbit food," she explained. "Salad with grilled salmon. Phil's a real comedian."

Gloria was the only married member of the Never Dullers. And from what I'd gleaned from Gabriella Nash's story on them, and Eric Chen's research, happily married to boot.

She had been born Gloria Ann Gillis. She'd moved to Hannawa from a coal-mining town in Western Pennsylvania when she was nine. "Daddy had what today they call black lung and had trouble keeping a job," she'd told Gabriella Nash for her story. "We moved from one rental to another. So I got to know about houses at an early age."

She'd bought her first home when she was only twenty-two. "All I ever wanted was a place I couldn't be evicted from," she'd told Gabriella. After a few years fixing up that first little run-down house on Baxter Street, she bought a slightly bigger and better house three doors down. That was followed by a pretty cape cod on Walhounding Avenue. "It was cute as a bug," she'd said, "but unfortunately it also had bugs—termites. That's how I met Phil."

They were married in October 1962. A month later they had their first of six children. In between babies Gloria got her real estate license and little by little she became one of the most successful Realtors in Hannawa. Even though she was well into her seventies and had plenty of money, she continued to sell houses.

"Cat and rabbit now being served in the grand hall," Phil announced in a horrible English butler's accent. We headed for the dining room table. It was long enough to land a 747.

Phil McPhee looked more like a Presbyterian minister than a retired pest exterminator. He was tall and thin with enough white hair on his head for a dozen men his age. His teeth were a little yellow and his nostrils a little fuzzy, but he was by and large a handsome man. According to Eric's research, he'd graduated summa cum laude from Ohio State University, with twin degrees in business and entomology. Eric had found an article on him in *Pest Control* magazine. "I was a practical young man," he'd said of himself, "who was more interested in making a lot of money killing bugs than no money studying them."

Phil kept us laughing throughout our lunch. And his salmon salad was as good as his jokes. After sherbet and coffee Gloria gave me a tour of the condo. The bedrooms were spectacular. Their bathrooms were too magnificent to use. Gloria and Phil both had an office—not converted spare bedrooms but actual offices with built-in bookcases, daybeds and massive desks. I particularly liked Phil's desk. It was an old roll top with three long rows of pigeonholes. I also liked his wastebasket. It was covered with hundreds of hand-painted ants going every which-away. "Our oldest daughter, Carol, made it for him. For Christmas. Probably ten years ago. She's an art teacher in Buffalo of all places."

I took a closer look at the ants. They were all wearing little gas masks. I also took a closer look at what was in the wastebasket. Nothing but several little tightly rolled balls of fur.

16

I was determined to have an easy day. I'd mark up the weekend papers, dawdle over my mail, have a long lunch at Ike's, and then in the afternoon do a little personal research on the relationship between dogs, enlarged tonsils, and snoring. Dr. Menke usually knew what he was talking about—I'd been going to him for twenty-five years—but this business about James possibly causing my sleep apnea was a bunch of baloney.

Eric Chen quickly changed my plans. "I've got that stuff you wanted on the prince's brother, et al.," he said, falling in next to me as I headed back to the morgue with my morning tea. I'd only given him the weekend to investigate the Clopotar clan. I hadn't expected him to get it done that fast. "No there there?" I asked.

Before he could give me one of his smart-ass answers, Louise Lewendowski swept past us with a manic smile. "You guys hear?" she squealed. "The president is coming to Hannawa! On Thursday!"

I cringed. "This Thursday?"

She was nodding her head like a Pez dispenser with Tourettes. "Isn't it exciting?"

"With a capital E," I said.

Presidents don't generally come to Hannawa, Ohio. In fact you can count presidential visits to our city on one hand, even if you don't have a thumb: Abraham Lincoln visited twice, once

on his way to Washington to be inaugurated and once on his way
home to be buried. Calvin Coolidge once gave a commencement
speech at Hemphill College. Ronald Reagan once made a campaign stop at Hyker Hydraulics to tout American competitiveness.
Two weeks after Reagan's re-election, Hyker announced it was
moving all 1,300 of its well-paying jobs to Mexico.

Contrary to popular belief, I wasn't at the paper for the Lincoln
or Coolidge visits, but I was here for Reagan's. Pandemonium
doesn't begin to describe it. For three days I had one damn
request after another. "What do we have on this?" "What do we
have on that?" "I'm on deadline, Maddy!" "I need it yesterday,
Maddy!" Good gravy! You'd have thought the four Horsemen
of the Apocalypse were spotted galloping up Main Street!

All of this over-kill reporting on the president's visit would
be coming right in the middle of our shameless coverage of
Violeta Bell's sex change. For Sunday Dale Marabout had written a 3,000-word analysis of how the revelation was affecting
the police department's investigation. That morning's paper
featured medical writer Tracy Winkler's snip-by-snip explanation
of gender reassignment surgery. For Tuesday Tracy was examining the psychological impact of such surgery on family, friends,
co-workers, and neighbors. A feature on a local transgender
college professor was slated for Wednesday. A huge package of
stories was being planned for the weekend. The working title:
JUST WHO WAS VIOLETA BELL? No doubt about it, my plans
to take it easy were out the window.

By ten o'clock no less than eight different reporters had come
crying to me about the stories they'd been assigned to write about
the president's upcoming visit. Gabriella's request was the worst
of all. "They want me to do a story on how the paper covers
a presidential visit," she whined as I scrolled through another
indecipherable roll of microfilm. "I thought maybe you could
give me a quote."

"There's nothing I can say that the paper could print."

"Perfect," she said. She scribbled it down and scampered
back to her desk.

It took Eric and me until two o'clock to make everybody happy. Then we went out to lunch. To the Midas Muffler shop on Orange Street. If I wanted an update on his research on the prince's family, I'd have to sit with him in the waiting room, eating stale snacks from the vending machine, while the rusty belly of his old Toyota pickup truck was fitted with a new exhaust system.

Eric's lunch consisted of Strawberry Twizzlers, Chili Cheese Fritos, and his umpteenth Mountain Dew of the day. I chose the Fig Newtons and a slurp of tepid water from the drinking fountain next to the restrooms. We found a pair of empty chairs by a pyramid of windshield wiper fluid and got to work.

Eric licked the chili cheese off his fingers and opened the geeky backpack he'd brought with him. He handed me copies of the news stories and police reports on Petru Clopotar's drowning. "Looks like they never found the guy's body," he said.

"And yet they ruled it accidental?"

"The anchor was missing along with him."

"Well, isn't that interesting," I said, nibbling on my cookie. "Prince Anton told me the anchor had been tied around his brother's feet."

Eric tore open the Twizzlers package with his teeth. "The police figured he must have gotten tangled up in it and fell overboard."

"Accidents do happen."

"There were also fishing poles and live minnows on the boat," he added. "And there was a cooler with sandwiches and beer."

I shook the cookie crumbs off the police report. Mixing lunch and work is never tidy. "It makes you wonder why the prince insists it was a suicide, doesn't it?"

"Maybe he's afraid that his brother's bones will still be found some day," Eric suggested. "With a bullet rattling around in his skull or something."

I finished his thought. "Which would make it either suicide or murder."

Eric finished mine. "So the prince killed his older brother and made it look like a suicide. So he would be the heir and not just the spare."

I told him about my own research. "When Petru went overboard in the fifties, there was real hope that the Communists would be driven out of Romania. Hungary was in open revolt. People in other Eastern European countries were grumbling. It would be just a matter of time before the monarchy was restored. That was only pie in the sky, of course, but nobody knew that then."

"What about now? It's still pie in the sky, right?"

"Where there's sky there's pie. Now, what about the prince's father? Dumitru. Where, when and how did he die?"

Eric handed me an old Associated Press story. "Heart attack. January 1968. Skiing in Austria with his son, Prince Anton."

My cynicism—as it has a tendency to do—was soaring like a runaway birthday balloon. "Father and son all alone on a remote slope in the Alps, no doubt." I read the AP story. I hadn't been that far off. The prince had found his father's body on the floor of his hotel room when he went to get him for dinner. "What about the prince's mother? She can't possibly still be alive."

"Old age. June, 1996."

"And the prince's three sons? Anything about them we need to know?"

Eric handed me his research. While I read, he gave a thumbnail sketch of each son: "Christopher. Age fifty. High school science teacher by trade. Currently Labor Party member of Parliament. No public views on Romanian monarchy....

"Anthony. Age forty-three. Assistant deputy minister of tourism for Ontario. No public views on Romanian monarchy....

"Simon. Age thirty-eight. Hosts an all-night bluegrass radio show in Saskatoon, Saskatchewan. No public views on Romanian monarchy."

I didn't know whether to feel disappointed or relieved. "Two politicians and a ne'er-do-well. They don't sound very sinister, do they?"

Eric moved on to another one of my requests—whether Prince Anton had left Wolfe Island shortly before Violeta Bell's murder. "The ferry operators know him well. They don't think he's been off the island since his wife died."

I wasn't about to let Eric off that easy. "I suppose he could have his own boat."

He was more than ready for me. "Nope. Nope. And nope."

"What questions do the last two nopes belong to?"

"Nope there isn't an airport on Wolfe Island—not even for puddle jumpers—and nope he doesn't know how to swim."

I laughed at him. And myself. "You're making that last nope up, aren't you?"

"Yep."

The mechanics lowered Eric's truck from the rack. We drove back to *The Herald-Union* for more insanity. Among the oodles of phone messages waiting for me was this one from Detective Grant: *"You were right, Maddy. We had an expert look at that stuff from Eddie's apartment. All fakes. Thanks."*

When I got home, Ike had supper waiting. Green pepper and onion omelets made with fake eggs. Sugar-free lime Jello topped with sugar-free Cool Whip. We walked James. We watched TV. We went to bed.

At two o'clock I was still awake, listening to *Coast to Coast* on the radio. You can't believe a word that anyone on that show says but I just love it. It's a welcome relief from real life where you're not quite sure whether you should believe someone or not. George Noory's guest was an Indian medicine man named Red Elk who said alien lizard people were living inside the earth. Occasionally these lizard people snatch humans and grind them into a powder that makes them live longer.

I was afraid to go to sleep. Not because the lizard people might crawl up through the heating ducts with their mortars and pestles. Because I'd start snoring like a Clydesdale. I'd wake up Ike and he'd start pestering me to have my tonsils out. Which I was not going to do.

So there I lay, hands folded on my belly like a corpse, listening to Ike's soft breath and Red Elk's unbelievable stories, thinking about Violeta Bell.

All of Hannawa was buzzing about the sex change thing and Detective Grant seemed to think it could have something to do with her murder. Which I did not think. There was no evidence that Violeta had a boyfriend. Or a girlfriend. Or any other kind of friend or friends that would be so psychologically discombobulated by learning she had once been a he that he or she or they would kill her. No, there was no evidence like that at all. There was, however, strong evidence that she was trafficking in fake antiques. But would someone kill her over a fake fireplace mantel?

Could Eddie French be the murderer after all? He was in business with her. Presumably he knew more about her dark ways than most. But Violeta Bell hadn't been stabbed or strangled or knocked over the head. She'd been shot. And Eddie had an aversion to guns. Or did he?

Kay Hausenfelter, on the other, was very comfortable around guns. And Gloria McPhee was the executor of her estate. And Ariel Wilburger-Gowdy paid Eddie's bail. And wouldn't you think at least one of them would be in an emotional dither about Violeta's secret past? Their unruffled reaction to the news simply wasn't believable. Good gravy, I had a harder time accepting that Ike was a Republican than they were having with the coroner's revelation that Violeta had been born with a you-know-what.

And what about Prince Anton? A few days after Violeta told the world she was the queen of Romania she was dead. Could she really have been a Romanian royal? Surely her claim was as fake as the antiques she sold. As fake as the name on her driver's license. But what if it were true? And what if Prince Anton knew it? Had he so wanted to be king—if ever there was to be a king—that he killed her? Or had her killed? Two other pretenders to the throne standing in his way had met mysterious deaths. His brother and his father.

Of course if the prince knew that Violeta Bell really was a royal, then he also would have known who she really was. That once upon a time she'd been a he. Was she a cousin perhaps? Distant or otherwise?

When the person Hannawa knew as Violeta Bell changed his sex, he also changed his name. He took the name Violeta. Prince Anton's great-grandmother was named Violeta. But where did the name Bell come from? Bell wasn't a Romanian name. Why would someone who wore their Romanian ancestry on their sleeve adopt such a non-Romanian last name? Could Violeta have been married to some guy named Bell before coming to Hannawa? Could she have chosen it out of thin air?

I slid out of bed, stepped over James, and padded into the kitchen. I called Eric. "You asleep, Mr. Chen?"

"I'm in the middle of a chess game with a guy in Rawalapindi, Pakistan."

Eric was a chess player. When not playing with his goofy friends at Borders, he played with goofy strangers on his computer. "Hurry up and lose," I said. "I need you to Google something for me."

Suddenly sleep mattered to him. "Do you realize what time it is?"

I was adamant. "It's time for you to lose."

The guy from Rawalapindi was more cooperative than Eric. "Damn!" Eric squeaked. "He checkmated me with a pawn!"

"Good. Now say good-bye and get ready to Google."

Eric fussed and fumed but he did as he was told. "Okay, shoot."

"I need you to do a translation for me," I said. "You can do translations, can't you?" I asked.

I head a *clickety clickety click*. "What to what?" he asked.

"English to Romanian."

Clickety clickety click. "What's the magic word?"

"Bell."

Clickety clickety click. "Bell—*clopot.* Oh, Morgue Mama! You are soooo good."

"Now translate Clopotar into English." I spelled it for him. "C-l-o-p-o-t-a-r."

Clickety clickety click. "One who rings a bell."

17

Thursday, August 10

Ike and I were in separate but equal pickles. Ike's pickle was philosophical. Should he, as a good patriotic Republican, close his coffee shop at noon to attend the president's speech at City Hall? Or should he stay open and sell as much coffee to the crowd as he could? My pickle was more practical. How was I going to get through that crowd for my very important tête-à-tête with Detective Scotty Grant?

Ike, after much stewing, decided to stay open. Not to make as much money as he could, mind you, but to serve his fellow citizens during their time of need. "Whether you're the president or just pouring coffee, people need to know you're there for them," he explained. For my part, I decided to charge straight ahead, supporters, protesters, police barricades, and Secret Service agents be-damned.

I left the morgue at noon. The sidewalks along Hill Street were clogged with people. There was an American flag on every light pole. The police had already stopped traffic at both ends of the downtown. There were sirens blaring in the distance. Any minute now the president's motorcade would be arriving. It took me ten minutes to get to Ike's. I waved at him through the window but he was too busy to wave back. He just flashed his happy Republican smile at me and went back to making change.

I fought my way up the hill toward City Hall. That's where the president would be speaking and the crowd was being sucked in that direction, like dust bunnies into a vacuum cleaner. At Hill and Spring I encountered a row of barricades. To get on the other side you needed an invitation. I showed the policeman the one Ike got from the Chamber of Commerce while he was still dithering whether to attend. The policeman let me through. Apparently I looked like an Ike to him. I squeezed through the crowd to Hill and Court and another row of barricades. From here on you needed a VIP invitation. Ike hadn't gotten one of those. "Sorry ma'am," the man in the suit said. From his buzz-cut and sunglasses I gathered he was a Secret Service agent.

"I've got to get through," I said, "I have an appointment at police headquarters. With Detective Scotty Grant. About a murder."

He folded his arms, so his elbows were level with my ears. "This is City Hall, ma'am."

"And police headquarters is on the other side," I said.

"Then you'll have to go around."

My civility was waning. "There are barricades on that side, too. And a goon worse than you, more than likely."

"Please move back, ma'am."

Now my common sense was waning. "For Pete's sake! Do I look like the kind of woman the president needs to worry about?"

Two of the agent's clones appeared out of nowhere. They let me through the barricade, all right. But not before confiscating my purse and clamping a pair of handcuffs on my dangerous wrists. A minute later I was in a trailer behind City Hall, justifying my very existence to this pair of extremely unfriendly young men. Their names were Canfield and Morris. They took turns bouncing questions off me, like I was a Ping-Pong table.

"My name is Dolly Madison Sprowls," I said. "Although I go by Maddy—for obvious reasons—and I'm the head librarian at *The Hannawa Herald-Union*—that's the newspaper here."

"You have some proof of that?" Agent Canfield asked.

I pointed to my purse, which he was cradling on his lap. "No, but you do."

He blushed and dug out my wallet. He studied my business card and my driver's license and all the rest. He asked me if I knew my address and my phone number and my Social Security number. I rattled off all three.

"Why did you threaten the president?" asked Agent Morris.

"I did not threaten the president," I said. "I merely asked the other agent if I looked like the kind of woman the president needs to be concerned about."

Agent Canfield corrected me. "You said 'worry about,' ma'am."

"I suppose in your business *worry* sets off more alarms than *concern*," I conceded. "In mine they're pretty much tweedledum and tweedledee."

"So you had no intentions of confronting the president?" Agent Morris asked.

"Absolutely not."

"The agent at the line felt you were exhibiting anger," said Agent Canfield.

"Poop! I was just worried—*concerned*—about getting to my appointment with Detective Grant."

Asked Agent Morris, "And who is Detective Grant?"

"Chief homicide detective with the Hannawa Police," I said.

"And why was it," Agent Canfield wondered, "that you wanted to see a homicide detective at the very location where the president was about to speak?"

"I'm helping him solve a murder."

"This Detective Grant needs help solving murders, does he?" asked Agent Morris.

"All the help he can get," I said.

I was convincing enough that Agent Canfield called Detective Grant to confirm our meeting. Which was, as they say, problematic. I didn't actually have an appointment with Grant. I'd just planned to pop in and ruin his lunch, as usual.

Canfield put the phone down. He pulled his sunglasses down so I could see his cold eyes. "He said he's never heard of you." Then he smiled somewhat humanly. "Actually, Mrs. Sprowls, he's on his way to take custody of you."

"Take custody! What do you mean take custody?"

Ten minutes later Grant and I were fighting our way across the front of City Hall. The president's motorcade had just pulled up and the crowd was going nuts. "Had you bothered to call for an appointment, you would have found out that I was on security detail today," Grant yelled into my ear.

"Does this mean we can't talk?" I yelled back.

"We can talk," he assured me. "If you don't mind sharing the stage with the president of the United States."

"If the president doesn't mind, I don't mind."

And so my meeting with Detective Grant was held on the top step of City Hall, surrounded by the Hemphill College Marching Bear Cat Band. On a makeshift stage fifty steps below us stood the president, the governor, the mayor, two U.S. senators, a gaggle of congressmen, a herd of local politicians. Below them was a great horseshoe of Hannawans, some with signs, some with children on their shoulders, all thrilled to pieces to be participating in this unimportant historic event. I waited until the president got to the podium then got to the business at hand. "So, Scotty—have you questioned Eddie again?"

Grant's eyes were on the backsides of the politicians in front of us, but at least his mind was on me. Some of it, anyway. "Again and again," he said.

"But nothing new to report?"

"Nothing new to report."

The president was getting a resounding cheer about something. I raised my voice. "What about the sex change thing? Getting anywhere with that?"

"We're still working it."

"In other words, nothing new there either."

"Nothing new there either."

The president was now saying something about the American can-do spirit. The crowd was wildly agreeing. "You know what your problem is, Scotty?" I said. "You're getting too much sleep. It makes the mind sluggish."

He knew I was playing with him. And he knew he had no choice but to play along. "Been lying awake nights, have you?"

"Thinking and thinking."

"I've been meaning to try that myself."

"You should. It can help you unravel the most interesting mysteries."

"For instance?"

Now the president was saying something about the future. The crowd was all for it, apparently. "Well, for instance, who Violeta Bell was before she was Violeta Bell."

Grant was done playing. "You know for sure?"

"Not 100 percent sure," I admitted. "But I think there's a very strong possibility that the late Violeta Bell was, once upon a time, the late brother of Prince Anton Clopotar, pretender to the throne of Romania."

It was as if I'd just told him he'd won the state lottery and then explained that it was a $5 scratch-off ticket. "Good God, Maddy, you're not still climbing that family tree, are you?"

First I told him what I knew for sure. That Prince Anton lived on an island in the St. Lawrence River. That *clopot* in Romanian means bell. That the prince's great-grandmother, Violeta, had married a man named Clopotar. That fifty years ago the prince's older brother, Petru, took the family boat out on the river and was never seen again. That the Canadian police ruled it an accidental drowning even though they hadn't recovered a body. That the prince, after half a century, still continued to insist that his brother's death was a suicide. That while there was little chance Romania would ever restore the monarchy, the Clopotar family was in the running if they did.

Then I got to the fun part—my theory. "Until a couple of days ago I thought maybe the prince had killed his brother to get him out of the picture. And then learning that another pretender to the throne was alive and well and living in Hannawa, Ohio, made sure that she, too, was out of the picture. The prince's father died a bit suspiciously, too, by the way."

The president was now warning some country or the other to stop doing whatever it was doing, lest we be forced to do something about it. I waited for the applause to die down. "But obviously, the prince couldn't have killed his brother back then if his brother was also Violeta Bell," I said.

"It wouldn't be the easiest thing," Grant agreed.

He was being a smart ass. I ignored him and went on. "I now think the prince really believed his brother drowned. And I think he really believed it was suicide. Petru must not have been very happy in his own skin. But instead of wrapping himself in an anchor and jumping overboard, Petru only made it look that way. He swam to shore. He went somewhere and had a sex change. Took the name Violeta Bell. Moved to Hannawa and opened an antique shop."

Grant seemed more relieved than intrigued. "So, the prince didn't kill his brother fifty years ago."

"That's right."

"And there's no evidence he killed his father."

"Well, no."

"Which means you have no evidence that Prince What's-his-name is the murdering type."

"I never said I did."

"Which means you're finally off this royalty stuff."

"Not at all," I said. "What if the prince had been happy that his brother drowned? Even if he had nothing to do with it? Then all these years later he realizes his older sibling still might be alive. He does some digging. Figures out what I've figured out."

Grant corrected me. "What you *think* you've figured out."

And I corrected him. "I'm sure the prince knows his Romanian. How many nano seconds after he saw the name Violeta Bell in Gabriella Nash's story would it take his frontal lobes to start flashing Violeta Clopotar?"

"I suppose it's a possibility."

Both the president and I were really feeling our oats now. "You bet it's a possibility," I snapped over the roar of the crowd. "And if the prince wasn't surprised that his brother committed suicide, he might not be surprised to learn he faked his death and had a sex change."

"And the prince liked it better when his brother was dead and so he kills him now?"

"Kills her—but yes, that's what I'm saying."

Grant now reminded me why he was the detective, and I a lowly librarian. "It's a nice theory, Maddy, I'll give you that. But you've no real evidence. Not that the prince killed Violeta Bell. Not that Violeta Bell was really his sister or brother or whatever."

It was time to confess. "I may have gone to see the prince during my vacation."

I could see the headache wiggling across his forehead, like a million invisible worms wielding tiny sledgehammers. "Judas H. Priest! Were you trying to get yourself killed?"

"I was curious. And I wasn't killed."

He almost screamed at me. "You've just spent twenty minutes telling me what a cold-blooded killer the prince is!"

I pressed my finger across his lips to shush him. "Good gravy, Scotty. The Secret Service is going to wrestle you to the ground." I gave him a few seconds to cool down. "I know I shouldn't have gone. But you've been pooh-poohing the Romanian thing from the get-go. And I had to get a read on the guy—"

Grant started raking his eyebrows with his fingernails. "A *read* on the guy?"

"That's right. And maybe stumble and bumble into some-thing important."

Grant was wilting in front of me like a bone-dry petunia. "And did you, Maddy? Did you stumble and bumble into something?"

"Well, for a few seconds there I thought he was going to give me a nice sample of his DNA."

"His DNA? Judas H.—"

"To compare with Violeta's," I explained. "To see if they were related." I took the photo the prince had given me from my purse. I handed it to Grant. "He almost licked the envelope. But then he didn't. You can get DNA off an envelope, can't you?"

Grant pulled the photo from the envelope and studied it. "Yes, you can."

"And I imagine you have Violeta's DNA."

"The coroner routinely takes a DNA sample during an autopsy," he said, beginning to un-wilt a bit. "In fact, we used Violeta's DNA to back up the coroner's finding that she'd once been a he. All that X and Y chromosome stuff I've never understood."

"Well, it's too bad the prince didn't lick the envelope," I said. I reached back into my purse. I pulled out a Ziploc sandwich bag. "Of course he did lick this teaspoon. Can you get DNA off that?"

Grant took the bag. Held it in front of his face. "You'd think it would be impossible. Slick surface and all. But sometimes you can."

I pulled out another bag. "Surely you can get some from this." It was one of the prince's smoking pipes. "There's enough stinky old spit in the stem to gag a buzzard."

Grant was a much happier man now. "I suppose the prince just didn't give these things to you."

"I realize you probably can't use any evidence from them in court," I said. "But if you can have the DNA checked—well, we'd at least know if I was on the right track, wouldn't we?"

The president had finished speaking. The crowd was going insane. The Marching Bear Cat Band was blasting the theme from *Rocky*. "That we would," Grant bellowed. "That we would."

The president waved good-bye to the crowd. Started moving up the steps toward us, fervently shaking hands with all the local pols and their well-scrubbed families. Before I could get out of the way, the president was eyeball-to-eyeball with me, smiling like I was a favorite sister. "So good to see you," the president said to me.

I don't have much patience with politicians. No matter how high an office they hold. But I couldn't help myself. I grabbed the president's hand. "And good to see you—Madam President."

◇◇◇

By the time I got back to the paper I was shaking like a maraca. I'd just met the president of the United States. I'd been hassled by Secret Service agents. Been serenaded at close range by a marching band. I got off the elevator and headed straight for the women's room.

Eric stopped me in the hallway. I was trying not to look like I needed to get there in a hurry but he'd worked with me long enough to know I did. "I'm done checking into that bread truck business," he said.

With everything that had happened in the last two weeks, I'd forgotten all about that old Hausenfelter bread truck that Eddie French claimed no one owned. Of course, I wasn't going to admit it. "And?"

Eric leaned against the wall to block my escape. He slowly opened his notebook and studied his notes. "Let's see now— Hausenfelter Bread Company maintains a fleet of thirty delivery trucks. It routinely replaces five every year. The old ones are sold to a used truck dealer on Cleveland Road. W. E. Richfield & Sons."

"Did you call them?"

His deadpan face told me he was enjoying my discomfort. "Of course I called them, Maddy. I'm an enterprising young man. A self-starter extraordinaire. Not to mention a multi-tasker of the highest order."

"What you are is an idiot," I snarled. "Just tell me what you've got before I explode."

He dragged out a long, long, "*Welllllllllll*—if the good ole boys at Richfield & Sons don't sell the trucks in a year they put them in the crusher and sell the metal for scrap."

"So obviously someone bought that old truck Eddie drives," I said.

"Obviously. But they wouldn't give me any names. Company policy."

I tried to step around him. "Check the title bureau."

He moved to the middle of the hallway, blocking me again. "Already have. But there's no record of Eddie French ever buying a truck from the Richfields or anywhere else."

Another thirty seconds of this torture and I'd be dancing like James before his morning walks. "So we have no idea who owns that truck in his backyard?"

His straight face was beginning to warp. "We don't know for sure about that particular truck. But somebody interesting did buy a used Hausenfelter truck from Richfield & Sons eleven years ago."

I crossed my fingers that it wouldn't be Kay Hausenfelter. I liked her too much for her to be the murderer. "Who bought the bread truck, Eric?"

"Jeanette Salapardi."

"No!"

"She also buys the license plate stickers every year."

"No!"

18

I wasn't exactly having the easiest of weeks. Oh, don't worry. I was still keeping to my in-at-nine-out-by-five work schedule. And I was still taking my good old time getting back from lunch. But a multiplicity of intertwining troubles, all of my own making, were beginning to take their toll on my already shaky disposition.

First of all, I was still getting grief about my run-in with the Secret Service. The paper had actually reported it as part of their coverage of the president's visit. It was a little story on an inside page—SECRET SERVICE STOPS HERALD-UNION STAFFER—but everyone saw it. Everyone in the newsroom saw it. Everyone on my street saw it. All the clerks at the supermarket saw it. That right-wing nut on the radio, Charlie Chimera, saw it. Even the clucks at TV23 saw it. I was the laughing stock of Hannawa, Ohio.

Managing Editor Alec Tinker, to his credit, did have the good sense to warn me of his decision to run the story. "If anyone else in our circulation area had been held by the Secret Service we would have published it," he said.

"But it was just a stupid misunderstanding," I argued. "They let me go right away."

"We have to demonstrate that we're a part of the community," Tinker said. "Not above it."

The other thing churning away at my insides was that damn DNA sample. Detective Grant had warned me that the results probably wouldn't be back from the Ohio Bureau of Criminal Identification for a week. "It might even take longer if things get backed up over there," he cautioned.

I growled at him like a bear that hadn't eaten all winter. "Can't you tell them it's important?"

"Oh, we will," he said. "And so will every other police department in the state about their samples. Everybody wants it yesterday. So my advice, Maddy my dear, is to take a chill pill and wait for the test tube elves at BCI to do their magic."

On top of those two things, Bob Averill was continuing to pester me about Eddie, and Ike was continuing to pester me about my tonsils. So I couldn't get away from the morgue fast enough that noon.

I pulled into Speckley's ten minutes late. I hurried inside and scanned the crowded booths. Kay Hausenfelter was already there, studying the menu while everyone else was studying her.

Kay was actually dressed somewhat conservatively for our lunch—for Kay that is. She'd squeezed her ample top into a pink scoop-neck jersey and hidden her equally plentiful bottom under a red peasant skirt. Her hoop earrings were big enough for a gymnast to perform on. The straps on her sandals were trimmed with glass diamonds. Her fingernails matched the jersey. Her toenails matched the skirt.

I apologized for being late and recommended the house specialty to her, the meatloaf sandwich, au gratin potatoes on the side. She wrinkled her nose and asked me if the Cobb salad was edible. "I've never had it," I said. "But if it's on the menu it's probably good."

We engaged in the usual Ohio small talk until our lunches came. How hot the summer has been. How the fall is our favorite time of the year. How winter's always a bitch.

It was Kay who finally got the ball rolling. "I suppose you invited me to lunch to talk about something more than the weather."

I folded my hands and got as comfortable as I could. "I thought maybe we could talk about sex."

Kay Hausenfelter forked a slice of avocado and snipped off the end with her perfect whiter-than-white teeth. "My favorite subject," she said.

I took a bite of my meatloaf. "I don't want you to think I'm talking to you about this because—"

She could see I was having trouble finishing the sentence. She laughed. Devoured the rest of the avocado. "Because I dress like a hootchie?"

"Because I figured you'd be more comfortable with the subject than Ariel or Gloria."

She laughed again. Went after a sliver of radish with her fork. "You're obviously a good judge of people."

It was a good opening and I jumped right in. "I doubt as good as you. And I guess that's why I still find it strange that you didn't realize Violeta was a man."

Kay was suddenly defensive. "She wasn't a man."

I retreated. "Well, you know what I mean."

She softened again. "I do know what you mean. And no, she wasn't mannish. Not physically or mentally. She looked like a woman. She walked like a woman. She talked like a woman. She was a woman. A born woman."

I started down the long list of questions in my head. "Was she interested in men?"

"Not as interested as me," Kay said with a wink. "But she liked the company of the opposite sex. You couldn't get her off the dance floor on our cruises. She could really cha-cha-cha."

It was hard not to like Kay Hausenfelter. She was funny, brash, what they used to call saucy. If she were fifty years younger she would be one of those girls shaking everything the good lord gave them in those awful music videos. "The police think maybe she was killed by a boyfriend who found out she was a man and went nuts," I said.

"That Detective Grant is a cutie, isn't he?"

"So he's talked to you about this?"

"Honey, he's talked to me about everything twice."

The trouble with au gratin potatoes is that they can get cold pretty quick. And there's nothing worse than gooey cold potatoes. I had no choice but to talk with my mouth full. "So what do you think about his boyfriend theory?"

"He's the detective."

I ate more potatoes. "It's possible then?"

"It's possible that it's possible."

I had a sense from the way she was dragging a cube of chicken back and forth through her Roquefort dressing that she was struggling with that same moral dilemma that has plagued womankind since Eve wiggled out of Adam's rib—she wanted desperately to talk about things she knew she shouldn't talk about. I was empathetic. I'd been there a few times myself. But my job was to uncover the naked truth about Violeta. That meant to hell with sisterhood. That meant playing the serpent. Tricking her, if possible, into feasting from the Tree of Gossip. "I'm sorry," I said. "I know there are probably things you told Detective Grant that you might not feel comfortable telling me. About her boyfriend especially."

Kay Hausenfelter was no innocent Eve. "Good try."

"Apparently not good enough."

My admission freed her. She speared the chicken cube and swallowed it after a few quick chews. "There was no boyfriend, Maddy. Not unless she'd been creeping down the halls again."

I repeated half of what she said. "Creeping down the halls again?"

"I know everybody thinks of the Carmichael House as a warehouse for dried up old prunes," she said, swinging her eyes toward the two workers from the city water department who had just sat at the counter across from our booth. "And to a certain degree that's true. But there's some hanky panky, too."

"When you say hanky panky—exactly what do you mean?"

She swung her eyes back toward me. "You can't possibly have forgotten what hanky panky is!"

We laughed. Me, uncomfortably. "I guess I'm asking if Violeta was creeping to meet somebody's husband."

"It was years ago, Maddy."

"And the husband in question will forever remain anonymous?"

"Forever dead, too."

"I see—and the wife is still very much alive."

"A very nice gal who doesn't have a clue."

"I understand. No more questions."

We finished our lunches. We spent an enormous amount of time discussing the dessert menu. We gobbled our respective slices of strawberry pie. Hugged in the parking lot. Drove off in our respective cars. Kay in a little red car that looked both expensive and foreign. Me in my old Dodge Shadow.

The minute I got back to the morgue I summoned Eric and his bottle of Mountain Dew to my desk. He pulled up a chair with his foot and slumped into it. "Whatever you're working on, shelve it," I told him. "I just had lunch with Kay Hausenfelter and I'm dying to know if I learned anything." I gave him his marching orders. "First, I need the name of every married couple that's lived at the Carmichael House during the last eight years. The number of their condo unit and whether they still live there."

Eric, as I expected, went apoplectic. "No-no-no-no. That building is a regular stairway to heaven. That could take days and days."

I put my foot down. "You can do it in an hour. Check the county tax records. I need first names of both the husbands and the wives. List them by year. Alphabetically by last name. That will make the next step easier."

This time his protest was perfunctory. "The next step. Sheeeesh."

"Another hour," I assured him. "Two at the most. Check the husband's names against our obits for the same eight years. I want to know who's dead and who's not. And I want copies of the obits for the dead ones."

He looked at me like a wild-eyed cat that had just spent a week trapped in a dresser drawer. "Do you have any idea how many obits we run in a year, Maddy?"

"Eight thousand. Now get your lazy carcass off my chair and get to work."

He slowly unhinged. Stood up straight and stretched. "And what will you be doing while I'm having my nervous breakdown?"

"I'm the head librarian of a major daily newspaper," I said. "I've got major administrative duties to perform."

Eric dragged himself back to his desk. I hurried to the cafeteria to make my afternoon tea.

Why, if I liked her so much, did I think Kay Hausenfelter was lying to me? To tell you the truth, I didn't know if she was or not. She admitted that Violeta once had an affair with a married man right there in the Carmichael House. She admitted that Violeta might have been "creeping down the halls again," as she put it. She gave in to the temptation of answering my questions after resisting me only minutes earlier. Were those signs of an honest woman? Or were those signs of a devious woman? Did she tell me those things because she wanted me to share Detective Grant's suspicion? Grant had already questioned her about the possibility of a boyfriend gone mad, so certainly she knew what I was getting at from the get-go. Did she want me to snoop as far away from the real reason for Violeta's murder as possible? Yes, she'd been a stripper in her early days. Yes, she'd been called a gold digger. Yes, she'd been accused of rewriting her husband's will as he lay on his deathbed. Yes, she'd been accused of being adulterous and uncouth. And yes, she was handy with little guns. But did that make her a liar? Did that make her a murderer? Somebody I couldn't trust? Somebody I should fear?

My water came to a boil. I poured it over my teabag. Just the smell of those soaking Darjeeling leaves sweetened my mood. Then Gabriella Nash found me. She was crying. Again.

"Good gravy, Gabriella! Don't you know we've got a woman president? Buck up!"

"They want me to do a column," she said.

"So those are tears of joy."

She started *waaaah-ing* like Lucy Ricardo. "No they aren't."

I felt like strangling her. I strangled my teabag instead. "Let's get this straight—you've been at the paper for two months and they've given you a column? And this is bad news? Most reporters have to wait for twenty years."

"It's for the Saturday Home & Garden section."

"Oh."

"On pets."

"Oh dear."

She pulled a paper towel off the roll on the counter and wiped her nose. "I didn't go to journalism school to write about cats and dogs. Not to mention tropical fish."

"You'll still be able to write your features won't you?"

"Well, yes."

"See there," I said. "It's not as bad as you think. Continue to write your features as well as you can and make the column as unreadable as you can. When the veterinarians and dog groomers start to bitch, they'll give the damn thing to someone else."

"I guess that's a plan."

"You bet that's a plan," I said. "Meanwhile I'll give you an idea for your first column. Does your dog make you sick?"

"That's a stupid idea."

I headed for the door. "You think so? Do you know that dog hair can make your tonsils swell up like basketballs? Make you snore? Ruin your last chance at love?"

"Love, Mrs. Sprowls?"

I gave her my best Morgue Mama scowl. "That was an unfortunate slip of the tongue, Gabriella. And if you ever tell anybody, I'll see to it that your next job is writing want ads."

The afternoon crawled like an 800-year-old Galapagos turtle. Finally, at 4:30, Eric reported what he'd found. He was quite proud of himself. "There are 120 units at the Carmichael House," he said. "The turnover rate during the eight years

Violeta Bell lived there averaged 7.9 percent a year. That's 183 owners, total. Seventy-two percent of those owners were single women. Four-point-four percent single men. Married couples, happily or otherwise, 23.6 percent. That's forty-three couples if you can't do the math in your head." He handed me the list I wanted with all the married couples' names.

"Alphabetically, too," I said, pretending to be impressed. "Now what about the obits?"

He continued his geeky presentation. "Assuming we ran all their obits, a grand total of eight married men passed on to their heavenly reward during the last eight years." He not only gave me copies of their obituaries, but a cover sheet listing their names and dates of death.

I sent him back to his desk and got to work on the obits. One husband had died the same month Violeta moved in, so I eliminated him as the likely lover. That left seven. Two had died in nursing homes, which meant they had probably been out of their condos for some time. So I eliminated them. That left five. One of the husbands was ninety-seven when he passed. Men being men, I couldn't totally eliminate him, but I did put him in the unlikely category. That left four.

I checked those four against the first list Eric gave me. Two wives had sold their units after their husbands died. Two still lived there. Was one of them the nice gal who didn't have a clue her husband had an affair with Violeta Bell? Or was Kay Hausenfelter lying? Was that husband still alive? And did his wife actually have a clue? Was Kay covering up for her? Or was Kay telling a much bigger lie? Was Kay Hausenfelter covering up for herself? Sending me on a wild goose chase? Looking for a goose that didn't exist?

And there was an even bigger question: How in the hell was I going to find answers to those other questions?

I fled the morgue at five. Drove straight home. I gave James a quick walk. Boiled a packet of Tabatchnick's Golden Cream of Mushroom Soup for my supper. Thank God it wasn't an Ike night. I watched a couple hours of TV, flipping back and forth between the *Everybody Loves Raymond* marathon on Channel Nine and *The Naked Archeologist* on The History Channel. I was slipping into my pajamas when the phone rang. It was Detective Grant. "Don't tell me you're home from work already," he said.

I knew he was yanking my chain. "I just walked in the door."

I was standing in my dark bedroom with one leg in my bottoms and one leg out, but I could see the grin on his big round face. "Well, Mrs. Sprowls," he said ever-so-nonchalantly, "I'm sitting here behind my big policeman's desk with a very interesting report from my pointy-eared pals at BCI."

I hopped into the second leg. "And?"

"Looks like Prince Anton and Violeta Bell are siblings. A ninety-percent likelihood, anyway."

"A ninety-percent likelihood? That's the best you can do?"

There was a long silence. Then the sound of something being slurped. "Apparently testing for *siblingship*, as the elves call it, is not as conclusive as other types of DNA testing. Especially when you don't have a mother or father to test. Which in this case we don't."

To say the least I was disappointed. "Can't they squeeze out another ten percent?"

"We're not talking about making lemonade, Maddy. Be happy with the ninety. It's as close to a slam-dunk as you can get. Then, of course, there's the scrapbook."

"The scrapbook?"

"Yeah—she had a scrapbook. Mostly birthday cards and Christmas cards and gooey crap like that. But there are several pages of clippings on Prince Anton and his sons. From Canadian newspapers and magazines."

I screeched at him like a cuckolded wife. "And you've had this all along?"

He hemmed and hawed. "Actually—no. After I got the BCI report this afternoon, I went back to Violeta's condo. To make sure we hadn't overlooked something. Seems we weren't as thorough as we should have been."

I forced myself to simmer down. Not an easy task. "So, the DNA and the scrapbook pretty much make the case?"

"Yes, they do."

"And I was right."

"Yes, you were."

"And you were wrong. Not to mention sloppy."

"Yes and yes."

I had oodles of questions for him. I asked the only one that counted. "What do we do now?"

Said Grant, "That was going to be my question to you."

"I suppose the polite thing would be to tell the prince first," I said. "Before you leak it to the media."

"I agree."

"To see how he reacts to the news."

"Absolutely."

"That's what we'll do then."

Grant tickled my eardrum with his happy little laugh. "No—that's what you'll do. You already know the man. You can better judge his reaction."

Now I laughed in his ear. "You still don't believe it's possible that Violeta was killed because of her royal blood, do you?"

There was another long silence. Another slurp. "Frankly, your theory is just too far-fetched for me to devote my department's resources to it," he said. "Especially since I've got a couple of much better leads to spend the city's money on. And then there's the political ramifications of the thing."

"Political ramifications? Who gives a flying frog about political ramifications?"

His irritation was growing. "He's a Canadian, Maddy. And Canada the last time I checked is another country. And I'm not too crazy about getting our fair city into an international brouhaha unless it's absolutely necessary."

"And I'm not too crazy about getting myself killed," I snarled.

He snarled right back. "Do you really think I'd let you go ahead with this if I thought you were in any danger?"

"Yes, I think you would," I said, joking but not joking. "I've been nothing but a burr in your saddle since the day we met."

"Actually well before that happy day," he said, also joking but not joking. Then he turned into a teddy bear. "Look, Maddy, I don't think you're going to be the one finding the murderer this time—the gods do owe me this one—but your interference in the case has already done a lot of good."

"Good? I haven't discovered diddly."

"But you have, Maddy," he said. "You discovered who Violeta Bell really is. Or really was, I should say. And you found out what actually happened to the prince's brother. He'll be grateful as hell. Probably fall head-over-heels in love with you and whisk you away to some smelly old castle in Transylvania."

It's always fun sparring with Scotty Grant on the phone. Especially when I get the last jab. "So, while I'm writing my *guess-who-your-brother-was* letter to the prince, you'll be following up on your other much-better leads?"

"That's my plan."

"Including which one of those two dead husbands was Violeta having an affair with?" I asked. "And whether they're really dead?"

I'm sure if a cringe made a noise, my ear would have been ringing like the Liberty Bell. "Actually, when I went over the list I counted three husbands," he said.

"You're counting the ninety-seven-year-old?"

19

Dear Prince Anton,

Thank you so much for your hospitality the other day. And for the autographed photograph. Given that I showed up at your door like a beggar, you didn't have to be so kind. You were truly a gentleman.

Sorry to say, I was not exactly a lady. When you weren't looking, I stole one of your teaspoons and then one of your pipes. I'll return both when I get them back from the police.

I gave them to the police to have your DNA checked. Not because I doubted your royal lineage, mind you, or suspected that you might be somehow involved in Violeta Bell's death. I just wanted to see if Miss Bell was truly a member of the Romanian royal family, as she claimed before her murder.

As it turns out, you and Miss Bell are siblings.

It's all very complicated, but the coroner's autopsy found that Miss Bell had undergone a sex change operation. Which means your brother faked his death and then sometime afterward had the aforementioned surgery.

I realize that this startling news will be hard for you to believe. And while it would be impolite to discuss the details of my research into the life and death of your brother/sister in this letter (some of those details are a little on the disappointing side, I'm afraid) I will be more than happy to share what I've learned with you, should you be interested.

Dolly Madison Sprowls
Head Librarian
The Hannawa Herald-Union

20

Ike and I arrived at the Salapardis' at six. The invitation was for five. We parked on the street and hiked up the winding asphalt drive toward the house. It was one of the biggest houses in Yellow Creek Township. Which was saying a lot. Yellow Creek is where Hannawa's new money lives. In houses so showy that even the old money shakes its head.

Most of the new homes in Yellow Creek are fanciful reproductions of the golden past—plantation-style colonials, pointy-roofed Tudors, Victorians with gobs of gingerbread. The Salapardis' house, however, was quite modern. It was comprised of a dozen or so glass boxes stacked this way and that like the pieces in a Jenga game.

The invitation said it was going to be a backyard barbecue, so we followed the cobblestone walk around the side of the house. "I'll probably be the only black person here," Ike grumbled.

I squeezed his arm. "And I'll probably be the only Democrat."

He smiled at me the way I wished he wouldn't. I smiled back at him the way I wish I wouldn't. We had a way of grounding each other—unfortunately. "Don't worry, Sweetie," he said. "I'm sure the serving staff will be Democrats."

We laughed our way toward the enormous flagstone patio behind the house. Just below the patio was a swimming pool. Below the pool was a horse barn and fenced-in riding ring. Below that was a long sloping lawn sprinkled with dogwoods and blue spruce. Below that was a lake lined with yellow willows.

We climbed the stone steps to the patio. Both of our fears proved to be unfounded. Ike quickly counted three other black guests and I spotted one of the most prominent Democrats in the city, Ariel Wilburger-Gowdy. All-in-all there were maybe a hundred people there, dressed casually but expensively, mingling like a hive of honey bees. Bustling among them were those Democratic servers Ike had joked about, in crisp white shirts and black slacks, some balancing big trays of finger food on their palms, some toting wine bottles the size of artillery shells.

Jeannie Salapardi saw us and came running with her fish-bowl-sized margarita. "Maddy! I'm so glad you could come." She smooched the air a foot from my cheek. She stuck out her hand for Ike. "And you're Mr. Sprowls?"

"So far I'm still Mr. Breeze," he said. "Ike Breeze."

"Well, Mr. Ike Breeze, don't you let Maddy escape," she said. "She's one of a kind."

"Thank God for that," said Ike.

Now Jeannie got as serious as her margarita would allow. "Even though it didn't work out exactly as we wanted, Eddie and I are still grateful for your help. My husband, too."

"I'm looking forward to meeting him," Ike said.

"Ike's a businessman, too," I explained.

Jeannie pouted apologetically. "Then you know how it is. Work-work-work, 24/7. But I'm hoping he'll be here later."

Jeannie hurried off to welcome another couple coming around the corner. Ike and I headed for the lemonade.

That night's party was for Eddie. Sort of a combined going away and going straight party. After several meetings with the prosecutor's office, Eddie had agreed to plead guilty to a single charge of aiding and abetting. In exchange, he agreed to tell everything he knew about Violeta Bell's fake antique business. That had led to the arrest of antique dealers in Tuckahoe, New York and Brattleboro, Vermont. Also arrested were a pair of talented furniture makers in Buncombe County, North Carolina, a whiz-bang metalworker in Mckeesport, Pennsylvania, and a crafty potter in Zanesville, Ohio.

The antique dealer in Tuckahoe confirmed that on the night of July 4, just four hours before Violeta Bell was murdered, Eddie was at his store unloading a shipment of just-made 19th century mantle clocks. The Tuckahoe Motor Inn confirmed that Eddie had checked in shortly before midnight and had watched one X-rated pay-per-view movie after another until dawn. Another establishment in that leafy New York City suburb, G.W. Moley & Son Auto Repair, confirmed that on July 5 a yawning man wearing a bright orange baseball cap paid in cash to replace the muffler on an old bread truck.

So that coming Monday Eddie French was going to court. To plead guilty and start doing the twenty-four months in state prison the prosecutor's office promised him.

Eddie, by the way, wasn't the only member of the French family to have a heart-to-heart with Detective Grant. His sister, Jeannie, confessed that she owned that bread truck Eddie used to deliver Violeta Bell's fake antiques. "My brother was broke, as usual, and was already driving his cab on a suspended license," she explained. "He was crying how he could get his life in order if he only had a truck. So I made sure he had one." She bought the old Hausenfelter truck from Richfield & Sons. She paid a mechanic at her husband's Mitsubishi dealership to pry the identification number off the dashboard. She bought new license plates and stickers for it. She made sure it was insured. She filled it with gas and had it parked behind her brother's apartment.

Eddie accepted the mysterious truck as a gift from the gods, just as Jeannie figured. No questions asked lest he be struck dead by a torrent of scruple-sized hail. He used the truck when he needed it. He wasn't the least bit territorial when others in the neighborhood did, too. Every year Jeannie bought new license stickers and stuck them on the plates when Eddie wasn't looking. "I know it wasn't exactly right," she told Grant. "But it wasn't exactly wrong either. He's my brother and, well, what can I say? I love him."

Ike poured our lemonade. We clinked our plastic tumblers together and sipped. It was not the sweetest lemonade. While I puckered like a goldfish, and Ike frantically searched for a sugar bowl, Eddie sauntered toward us. He had a bashful grin on his face. His hands were stuffed in the pockets of his Bermuda shorts. A baggy blue and green Hawaiian shirt was hanging off his shoulders. Instead of his orange ball cap, he was wearing a white straw fedora with a tiny Budweiser can stapled on the crown. He tipped it and gave me a cross-legged curtsy. "Quite an extravaganza, eh, Mrs. Sprowls?"

"The party or your shirt?"

He twirled slowly for me, like a model. "My sister insisted that I be dressed to the nines tonight," he said. "And how could I not oblige her wishes, me being the guest of honor, et al., and her picking up the freight credit card wise."

"She must be proud."

He laughed and twirled again. "She was appalled. But I said, 'Sis, you weren't exactly Grace Kelley before you became a Salapardi.'"

He was certainly right about that. According to Eric's research, Jeannie and Eddie had grown up in a working class family on Hannawa's east side. Their father worked in the city's sewer department. Their mother was an LPN at Hannawa General. While Eddie spent his youth getting in trouble, Jeannie spent hers getting As. That effort was rewarded with a scholarship to Kent State and an invitation to join one of the university's top sororities. After trying out majors in elementary education and English, she wisely switched to business. In one of her accounting classes she sat next to a Vietnam veteran named David Salapardi who had big plans for turning his father's used car lot into an empire. Unlike brother Eddie, she'd only had one scrape with the law. A speeding ticket in 1983. "Your sister obviously loves you very much," I told Eddie. "The way she's stood behind you through all this."

Ike had found some sugar cubes by the coffee maker. He gave us both three lumps. I introduced him to Eddie. "You're doing the honorable thing," Ike assured him as they shook hands.

"It's not like I haven't been in prison before," Eddie said. "Two measlies behind the Venetians will be a slice."

I could see that Eddie's choice of words had Ike's brain tied in knots. "Two years in a jail cell," I explained. "Piece of cake."

"I intend to mind my Ps and Qs in there, too," Eddie said. "Come out clean and live happily ever after, like a well-scrubbed clam in a fairy tale."

Ike looked at me for another interpretation. "You're on you own," I said.

All three of us laughed. Then Eddie's tough guy façade fell away. "I know you were forced into helping me," he said. "And for all your sneaking around and such, came up with pretty much *nada el grande.*"

He was right. I hadn't uncovered anything that helped exonerate him. Except for realizing that Violeta Bell's antiques might be fakes, I'd simply confirmed what Detective Grant already knew. "I was happy to try."

His apology—if that's what it was—apparently was just beginning. "And all you got from me was a hard time. Capital H. Capital T."

"I can understand your being a bit defensive."

"Defensive? I was the epitome of despicability. My only hope now is that my remorsefulness seems genuine."

"It does."

"That's good to hear," he said. "Because all I did that day you showed up unannounced at my abode was blow smoke in your face. Both literally and figuratively at the same time. My sister, too."

"She was just protecting you."

"And you were just trying to help," he said. He took an awkward step toward me. He took both of my hands in his hands. He rubbed his sweat all over my fingers. "The sappier moments in life don't come easy for me," he said. "But if it hadn't been for you, Mrs. Sprowls, I never would've given the police an accurate account of my who, what, when, where, and whys."

"I'm sure you would have eventually."

Said Eddie, "No I wouldn't've."

Ike tried to intervene on my behalf. "I'm sure you would have, too."

"Neither of you know me like I know me," Eddie said. He pulled me toward him, in a sweet, innocent way. He lowered his face until it was level with mine. His eyes were watering. Instead of the beer and cigarettes on his breath I expected, there was a powerful blast of Listerine. "You remember what you said to my sister that day, Mrs. Sprowls? 'Your brother is going to be twiddling his thumbs on death row if he doesn't start telling a more forthcoming version of the truth.'"

It was a pretty good line. I was impressed with myself. "I said that, did I?"

"I remember it word for word," he said. "Like it was one of those dirty parts in Deuteronomy or something." He let go of my hands. Stuffed his own hands back in the pockets of his baggy shorts. "It didn't turn me around right away, of course. I've been my own worst enemy for a long time. A real self-destructive sonofabitch. Capital S. Capital O. Capital B. But your words of wisdom eventually put my noodle in question mode. What if they don't find the real killer? What if I'm the best they can do?"

I patted his shoulder. "I'm just glad it's gone well for you."

Eddie the tough guy was back. "Damn friggin' straight! Those two measlies behind the Venetians will be a slice."

I liked Eddie French. But I also wanted to get away from him. Talk to a few other people before they brought out the steakburgers, or chicken legs, or whatever they were serving. "There is one little thing I'm still curious about," I began. "About Violeta."

Eddie blushed. "Like I've told you more than once, I truly never-ever expected that she'd been born with the male accouterments."

Smoke was rolling across the patio. The Democrats were taking things off the barbecue racks. Piling it on platters. We'd be eating soon. "It's not that," I told him. "I've reluctantly accepted the possibility that nobody had a clue about her previous gender. It's the fake antiques."

Eddie showed a little worry. "I've already told the gendarmes the brutal truth about that."

And for all I knew he had. According to the story Dale Marabout wrote about Eddie's change of heart, Violeta Bell didn't start trafficking in fake antiques until after she retired from her shop and moved into the Carmichael House. Dale quoted Eddie's statement to the police: "She was already hiring me to haul things around. Real things left over from her shop. Then every once in a while she'd sneak in something fake. Before long it was all fake. Some of the dealers called her on it. But others ate it up. Wanted all she could get." Eddie also opined that, "It's been my experience that there's good and bad in everybody, usually simultaneously, but sometimes sequentially."

"I know the facts," I said. "I was wondering how she felt about it."

Eddie shrugged. "She did it."

I tried to cool off my impatience with a long drink of lemonade. It was too sweet now. "But did she feel guilty about it? Some criminals do feel guilty about the things they do, don't they?"

"Crime is a very individualistic thing," he said. "Some do, some don't. Some both do and don't depending on what day it is. I, for better or worse, have always been one of those."

I was forced to take another long drink. It was either that or strangle the little man. "And Violeta?"

Eddie scratched his whiskers. "At first she exhibited the customary pangs of guilt," he said. "But as things went along, she started to get a kick out of it. I've been there myself. You say, 'Jesus, I can't believe I'm getting away with this.' The people you're rippin' off are the dummies and you're the smarty. Good for the ego."

I had another question. "Why did you think she was doing it?"

He looked at me like I was daft. "For the moola-boola!"

I had him in a lie. "But that day I visited your apartment, you said that you didn't know she was broke. You were downright flabbergasted in fact."

"I was flabbergasted," he admitted. "As downright as you correctly observed. I'd always assumed she was as comfy as the other three."

I was confused. "So, if you thought she was rich why would you also think she was doing it for the money?"

He shrugged. "Rich people keep working. Crooked people keep crooking. So sayeth Eddie French."

People were lining up at the serving tables. Getting their plates and silverware. Oohing and ahhing over the fare that awaited them. I locked one arm around Ike's elbow, the other around Eddie's. "What do you gentlemen say we get something to eat?" We headed toward the tables.

There were more than chicken legs and steakburgers. There were ribs. Blackened jumbo shrimp. Thick medallions of prime rib. Enormous brats ringed with bacon. Golden Cornish game hens almost too cute to eat. Ike and I went for the prime rib. Eddie loaded his plate with shrimp. He used his fingers to make a nest of them and plopped an entire game hen in the middle.

There were oodles of fancy side dishes, too. I limited myself to German potato salad and an ear of roasted corn. Ike chose roasted peppers, wild rice, stuffed mushrooms, and green beans. Eddie scanned the table with a disappointed frown and then went back to the meat table for more shrimp.

I was afraid that Eddie was going to latch onto us for the entire party. Instead he excused himself. "Sis will kill me if I don't spread my countenance about," he said. He headed off to the bar.

Ike and I strolled across the lawn, nibbling the best we could. It was a beautiful evening with just enough sun. We chatted with Kay Hausenfelter for a while. With Ariel Wilburger-Gowdy. With the Reverend James W. Bobbs. With Bob and Tippy Averill. With somebody named Penelope. With somebody Penelope introduced us to, whose name I never did catch. Then I saw Gloria McPhee's husband, Phil, strolling along the lake with his plate, by himself. "There's just the man I want to talk to," I told Ike.

"Alone, I gather?"

"I'm a one-man-at-a-time girl," I said. I headed for the lake.

I'd only seen Phil McPhee once before. At lunch, after my garage-sale juggernaut with the Queens of Never Dull. He'd cooked for us. He'd told way too many jokes.

I was half way down the lawn when Phil spotted me. I waved at him, hoping I didn't look too eager. I'm sure he wasn't thrilled to see me coming—he obviously wanted to be alone for some reason or the other—but he stopped and waited for me. He was sucking on a barbecued rib. He had sauce on his chin. On his white linen pants, too. "Feeding the fish?"

He smiled. "Don't tell me you abandoned that good-looking man up there to keep me company."

"He's not that good looking up close."

"Even if he's ugly I'm flattered."

Phil was quite the flirt. And that's exactly why I wanted to talk to him. At lunch that day he'd seemed a little too charming. A little too comfortable around women. "I think it's just terrific the way your wife and the others stood by Eddie throughout this mess," I said.

He went Groucho on me. Wiggled his eyebrows. "And Eddie is a hard guy to stand next to."

I pretended to like his joke. Then I got serious. "Then again, they spent a lot of time with Eddie over the years. I guess when you know someone that well, you know if they're capable of murder or not."

This time, no joke. "That seems to be the case."

"Seems?"

He tossed his rib bone in the lake. Lowered his eyebrows and smirked devilishly. "You didn't see that," he whispered, as if somebody was close enough to hear him.

He was testing me. Seeing if I was seducible. "I did see that."

"Do you want me to jump in and get it before the fish do?"

"Whatever your conscience will bear."

He laughed loudly. Sucked on a fresh rib. "I'm sure the girls are right about Eddie," he said. "The police seem to agree."

"But you don't?"

"I'm an exterminator," he said. "I know my wiggly little creatures."

He started walking along the bank again. I followed him. "I meet my share of those in my work, too," I said.

He finished sucking the meat off his rib. Made sure I saw him put the bone back on his plate. "You're a funny lady."

"And you're a funny man."

He grinned at me. Winked. Coming to the mistaken conclusion, I hoped, that I was indeed seducible. To improve the odds, I pointed out that he'd splattered more barbecue sauce on his pants. "And look there," I said. "You've got cat fur all over the place." I reached down and pulled a couple of the hairs off his knee.

"Gloria's cats have the run of the house."

"I noticed that day I was there."

"Well—I've learned to live with it."

I turned the conversation to Violeta Bell. "So, what did you think when all that icky stuff came out about Violeta's sex change? You didn't say anything about it that day at lunch."

He licked the sauce off his fingers. Tucked his arm inside mine. "What's there to say?"

"You weren't surprised?"

"Everybody was."

I was making him nervous. I kept going. "I figured a man might pick up on something like that. Quicker than a woman would, I mean."

"You think so?"

And going. "Was she, you know, feminine?"

"Yes. Sure."

And going. "Sexy?"

"She was no Maddy Sprowls."

And going. "Be serious. Was she the kind of woman that men, well, respond to?"

He found an opportunity to laugh. "She was of a certain age, you know."

"I'd be offended if I didn't know how you men are."

He playfully removed his arm from mine. Folded both arms across his chest. "Now I'm offended."

"Men like younger women. It's nature."

Back went his arm. "Men like women, period."

"That's better."

Ike and I stayed at the party until nine. Until the mosquitoes started biting and the bats from the woods starting buzzing the dessert table. When we got to my house, we took James for a late night walk. I held the leash. Ike held me. At one in the morning I slipped out of bed and went to the basement. For years now the paper has been computerizing the morgue's files. Little by little all those wonderful old clippings are being thrown out. I lug them to my car and bring them home. The wonderful old filing cabinets, too. I've set up my personal morgue right there in my basement. One hundred and thirty years of Hannawa history.

I went to the M cabinets. I looked up MCPHEE, P. There was a nice fat envelope of clippings on him. I sat down at the folding table by my washer and dryer. I clicked on my gooseneck lamp and read.

I found one item from 1951. It was a story on six local National Guardsmen getting married en masse at City Hall before they shipped out to Korea. Phil McPhee, age twenty-three, was one of them. Accompanying the story was a smudgy old photo showing Phil and his new bride saying their I-dos. Read the caption:

> **"I TAKE THEE** to be my lawfully wedded wife," says Pvt. Philip McPhee to high school sweetheart Lois Palansky. The McPhees were one of six happy Hannawa couples married Tuesday at City Hall by Mayor Dutch Schneider.

Another story was from 1959. It was from the business section. Phil McPhee, with the help of a government loan, was opening a new exterminating business in the blighted German Hill neighborhood east of downtown. The accompanying photo showed Phil and the city's new mayor cutting the ribbon with a big pair of cardboard scissors. Read that caption:

BUGS BETTER BEWARE: Mayor Merle D. Blackburn helps local exterminator Phil McPhee open his new headquarters on East Apple Street. McPhee's wife, Elaine, proudly looks on.

I stuffed everything back in the envelope. I clicked off the lamp and sat in the dark. "Two previous wives," I yawned. "Why am I not surprised?"

21

I took my mug to the cafeteria. I gave it a good washing in the sink, something I do every Monday morning. My goals for the day were modest. Mark up the weekend papers. Stop itching the mosquito bites on my ankles. Have Eric find Phil McPhee's first two wives.

Phil McPhee was clearly a ladies' man. He was more than likely a life-long philanderer. Just possibly he was the mystery man Detective Grant was looking for, the one who went bonkers and killed Violeta Bell when he discovered she'd once been a he.

While the water for my tea was coming to a boil, I read the crap stapled on the employee bulletin board. I was yawning like the MGM lion. Saturday and Sunday had both been sleep-over nights for Ike. So I was exhausted—from staying awake so he couldn't catch me snoring.

There was a letter on the board from Reporters' Guild President Will Canterbury on the upcoming contract talks with management. Given the paper's falling circulation and advertising revenues, those talks were going to be brutal. There was also a cute little poster with dancing hotdogs, inviting "friend and foe alike" to Dee Dee Killbuck's annual Labor Day patio party. An equally brutal prospect.

I made my tea and headed back to the morgue. Every few steps I stopped, closed my sleepy eyes and took a nourishing sip.

I hear that Eric does a hilarious imitation of me doing that, by the way, although I've never seen it myself. Anyway, I was half way across the sports department when I opened my eyes and over the steaming rim of my mug saw Prince Anton Clopotar standing in front of my desk with a long white box cradled in his arms.

I gasped. Spilled tea all over the front of my beloved Tweetie Bird tee shirt. The prince saw me, too. He hurried toward me. I retreated. My first thought was to take refuge in the ladies' room. Which would have been stupid. The man comes all the way from Wolfe Island to kill me and the social impropriety of going into a woman's toilet was going to stop him? Instead I trotted back to the cafeteria, where the only escape would be to dive through a fourth-story window.

"Mrs. Sprowls, please!" the prince called out. "I want to see you!"

The cafeteria was empty. I backed against the counter where I'd just made my tea. I reached into the utensil drawer and felt for a weapon.

The prince stuck his head through the open doorway. "Making me tea, are you?"

"I figured you'd want some."

He came in, smiling like Jack Nicholson in *The Shining*. He was wearing his blazer with the emblem on the pocket. His polka dot bowtie. A pair of beautiful gray slacks with a razor-sharp crease. Goofy tan-and-white saddle shoes. I wrapped my shaking fingers around a plastic butter knife. It was either that or a packet of McDonald's catsup.

He held out the box. "Friends?"

I let go of the fork. Took the box. "Not a dead fish, is it?"

"Roses, actually."

I removed the lid. It was roses. Yellow roses. A dozen of them.

"Friends," he said again.

I took the roses from the box. I was no longer afraid of being murdered. That crazy notion was gone. Replaced with embarrassment. "If I smell them will my nose explode?"

"I hope not," said the prince. "I've grown quite fond of that meddling proboscis of yours."

I smelled the flowers. I put them back in the box and put the box on the counter. I refilled the kettle to make him some tea. "Darjeeling?"

"Is there any other kind?" He sat at one of the empty tables. He leaned on his forearms while I washed out a mug for him. "Why would you ever think I meant you harm?"

"My letter! Stealing your spoon and your pipe! Involving you in a murder!"

He smiled at me. Not like Jack Nicholson in *The Shining*. Like Morgan Freeman in *Driving Miss Daisy*. "You found my brother for me. Or should I say my sister?"

"Does that matter to you? Petru having that operation, I mean?"

He frowned and rubbed his knuckles. "It is a hard thing to understand. But if it made him happier than he was, well, who can quibble with that?"

I poured the boiling water over the teabag in the mug I'd chosen for him. A big yellow one. I took it to him. Went back to the counter for the sugar and Coffeemate. "So you really thought he'd drowned himself in the river?" I asked.

He knew where I was going. "I never knew he wasn't happy being a man. Back then such a thing would never occur to you, would it? Not even today. But I knew he was confused to the bone about something."

I sat across from him. "So you assumed he committed suicide."

"We Clopotar men are known to take the unfairness of life head on," he said.

"And that's what Petru did," I said. "He burned his bridges and became the woman he should have been."

The prince smiled sadly. "I just wish he had let me in on it. I've missed him terribly all these years."

Memories of my own lost brother flooded my brain. I'd told the prince about him on Wolfe Island. "At least now you know

Petru went on to live a long life as Violeta Bell. And from what her friends tell me, a happy one."

"Until her murder," the prince said. "From what that detective told me, that must have been a frightening night for her."

I was surprised into silence. Not something that happens very often.

He winked devilishly. "Oh yes, Maddy, I've already talked to your favorite detective. Last night at the hotel. He showed me the DNA results. And the scrapbook."

"Did he now?"

"He is quite fond of you. Not to mention Irish coffee." He dropped the big bombshell. "In fact, Mr. Grant is upstairs as we speak. With Mr. Averill and some extremely unhappy fellow named Winkler or something."

I corrected him. "Alec Tinker."

The prince stood up and flattened the pockets of his sports coat. "Actually I volunteered to come downstairs and fetch you."

I found a horrible plastic vase under the sink for my roses. I trimmed the stems with that plastic knife I'd fingered in the drawer. He carried the roses back to my desk for me. We took the elevator upstairs.

Bob Averill's office was gray and austere. The no-nonsense domain of a powerful man. He was slumped into his enormous black leather chair, slowly swiveling back and forth. The only thing on his desk was a copy of that morning's paper. In front of him, on far more modest chairs, sat Detective Grant and Alec Tinker. There were empty chairs for the prince and me. The men were all wearing coats and ties. I was wearing baggy dungarees and that Tweetie Bird tee shirt with the big tea stain.

The prince was right on the money when he'd said how unhappy Alec Tinker was. And I knew why that was. Tinker had been left out of the loop. He hadn't known about my investigation. Or that Bob Averill had put me up to it. Or that Bob was in cahoots with Detective Grant.

"Now—where were we?" Bob Averill asked when we were seated.

Tinker glowered at him like a just-castrated bull. "You were about to answer my question. Am I managing editor of this paper or not?"

Bob responded calmly. "Yes, you are, Alec. And you will remain so."

Alec's response to that was not so calm. "Don't count on that, Bob!"

Said Bob, "There are plenty of starfish in the sea, Alec!"

Said me, "Let's not get into a pissing match, gentlemen." I turned toward Tinker. "Bob didn't ask me to look into Violeta Bell's murder for the paper. He asked me because his wife was on his back. And she was on Bob's back because her sorority sister, Jeannie Salapardi, was on her back. Because Eddie French was her brother. And so Bob got on my back. And I got on Detective Grant's."

Tinker wasn't appeased. "Sounds a little unethical, doesn't it?"

Prince Anton was amused. "Not to mention a little kinky."

We all laughed. And while everybody was still in good humor I tried to put things into perspective. "Alec," I said, "the only way it would have been unethical was if Bob had included you in our conspiracy. Bob is an ethical man. He would never blur the lines between editor and hen-pecked husband. That's why he turned to me. As a friend. And now you, Mr. Managing Editor, have one hell of a good story to cover." I turned to the prince. "Assuming that the prince doesn't mind sitting still for an interview."

"I've already told what little I know to Detective Grant," the prince said. "I've no objection telling it to you good people as well."

Bob Averill relaxed into his big chair and started playing with the uneven ends of his necktie. "The ball's in your court, Alec."

And so Tinker took over the meeting, demonstrating for the umpteenth time in two years why Bob had brought him in as managing editor. Tinker addressed his first question to Detective Grant. "You'd better wait outside."

Grant stood and bowed like a bad Shakespearean actor. "I'll get some coffee." He left the office.

Tinker then turned his attention to the prince. "Telling the media a different version of what you told the police can get you into trouble," he cautioned. "And there is still a murder investigation going on. By the police and apparently by one or more employees of this paper. So before you talk to us keep in mind that—"

Prince Anton interrupted him. "Everything I say can and will be used against me?"

"I just want you to go into this with a clear head," Tinker said.

I playfully leaned toward the prince and pretended to whisper. "We're going to do the story whether you talk to us or not. So you might as well give us your side."

The prince nodded that he understood. "The police don't suspect me of anything. And rightfully so. And I'm sure the people of Hannawa are as curious about Petru's old life as I am about his new one as Violeta Bell. We'll all fill in the blanks together."

Tinker nodded back at him. "We'll go ahead then."

Prince Anton was visibly pleased. He reached out and patted my hand as if to say thanks. "Is it my turn to exit stage right?"

"If you don't mind, we do have a couple of things to hash out," Tinker said.

The prince gave us an even grander bow than Scotty Grant had. He left.

I started to get up. "Time for me to bow out, too, I suppose?"

"Not so fast, Maddy," said Tinker. "You know more about this story than anybody else. We're going to need your wisdom." He turned to Bob Averill. "If that's okay with you, Bob."

Bob was still playing with his tie. "If it were up to me, I'd wear those clip-ons," he said. "But the wife says I'm too important a man."

That was Bob's way of playing Pontius Pilot, washing his hands of the whole mess. And why not? He'd been forced to get involved because of Jeannie Salapardi. And now Eddie was no longer a suspect. Jeannie had thrown a wonderful barbecue for him.

Tinker happily continued with his ideas for our coverage. "As I see it, the story is this: An exhaustive *Herald-Union* investigation uncovers Violeta Bell's shocking past. Finds her brother living on an island in Canada. A brother who, lo and behold, is a pretender to the Romanian throne. Which means Violeta's claim to be royalty was true. How will these revelations affect the police investigation? Which plods on with little success."

"Sounds more like a book than a story," I hissed.

"We'll give it all the space it needs," said Tinker, undeterred by my sarcasm. "And of course we'll do a story on you, Maddy. How your dogged research once again saved the day. We'll recap your work on the Buddy Wing and Gordon Sweet murders."

It was time to for me to rain on his parade. "Absolutely not."

Pontius Pilot was suddenly interested in throwing his weight around again. "You're a big part of the story, Maddy."

I wasn't intimidated. "Let me put it in the clearest English I can. No way, José."

Unfortunately, Tinker wasn't intimidated either. "To quote one Dolly Madison Sprowls, 'We're going to do the story whether you talk to us or not.'"

I looked to Bob Averill for mercy. His grin told me none was coming.

Tinker moved on with his plans. "It's not exactly a police story. But I think Dale Marabout's the guy for the job."

Dale Marabout is my best buddy at the paper. A terrific reporter, too. So I was as surprised as Bob and Tinker when I heard myself squeak, "Marabout?"

Said Tinker, "He's the best we've got when it comes to a big investigative piece like this."

I surprised myself again. "What about Gabriella Nash?"

"She's a gutsy girl," Tinker said. "But I don't think she's ready for something this complex."

His "gutsy girl" crack stuck in my craw. "You want me to cooperate, you give the story to Gabriella."

Tinker put his foot down. "I'm giving it to Marabout."

"Then I'm keeping my lips zipped," I threatened.

Pontius Pilot metamorphosed into Solomon. "You could put them both on the story, Alec."

Tinker immediately saw the wisdom of his suggestion. "Gabriella did interview Bell before her murder. And she could certainly add a lot of background color to the story. There's no question about that."

"And she is a gutsy girl," I added.

It was decided. Dale Marabout and Gabriella Nash would do the story together.

The next thing to do was break the news to Dale and Gabriella. I cautioned against it, but Tinker had them summoned upstairs together. And of course both immediately balked at working together. "I'm not a big fan of double bylines," Dale said.

I knew what his real objection was. Gabriella had not only cried when Violeta Bell was murdered, she'd had a hissy fit when Dale was given the story. "Gabriella will behave," I assured him. "Won't you, Gabriella?"

"I don't like double bylines either," she said, slumping back into an about-to-explode pout.

Bob Averill now played his best role. God. "We assign the stories. You write them."

Of course even God needs a little help from time to time. "I don't know beans about the news side," I said. "But couldn't they do separate stories? Dale a hard news story for tomorrow on Violeta's previous identity and how we found the prince. And then for Wednesday, Gabriella could do an in-depth feature on the prince. And then for Thursday Dale could write about the police investigation going nowhere. Friday you could run that worthless story on me you want, written, of course, by Gabriella."

Tinker loved my suggestion. "A four-day, page one series. Outstanding!"

Dale and Gabriella now quibbled about who should interview the prince first that afternoon. Gabriella said she should go first, since her feature was going to take a lot longer to write than Dale's hard news story. Dale saw it differently. Not only was he not a fan of double bylines, he wasn't a fan of "sloppy seconds" as he crudely put it. On top of that, he also had to cover Eddie French's court appearance at four o'clock. So he'd have two stories to write for tomorrow.

And so it was decided that they would interview Prince Anton together, in Tinker's office, in fifteen minutes, with him sitting in as a referee. I would sit in, too. His idea, not mine.

◇◇◇

We gathered in Tinker's office. There was coffee for everyone. Dale Marabout and Gabriella got their notebooks ready. Clicked their ballpoints. Tinker punched the button on his nifty little digital recorder. I sat there like the bump on the log I wanted to be. Yawning.

Dale Marabout asked the first question. "All these years you didn't know your brother was still alive? Is that right?"

Said Prince Anton, "I thought he'd drowned himself."

Gabriella asked her first question. "What was Petru like as a boy?"

"He was a wonderful big brother," said the prince. "He teased me, of course. But not as much as most younger brothers get teased."

Gabriella followed up. "How exactly did he tease you?"

"Knocked my toys about. Pinched my *bucă* when we were saying grace at the dinner table."

"*Bucă* meaning backend?"

The prince nodded and spelled the word for her. "B.u.c.a."

Asked Dale, "So you never knew he had a sex change operation?"

"Like I said, I thought he'd drowned."

Asked Gabriella, "Was he a good student?"

"Our parents insisted that we both be good students."

"Was he athletic?" she asked. "Did he play sports in school?"

"We both played tennis and football," said the prince. "Soccer you'd call it. And we both loved swimming and boating. We spent our summers on the island. So, we'd better."

Asked Dale, "So it's feasible that he faked drowning and then easily swam to shore?"

"There's no such thing as an easy swim in the St. Lawrence," said the prince. "Not out in the current where he left the boat."

"But he was capable of swimming to shore?" Dale asked more firmly.

"Yes, of course."

"Did you and your brother have a happy childhood?" Gabriella asked. "Your parents treated you well?"

"Poppy was quick with the strap if we talked back or shirked our duties, and mama was a stickler for etiquette. We were royals, after all, but no two boys had better parents."

Asked Dale, "Any hint that your brother wished he was your sister?"

"I never caught him trying on mama's delicates, if that's what you're getting at."

The interview went on like that forever. Dale asking hardball questions about Petru's disappearance and sexual orientation. Gabriella lobbing softballs. Out in the newsroom, the desks were filling up and keyboards were starting to click. The pace would pick up little by little throughout the afternoon, with total bedlam breaking out just about the time when the rest of the city was going home for supper.

"Was there an expectation when you were growing up that the Romanian throne would actually be restored?" asked Gabriella.

"Yes," said the prince. "There was real hope. Not only that the Communists would be booted out and the monarchy restored, but that the Romanian people would come to their senses and choose us Clopotars over King Michael's clan, those damn interloping Hohenzollerns."

"So in your minds, there was a real expectation that Petru would be invited home and crowned king?" she asked.

The prince gruffly corrected her. "The expectation was that my father would be invited home and crowned king. Petru's reign would come many years later."

Gabriella apologized. "Of course."

Dale was ready with his next question. "Did your brother like girls?"

"What's not to like about girls?" the prince asked back, winking at me as he did.

Dale tried again. "Did he date in high school?"

"Oh, for Pete's sake," I yowled at Dale, remembering the nerdy mess he was when he came to work at the paper. "You didn't even date in college."

"If my brother did consider himself a woman, then he wouldn't have been a homosexual if he were attracted to boys," the prince said calmly. "He would have been just as hetero as you, assuming that you are, Mr. Marabout."

Dale winced. Everyone else laughed. I knew that Dale had to ask those kinds of questions. That reporting wasn't a popularity contest. But I was sure hoping the interview would take a less contentious direction.

Gabriella gave me hope. "Why exactly did you come to Hannawa?"

Prince Anton's mustache lifted, like a Canada goose taking wing. Apparently he was as pleased with the question as I was. "I suppose for many reasons. All under the rubric of being a good brother. Doing the right thing, as you Americans would say. I want to visit her resting place. Pay my respects and make sure all the final expenses are taken care of. And I certainly want to help the police find the murderer. Not for revenge, mind you. To make sure no one else is harmed." He stopped and chuckled to himself. Winked at me again. "I did not come here to strangle Maddy for stealing my teaspoon and pipe."

Dale turned his attention—not to mention his pen and reporter's notebook—to me. "You stole the prince's teaspoon and pipe?"

I had no choice but to explain. Both Dale and Gabriella scribbled furiously. Tinker made sure his recorder was getting my every word. "And so when the DNA report came back showing that Prince Anton was Violeta Bell's brother, I immediately wrote him a letter apologizing for my—"

Prince Anton helped me out. "For your dexterity," he said. "Which brings me to another reason for my visit. To personally thank Maddy for caring so much about the truth. Even though she suspected I might be the one who did poor Violeta in. To protect the throne for myself. For all I know she still suspects that."

Before I could lie and assure him that I had no such suspicions, he went on with his long list of reasons for visiting. "I also wanted to see the city where my sister made her life. Meet her friends. Do my best to understand why everything happened as it did."

It was a wonderful bittersweet moment quickly despoiled by Dale's next question. "Your sister ran a rather far-flung fake antique ring. Did he, she, or whatever exhibit any larcenous tendencies as a kid?"

Before the prince could answer, Gabriella asked the same question in a more sensitive way. "She lived such a respectful life. So many people loved her. I can't understand why she would resort to selling fakes instead of asking for help."

The prince started to answer. "Well, Miss Nash—"

Dale stopped him. "How about answering my question?"

Gabriella's eyes narrowed. They'd been tripping over each other's questions for a good hour. "It's the same question," she growled.

Dale slowly swung his head and shoulders toward her. He was equally peeved. "Except that I asked it the right way."

"A question does not need to be disrespectful," she snapped back.

Dale was suddenly Mount Vesuvius, a trembling lump about to blow. "But a question does need to be a question! Not an admission of your own befuddlement!"

"Befuddlement?"

"Baffled. Bewildered."

"I know what it means, you condescending dick!"

"Condescending dick?"

"Patronizing. Penis."

Prince Anton shouted at both of them. "For God's sake! Will the two of you button up?" Tinker hit the stop button on his recorder. The two reporters shriveled. I—well, I yawned.

The prince now answered both of their questions. "Petru never stole anything when he was a boy, Mr. Marabout. Except his brother's heart. As to Gabriella's question about why in later life she resorted to selling fake antiques, I can only tell you what Maddy and the police have told me. She sought to maintain her lifestyle. And she became desperate. And little by little got in over her head. There is no pride more self-destructive than the foolish pride of a royal."

Gabriella then asked what I considered a very good question. "Was Petru always interested in antiques?"

Apparently the prince considered it a good question, too. He gave her the best quote of the interview. "We Clopotars are antiques ourselves. It must have seemed a natural enterprise for her. The family business as it were."

The interview went on. Both Dale and Gabriella minding their Ps and Qs. I'm not sure of every question they asked because—well, good gravy—because I fell asleep.

It was the prince who gently shook me awake. "Maddy," he whispered. "You're snoring."

22

Monday hadn't been an Ike night. But I was still pooped the next morning. After that three-ring circus in Tinker's office with Dale Marabout, Gabriella Nash, and Prince Anton, I'd spent another hour bringing Dale up to speed on my investigation. Then I'd spent a couple of hours with Gabriella, helping her get "a mental picture" of the story she had to write for Wednesday. Then I'd gone back to the morgue and marked up the Friday, Saturday, and Sunday papers, all the while keeping an eye on Eric as he grudgingly researched Phil McPhee's many marriages. After that I'd been forced to have dinner with Bob Averill, Detective Grant, and Prince Anton at Stu Kenly's Grille, the city's swankiest restaurant. We'd dined on the street-side patio, they in their coats and ties, me in my tea-stained Tweetie Bird tee, the tiny white Christmas lights twinkling above us in the trees, the New Age music crackling through the speakers hidden in the geranium pots, the wrought iron fence that couldn't have stopped a runaway tricycle let alone any of the cars and trucks zipping back and forth on West Apple. Then I'd foolishly walked next door with them to Lenny's Pub for beer and stale nachos. Then thanks to the industrial-strength pee stain James left on my dining room rug—a well-deserved reward for my irrespon-sibility—I hadn't crawled into bed until one in the morning. And now it was nine o'clock Tuesday morning and thanks to my big mouth, I'd promised to spend the day showing Prince Anton our fair city.

Prince Anton was waiting for me at the paper, in the small, dusty downstairs lobby that immediately lets visitors know they have not exactly entered the hallowed halls of *The New York Times*. The prince was wearing white slacks, a blue-checked gingham shirt, argyle socks and sandals. His shirt pocket was bulging with a pipe and tobacco pouch. "I'm raring to go!" he announced.

I wanted to curl up on the little sofa and take a long nap. Instead I yawned and gave him our first destination. "There's a wonderful little coffee shop just down the hill," I said. "Best caffeine in town."

And so we got in my Dodge Shadow and drove down to Ike's. Ike shook the prince's hand and said the most inane thing: "Now don't go thinking you can steal Maddy away to that island of yours. She's already got a handsome prince."

"I shall resist the temptation," the prince promised.

We took our tea and muffins to my favorite table by the front window. There was a rumpled copy of *The Herald-Union* waiting for us, paid for by someone else and read by who knows how many people that morning. I'd already read Dale Marabout's story on Violeta's royal past at home, of course, and the prince had already read it at his hotel, but we both took turns reading it again.

Of all the facts Dale had stuffed into his story, the most important to me were these:

> Chief Homicide Detecitve Scott "Scotty" Grant refused to speculate about what impact the revelations about Bell's past might have on the murder investigation. "It could be important, or simply a bizarre turn of events that doesn't have anything to do with anything," he said, after meeting with the prince Monday at *The Herald-Union*.
>
> For his part, Prince Anton promised to assist the police in any way he could. "It's good to know what happened to my brother

after all these years," he said. "And it's
good to know that he, as Violeta Bell, had
a good life here. But the fact is, a member
of my family was murdered. And the one who
did it remains free as a goose."

"Be honest with me Maddy," the prince said, as he frowned his way through the sports pages. "So Maddy, do you think you'll ever find the murderer?"

"Actually, I think I'm pretty close."

"I hope not as close as the width of this table."

I smiled at him without answering.

We finished our tea and muffins and drove out West Apple to Puritan Square, the fancy-schmancy shopping center where Violeta's antique shop had been located. The storefront she'd occupied for thirty years now housed Madame La Femmes' Fine Frocks and Accessories. The prince stood on the sidewalk outside and absorbed every brick. "Would you like to go inside?" he finally asked. "Perhaps I could buy you something. To show my appreciation."

No way in hell was I going to let him do that. "I'm afraid my handsome prince would flip his crown," I said. I did, however, let the prince buy me a two-dollar sugar cookie at the little bakery two doors down.

I drove him around Hemphill College, my alma mater, Gabriella's too, and then circled around through the parkway to Meriwether Square. I pointed out Speckley's to him. He talked me into going inside for an iced tea. By noon I'd shown him everything there was to see in Hannawa. Told him more uninteresting history than any brain could absorb. Then we drove out Hardihood Avenue to the Carmichael House for lunch with the Queens of Never Dull.

It was at Gloria McPhee's again, and again her husband, Phil, did the cooking. In honor of the Romanian prince, Phil first poured us goblets of wine made in Transylvania. He pronounced the name of the wine like Bela Lugosi, *"Feteaca Regala!"* Then he served us *"supa cu brinza,"* which I found quite delicious until he told us that the stuff floating on top of the soup was grated sheep's cheese. Then he served us roast duck and baked apples. Then he served us walnut strudel, which he admitted he'd bought at the supermarket.

Needless to say, I was stuffed. And more tired than ever. Still I couldn't wait for Gloria to take us upstairs to Violeta's condo.

It was on the top floor, with an incredible view of downtown Hannawa and the abandoned factories beyond. All of the walls were painted a pale rose. Beautiful Persian carpets were placed here and there on the shiny hardwood floors like colorful islands. The furniture and bric-a-brac looked incredibly expensive. Knowing Violeta's penchant for fakery diminished my awe a little, of course.

Gloria had the key to the condo, so certainly she'd been there since the murder. And by the way Kay and Ariel were yakking about their upcoming Mediterranean cruise, they'd been up there since the murder, too. Prince Anton and I, however, walked around in silence, touching everything we could.

The prince motioned for me to join him at the mantle. He was examining a fuzzy old snapshot in a small, oval frame. "See that, Maddy," he whispered, on the cusp of crying. "That's Petru and me when we were boys. In the backyard. Right about where you and I had tea. Poppy took it, I think."

I squinted at the photo. The two boys were wearing matching blazers and ties and short pants. I pointed to the shorter of the two boys, the one who was smiling. "That's you?"

"Cute as a button, wasn't I?"

"Yes you were." I gently blew the dust off the picture frame. "It looks like she kept a special place in her heart for you."

"It does, doesn't it."

Gloria interrupted us. "So, Prince Anton," she said, putting her hand on his shoulder. "What are you going to do with all this stuff?"

He surveyed the living room. He seemed genuinely perplexed. "There will be a few legal hoops to jump through, I gather, proving to the courts I'm the rightful heir. But after that, well,

I suppose there will be a few things I'll want. Family things. Personal things." He picked up the little picture. "But do make a list of anything you'd like. You and the others. I'll do what I can." He put the picture in his jacket pocket. He grinned. Impishly. "I don't suppose the American judicial system would object, do you?"

"Not at all," I said.

We poked our heads in the bedrooms, the closets, the kitchen, all three bathrooms. Then we left.

I dropped the prince off at his hotel. He wanted to swim and work out in the gym. Check his e-mails and take a nap. We had another long evening planned. I desperately needed a nap, too. Not to mention some Pepto-Bismol. But I had work to do. I drove back to the paper. I called Phil's McPhee's second wife. The phone rang and rang.

Eric had also found Phil's first wife, his old high school sweetheart, Lois Palansky. Unfortunately he'd found her in Greenlawn Cemetery. After Lois divorced Phil in 1955—back then you had to have a reason to divorce somebody and the reason was adultery—she'd married a local Pepsi-Cola driver. She'd had three children. She'd died of lung cancer when she was fifty-seven.

Phil's second wife was still alive and living in a retirement community for well-to-do Lutherans, just forty miles away in Hiram Falls. She'd divorced Phil in 1962, after just three years of marriage. The divorce was granted on the grounds of his "utter desertion of the marriage." She remarried in 1965 and had a couple of children.

Finally someone picked up the phone.

"Is this Elaine Shoaf?" I asked.

"Yes." She sounded like a mouse with laryngitis.

"My name is Maddy Sprowls. I'm with *The Hannawa Herald-Union.*"

"Oh, my."

"I'm not a reporter," I said. "And I'm not trying to sell you a subscription. I'm the librarian. I'd like to talk to you about Phil McPhee."

"Oh, my."

"For research purposes. Nothing will appear in print."

"Did he die or something?"

"He's fine."

Elaine suddenly sounded like a *rat* with laryngitis. "That's too bad."

"But he may or may not be in a little trouble."

"I hope so."

I took that as permission to ask my questions. "I'm interested in your divorce. He deserted you, is that right?"

"His girlfriend was pregnant."

"Gloria Gillis?"

"That's her."

"Was she also your real estate agent?"

"That's how he met her."

I recapped. To make sure I had it right. "You and Phil were married in 1958. His second. Your first. Gloria was your agent when you bought your house on South Balch Street. He started having an affair with her. Got her pregnant. Deserted you. You divorced him and he married her two months before the baby was born."

"Very noble of him, wasn't it?" Elaine hissed.

I asked her a touchy question. "Did you know why his first wife divorced him?"

"I'm embarrassed to say I did."

My next question was downright rude. "Were you dating him when he was still married?"

"Absolutely not."

"So somebody else was the other woman."

"Knowing what I know now, I'd say there were probably several somebody elses."

She'd gotten to the point of my call before I did. "So, in your judgment Phil McPhee is—how should I put it—pathologically adulterous?" I asked.

She quickly let me know that was not the way I should have put it. "I'm not one of those who consider fooling around an addiction."

"I'm with you," I said. "I was married to a fooler-arounder, too."

My flippancy didn't go over well with her either. "You're sure none of this is going to become public? I've been happily remarried for a long time."

"This is just between you and me," I assured her. "I'm not even writing anything down." Which was the truth.

She softened again. "It was not an easy time," she volunteered. "You can imagine finding out that the friendly real estate agent who sold you your first little house was carrying your husband's baby. When you hadn't had one yourself yet." She analyzed what she'd said. "It's not that I was jealous. When I realized what a bum I'd married, I was glad it was her and not me with a baby in her belly."

"I understand."

Elaine swallowed her self-conscious giggle. "I haven't thought about this stuff for years. My marriage to George is just so good. We have the two of the best kids."

I was not interested in how happy she was. I was yawning like the bears in the zoo and all the food and drink I'd had in the last twenty-four hours was beginning to take its collective toll on my nether regions. "Phil and Gloria have been married for a long time. Do you think he's still that way?"

She didn't have to think for a second. "Of course he's still that way."

"Once a bastard always a bastard? Or do you know for certain?"

"Hannawa isn't the biggest city in the world," Elaine said. "Over the years I've had to warn three or four women about him."

My heart wasn't in it—not to mention my mind—but I got busy marking up the paper. At five on the dot I headed for the elevator. I pushed the button for the lobby.

Was I surprised that Barbara Wilburger might be having an affair with Phil McPhee? Not in the slightest. First of all, people of every disposition and description have affairs. And I'd picked up on a couple of signs that first day Gabriella and I met the professor at her mother's condo. They were small, incongruous signs to be sure, but revealing as hell in hindsight. One was the little BMW convertible she'd sped off in. Not your typical professor's car. But it was the kind of toy someone trying to break out of a life-long rut might buy. The other thing that struck me was her wristwatch. It was old and gold and obviously expensive. Not the utilitarian timepiece you'd expect to find strapped to the wrist of a woman like Barbara Wilburger. I'd asked her if it was a family heirloom. She'd said it was a gift. From a friend. It's doubtful that anyone who knew Barbara well enough to be called a friend would give her a watch like that. And Barbara would never wear a watch like that unless it came from a very special friend. One she wanted to keep. A lover. And if it were a gift from Phil McPhee, I wouldn't be surprised to learn that he'd bought that watch from his other lover, one Violeta Bell. Or that the watch was a fake.

Prince Anton and Detective Grant were waiting for me in the lobby. So was Gabriella. The four of us waited another ten minutes for Weedy. Just as I was about to call upstairs to the photo department to see where in the hell he was, he jiggled down the stairs with his camera equipment dangling from his shoulders and a cellophane bag of Cheez-its dangling from his clenched teeth. "Orry-ooh-eep-ooh-aiting," he said.

Outside, we piled into the long, black police van Detective Grant had requisitioned for our outing. "I feel guilty just riding in this thing," I said, as we drove off.

Our first stop was Swann's, Hannawa's legendary drive-in, where all of the car hops are muscle-bound college boys in matching green polos and khaki Bermudas. The minute you pull into a parking slot and click your headlights, they run to your car—actually run—and take your order.

So, for the next forty-five minutes our happy crew huddled inside the van wolfing hamburgers and onion rings and French fries and milkshakes, messing the upholstery and ourselves with catsup and salt and mustard and mayonnaise. It was great fun, even though the last thing my already roiling digestive track needed was a double cheeseburger and curly fries. Not to mention the pineapple shake. The prince graciously paid the bill. We hurried off to Bloomfield Township, to the Riverbend Moor Family Memory Garden, the cemetery where Violeta Bell's ashes resided, inside a pretty purple urn.

We climbed the long walkway toward the columbarium. It was a beautiful evening with only the slightest breeze. Prince Anton, however, looked like he was walking into a hurricane. He was bent forward. Each step seemed a struggle. If he were to be believed, he'd spent the greater part of his life thinking his reunion with Petru would be in heaven. Now it was going to be here on earth. Here and now. I took his arm. "It's quite a climb, isn't it?"

He put his hand over mine. "Yes, it is."

It would have been a wonderfully bittersweet moment if Weedy hadn't been orbiting us like a wobbly moon, clicking his pictures. Or if every few steps Gabriella hadn't stopped to scribble in her notebook. Their callous intrusions were the reason everybody hates the media. And why nobody would want to live without it. I apologized for their behavior nevertheless.

"They're just making their way in the world," the prince said, managing a weak grin. "Like everyone else."

We reached the columbarium. Detective Grant held the door open for us.

Our footsteps on the marble floor banged with a hollow sadness. Weedy stopped orbiting. Gabriella stopped scribbling. We reached the glass cabinets. We found the niche holding Violeta's urn.

The prince studied the urn in silence. It would have been impossible to know what he was thinking or feeling. But it was probably a lot of things. That's always been my experience at cemeteries. Right when you need them at their solid best, your heart and brain go schizo on you.

I watched the prince's reflection in the glass. His eyes were meandering from the urn to the objects that the other Queens of Never Dull had placed in the niche. I told him that the ceramic bell was from Kay, the classified section with the garage sales circled from Ariel, the small wooden box from Gloria. "Any idea what's in it?" he asked me.

I admitted that I didn't know. "I never saw," I said. "And Gloria never said."

"Probably something personal. Between the two of them."

"Very likely."

"Probably wouldn't mean a hill of beans to any of us."

"Probably not."

Prince Anton turned to Detective Grant. "Would it be possible to take a look?"

Grant rubbed his eyebrows. He pulled his thumb and fingers down the bridge of his nose. He stroked his chin. He ran the back of his hand back and forth on his double chin. The body language of an important man who didn't know what to say. "I don't have the foggiest what the law books have to say on matters like this," he finally said. "But if I had to guess, I'd say you don't have the legal right to touch anything until the probate court gives you custody." Then he shrugged and added this: "But, if I was in your shoes, well, I wouldn't give a shit about the law."

The prince chuckled. "So, you wouldn't feel compelled to arrest me?"

"Not particularly," Grant answered. "But there is a photographer and a reporter here. Not to mention the world's nosiest librarian. Whether they're as attitudinally *laissez faire* as me, I can't say."

"I don't see a photographer," Weedy said.

"I don't see a reporter," Gabriella said.

"And I don't see a librarian," I said.

"Well, then," said Grant, "let's go find the man with the keys. Whoever and wherever that may be."

The prince had another idea. "I could just jimmy the lock. Save a lot of time."

Grant offered three more useful foreign words. "*Que sera sera.*"

The prince gave him a quick, appreciative bow. Then he turned to me. "Wouldn't have a bobby pin, would you, Maddy?"

I dug into my purse and produced one. I handed it to the prince. He pried it open, and with the skill of a burglar, inserted it into the tiny lock on the niche's glass door. He wiggled it back and forth. Then up and down. Then sort of round and round. Clockwise then counterclockwise. Nothing. Grant took over. He, too, wiggled the pin every whichaway. With equal failure. I also tried—it was my bobby pin after all—but after two minutes of frantic jiggling handed the pin to Weedy. It took him about five seconds. "It's pretty much the same kind of lock they have on our vending machines," he explained.

Gabriella was shocked by his criminality. "You steal from the vending machines?"

"Not steal—get the candy I paid for."

The prince opened the glass door. Put his head inside and lowered his nose over the little box. He lifted the lid. Without a smile or a frown he whispered, "Oh my!" He closed the lid. He pulled back his head. Moved his hands to the urn. He stroked it. Then he gently lifted it. Then he cradled it against his chest and kissed the shiny purple lid. "I wouldn't have expected it to be this heavy," he said. "Not that I ever held one before."

That's when Detective Grant had his epiphany. "Oh shit!" He coaxed the urn out of the prince's hands and gently put it on the floor. He got on his knees and bent over the jar. The rest of us bent over him. He unscrewed the lid. He took a pair of latex gloves from his jacket. He wiggled his fingers into them. He undid the twist-tie on the plastic bag inside the urn. He held his breath and pulled the bag open. He slowly drilled a finger into the ashes. He slowly pulled out a small pistol.

Prince Anton had been a regular Rock of Gibraltar since the day he arrived in Hannawa. Sweet and patient. A gentleman. Now he went crazy.

And why wouldn't he go crazy?

Can you imagine standing in that cold columbarium looking at the ashes of someone you'd missed horribly every minute of your life for fifty years? Then see that pistol emerge through those lifeless ashes like some ghastly demon? Good gravy, can you imagine it?

"What the hell kind of a country is this?" he screeched. "What kind of people?" He was grabbing at the pipe in his shirt pocket. I swear if it had been a knife he might have driven it through his heart.

Grant held the pistol just above the bag of ashes while Weedy snapped his pictures. While Gabriella furiously took her notes. I tried to comfort the prince. "What a horrible shock," I kept repeating. I walked him to a pair of wrought iron chairs by the window overlooking the outside garden. He covered his face with his hands and cried. "I'm taking Petru home, Maddy."

"Yes—you should."

"Such a vile thing, Maddy."

"Yes—it is."

"I'll sprinkle those damn ashes from one corner of Romania to the other."

I pulled him up by the arm. Pulled him toward the others. "Come on."

He pulled away. "No—I can't stand to look."

I let go of his arm. Called to Gabriella. "Bring your notebook over here. The prince has a quote."

Gabriella knew enough to come.

I pinched my thumb and forefinger on the prince's chin and swung his face toward mine. "Tell her exactly what you just told me," I commanded.

The prince started stammering, unsure of what he'd said.

I gave him a hint. "About sprinkling."

"Maybe it isn't such a good idea that I say anything right now," he stammered, trying to retreat.

I refused to let him. "Maybe it is. Tell her!"

He obeyed. "I told her I'm going to take Petru's ashes home. To Romania. And sprinkle them from one corner to the other." Now he embellished a bit. "It's what she would want, I think."

I waited until Gabriella stopped scribbling. "You get it all?"

"Of course I got it all," she said.

Now I called Detective Grant over. Weedy came with him, snapping pictures like a frog in a swarm of flies. "Now Gabriella," I said, "read your quote to the detective."

She refused. "I don't have to run my quotes by the police."

"This one you do," I said. "Read!"

And so she read: "I'm going to take Petru's ashes home. To Romania. And sprinkle them from one corner to the other."

I looked at Grant. Mentally crossed all my fingers and toes that he knew where I was going. Luckily he did. "There's nothing I can do to stop you from reporting that," he said to Gabriella. "But—so there's no confusion—finding the gun in the ashes is part of an ongoing police investigation and strictly embargoed until I say so." He looked squarely at Gabriella. "Agreed?"

Gabriella, by now, of course, knew that something was up. Something conspiratorial. More than likely unethical. "I think I'd better call Tinker before I agree to anything," she said.

I set her straight. "The only call you're going to make is to the metro desk. You're going to have them insert Prince Anton's quote into your story for tomorrow."

She started raking through her purse for her cell phone. "I'm calling Tinker."

I had to act fast, as they say. "And of course when they arrest the killer, tomorrow or the next day, Detective Grant will make sure you're the one who gets the story. Even though Dale Marabout is the police reporter."

That Gabriella understood. "Well, I can't muck up an ongoing investigation, can I?"

"No you can't," I said. "And neither can you, Weedy."

Weedy stopped snapping. He knew how to play the game. "It would be great to be on hand when the arrest is made."

Gabriella called the metro desk. With my help, she gave the night editor a couple of paragraphs to insert in her story for the morning paper. We didn't have to rearrange the facts much at all:

On an emotional visit yesterday to the Riverbend Moor Family Memory Garden in

Bloomfield Township, Prince Anton announced his intention to take his sibling's ashes back to their Eastern European homeland.

"I'm going to take Petru's ashes home, to Romania," he said, staring sadly at the purple urn and other mementoes inside the glass-covered niche in the columbarium. "And sprinkle them from one corner to the other. It's what she would want, I think."

23

Ike shook me awake at three o'clock, just like I'd asked. I took a quick shower and dressed. Dungarees. A tee shirt. A peelable sweat shirt over that. I drank half a mug of much-too-hot tea. I shook Ike awake and reminded him to take James out for his six a.m. pee. Then I drove to the paper. West Apple was empty. It had rained sometime after I'd gone to bed. The dark city glistened like a glazed chocolate donut. Something I wished I had right then, along with the rest of my tea.

Detective Grant was waiting for me when I pulled up. He didn't have the police van this time. He was driving his own car. It was one of those enormous station wagons they don't make anymore. I opened the back door. Gabriella, Dale Marabout, and Weedy slid over. Their sleepy, bugged-out eyes made them look like hallucinating toads. Weedy offered me his open box of Entenmann's Mini Muffins. I took the last three. "God bless," I said.

Prince Anton was in the front with Detective Grant. He twisted his head and blew me a playful kiss.

Grant sang out, "Wagon ho!"

We pulled away from the curb, made a wide, illegal U-turn and headed out of the city, everyone slurping from a plastic travel mug of something except me.

We were on our way to Bloomfield Township, to the cemetery, to catch Violeta Bell's murderer. And we were driving there in the middle of the night because we wanted to be in place before the murderer could read the morning paper, then drive like a maniac to the cemetery and remove the little .22 pistol from the ashes.

It could take weeks for the prince to clear all of the legal hurdles, of course, but Detective Grant and I were working on the assumption that the murderer would panic and want to get the gun out of those ashes as fast as possible.

The murderer had put the gun there thinking it was the best place in the entire universe to hide it. And it was a dandy hiding place. Cops search garbage dumpsters. Cops dredge rivers. Cops scrounge around in ditches and dig up backyards. But poke into the ashes of the deceased? When is the last time you heard of a cop doing that? But then a pretender to the Romanian throne shows up in town. And he's the brother of the person you've killed. And he plans to take those ashes off to his homeland and sprinkle them over hill and dale. And the gun would come tumbling out.

And presumably that gun would be traceable to the killer in some way. Given the planning that must have gone into Violeta's murder, you wouldn't think the killer would have been dumb enough to leave fingerprints on the gun. Or a paper trail. But if the killer did show up to retrieve the gun, then most surely there was something that could link the killer to it. It was still dark when we reached the cemetery. We took the looping drive to the maintenance building. We parked behind it, alongside a stack of burial vaults. A couple of cars were already parked there. "Looks like we're the last to arrive," Grant said.

We hurried to the columbarium. We used the back door, entering directly into the superintendent's office. The first thing I noticed was that there were only two chairs in the little room. And both were already occupied by uniformed officers. One officer—the one not monitoring a trio of small video screens—jumped up and offered his chair to Detective Grant. Grant immediately offered it to Prince Anton, who immediately offered it to me. Not being a total fool, I immediately accepted his offer. Grant sat on the corner of the superintendent's desk.

Weedy, Gabriella, Dale, and the prince were forced to sit on the floor.

Grant folded his arms and dug his chin into his chest. "Let me give you a brief overview of our plans this morning. We've got one camera fixed on the entrance and another on the exit. Who knows which way the suspect might come in. The other camera is in the ceiling above Violeta's niche. The only caveat we face is the possibility that the suspect might park somewhere else and come up through the river valley, or the woods on either side. That's why, as of right now, there'll be no talking or coughing or sneezing or farting or anything."

Weedy immediately broke the rules. "No farting?"

I broke the rules, too. "If the murderer is who I think it is, then we won't have to wait long."

Grant shushed us and the wait began. It was five o'clock. All over Hannawa drivers were dropping off bundles of papers. The route rats who delivered those papers at fifteen cents per were busy filling the back seats of their cars.

The truth of the matter was that I didn't have one suspect in mind that morning. I had two. One was just as likely to pop up on the video monitor as the other.

After ten minutes or so, Gabriella, Weedy, and the prince rested their heads against the cement block wall and closed their eyes. I would have loved to scrunch down in my chair and take a nap myself, but I figured snoring was another one of Detective Grant's verboten noises.

For a while I watched the second hand on my watch slowly circle Betty Boop's sexy cartoon face. I'd bought the watch from the National Public Radio catalog that comes every fall. Every year I feel guilty and order something dumb I don't need. That past fall, I'd actually ordered a couple of dumb things, the watch for myself and a pair of green Mountain Dew "Do The Dew" boxers for Eric Chen. I know that underwear is the last thing you should buy a subordinate, but how could I have resisted? Given his addiction to that horrible stuff? Anyway, it was a big mistake. Every time he wears them, which is at least twice a week, he pulls up the elastic and snaps it. "Got your undies on," he says.

After watching my watch, I watched Detective Grant's dangling feet. Either he had some terrible twitch or he was keeping time to some crazy tune in his head. I also watched the officer who'd dutifully given up his chair. He was leaning against the wall next to the inside door. The tips of his fingers tucked into the front of his thick gun belt. His eyes were fixed on Gabriella. His mind was, well, you know where his mind was.

My own eyes eventually focused on the calendar on the wall. It was one of those pathetic calendars that men insist on putting up in their workspaces. This one featured a girl in short-shorts suggestively perched on a giant riding lawnmower. Each month's photo, I supposed, featured a different half-naked nymph with another gargantuan piece of lawn-care equipment. Admittedly, mowing a 200-acre cemetery must be a lot more mind-numbing than mowing your grass at home, but never once while mowing my eighth of an acre have I fantasized about sex.

I slid my eyes to the other purpose of the calendar, the dates. I tried to see how many of them I could connect with somebody's birthday, or death, or wedding, or divorce. I came up with only six. Then I remembered Gabriella's very first story on the Queens of Never Dull. In that story Violeta said she was going to be seventy-three on August 17th. I dug a piece of paper out of my purse—a bank ATM envelope—and wrote a note to Prince Anton: *What was the day and month of Petru's birth?* I handed him my pen along with the note.

The prince scowled at me then scribbled his answer. He handed the envelope and pen back to me. His answer: *8 February.*

I smiled thanks and averted my eyes so I couldn't see his. We already knew that Violeta had lied about her age, that she was not seventy-two at the time of her murder, but seventy-eight. And we knew she'd lied about a ton of other things. So it was not surprising that she'd also lied about the date of her upcoming birthday. Or had she lied? Was the 17th of August indeed her birthday? The day Violeta Bell was born? The day of her sex change surgery? None of this mattered, of course. Violeta was dead. Prince Anton was her brother. But when you're waiting for a murderer to show up—well, you have to nip your anxiety in the bud with something, don't you?

Another equally useless thing came to me while we waited. It was my own version of that tasteless ethnic joke about how many whatevers it takes to screw in a lightbulb. I'm sure you've heard it. Three. One to hold the bulb. Two to turn the ladder.

My version of the joke was this: How many people does it take to catch a murderer? The answer was eight. One old Romanian prince. Three policemen. Two reporters. One librarian. One photographer to capture all the fun.

And why did Detective Grant allow so many unnecessary people to come along on his stakeout? He told me he wanted Prince Anton there so he could keep an eye on him. He said there was still a remote chance that the prince was the murderer. "I don't want his highness sneaking off while I wait for nobody," Grant told me when he called me at midnight to make sure I didn't oversleep. Weedy was there because both Grant and Alec Tinker wanted plenty of pictures. And if there's a photographer, there's got to be a reporter to make sure everybody's name is spelled right. And why two reporters? Both Gabriella and Dale Marabout? Because there would be a very easy murder to solve if only one of them were invited. And why was I there? Because I'm Morgue Mama.

"Car."

Grant twirled off the desk and leaned over the officer watching the monitors. "Very nice," he whispered. "It's show time."

I checked my watch. It was only 6:15. There was no way in hell the killer could have gotten the paper at home, read Gabriella's story, digested the gravity of it, and then driven way out there by a quarter after six. Which meant one of three things. One, that the killer was not one of the two people I thought it was, but an employee of the paper. Two, that the killer had been tipped off. Three, that the murderer was one of that ever-growing percentage of Hannawans who read the paper for free on our website. My betting was that it was three. The murderer got up early, as always, went online to read hellohannawa.com, as always, and got a big, big surprise.

I leaned back in my chair and tipped my head back until I could see the video monitors. I remained frozen in that awkward position for a good five minutes until the camera hidden above Violeta's niche showed a blurry but very recognizable Barbara Wilburger. Ariel Wilburger-Gowdy's totally unlikeable, tight-assed professor daughter. I gave myself a pat on the back. Not a real one. An imaginary one. I'd been right. She was one of the two possible murderers I'd expected to show up to dig the pistol out Violeta's ashes. The other, of course, was Phil McPhee.

Barbara stopped in front of Violeta's niche. She looked this way and that, like a school kid about to cross a busy street. She was wearing jeans and a man's oxford shirt with the tails hanging out, the kind of outfit a woman wears when she's going to repaint the bedroom. She was carrying a canvas beach bag.

Now, why did I suspect Violeta Bell's murderer was either Barbara Wilburger or Phil McPhee? Like Detective Grant, I'd found no direct evidence. But I had found those little balls of pet fur. First, in Ariel Wilburger-Gowdy's condo. In that beautiful brass wastebasket in the foyer. Second, in Phil McPhee's office. In that kitschy wastebasket with the hand-painted ants. The common denominator, of course, was Barbara. That day Gabriella and I had visited Ariel's condo, Barbara had made a huge, unnecessary fuss over the cat fur. She'd rolled the fur she'd raked off the sofa into a tight tiny ball. The peculiar habit of someone visibly uptight and angry. Someone with a high opinion of themselves and a correspondingly low opinion of others.

So when I later spotted those tiny balls of Shih Tzu fur in Phil McPhee's wastebasket, I knew Barbara Wilburger had been there. And not just once. You don't roll dog fur into tiny balls on your first visit. No, Barbara felt very much at home in the McPhees' condo. Specifically in Phil's office.

Phil McPhee was an experienced philanderer. He knew the dangers of romancing his lovers in the bed he shared with his wife. The daybed in his office was a much safer venue. And so were the mats in the fitness room. I was sure that's why Violeta Bell showed up down there in the middle of the night in her frilly underwear. She was expecting to find Phil. Instead she found Barbara. And Barbara made her take off her robe. And she wrapped it around her little .22 pistol. And she shot Violeta Bell dead.

Phil McPhee was a lot like my late husband. Way too much testosterone. Precious little conscience. Multiple mistresses were the norm. If my theory was right, Phil was carrying on with Barbara Wilburger and Violeta Bell at the same time. Violeta was hardly a spring chicken and Barbara anything but sexy. But a snake like Phil would get a thrill out of bedding one of his wife's best friends at the same time he was bedding the daughter of another friend.

At some point, Barbara found out about Phil and Violeta. Instead of dumping Phil, or murdering Phil, although either in my book would have been the sensible thing to do, she opted to murder Violeta. Clearly the professor of business ethics was not one of those people who practiced what they preached.

And the fitness room was the perfect place to kill Violeta. If indeed it was where Violeta often met Phil for their monkey business, all it would take to get her there at that hour, on the Fourth of July when firecrackers were booming all over Hannawa, was a note under the door, or an email, or whatever signal Phil used to summon Violeta to the mats. Barbara certainly had a key for the Carmichael House, and from what Gabriella and I saw that day we visited, permission to use the parking garage. Barbara also would have known about all the skeleton keys hidden all over the place. Oh yes, the fitness room was the perfect place.

And not only because of the ease in luring Violeta there. It would let Phil know in no uncertain terms that hence forth, his only woman on the side would be one Barbara Wilburger. Forever and forever. And now a hidden camera was about to catch Barbara remove the gun she used to commit murder from the ashes of the woman she murdered.

Grant and I watched as Barbara struggled to get something out the front pocket of her jeans. It was a key. She put it between her teeth for safekeeping. She took a pair of rubber gloves from her bag. They weren't the surgical gloves you'd expect a murderer to wear. They were the bright yellow kind you buy in the cleaning aisle at the supermarket. She wiggled her fingers into them. She took the key from her teeth. She unlocked the glass door covering the niche. She put the key back between her teeth. She knelt on the floor. She pulled a black trash bag from her beach bag. She shook it open and arranged it on the marble floor, so that the bottom of the bag was flat and the sides stuck up about a foot. She removed Violeta's urn from the niche. She carefully lowered it into the trash bag. She got on her knees again. Looked this way and that again.

Grant reached under his jacket and took out his gun. The uniformed officer leaning against the wall by the door readied his gun.

Barbara took the lid off the urn. She carefully put it next to her knee. She untied the twist-tie. Inserted it between her teeth, next to the key. With her thumbs she spread open the plastic bag inside the urn. She drilled into the ashes with her index finer. She slowly lifted the gun out. She lowered it into the trash bag. She took the twist-tie from her teeth and refastened it on the plastic bag. She put the lid back on the urn. She took the key from her teeth. She bent over and blew off whatever ashes may have floated onto the urn. She put the key back between her teeth.

Weedy readied his weapon of choice, a big shiny digital camera that could click a zillion pictures a second. Gabriella clicked her pen and scribbled on the cover of her notebook, to make sure she had plenty of ink. Dale Marabout looked at her with disdain.

Barbara put her hands around the urn. She slowly stood up.

Prince Anton couldn't see what was happening on the monitor. But he could watch us watching. His eyes were bouncing back and forth between Grant and me like one of those Kit Kat clocks with the big Ping Pong ball eyes.

Barbara put the urn back in the niche. She took the key from her teeth again. She locked the niche door. She slid the key back into her jeans. She knelt and pulled the sides of the trash bag together. She rolled the bag up around the gun. She put it in her beach bag.

Detective Grant whispered "Go!" The officer by the door reached for the knob. He gave it a hard twist and yanked the door open. Grant, already in motion, rushed out. The officer followed him. Weedy, too.

Weedy wasn't supposed to follow them. He was supposed to do what the rest of us were doing. Crowd around the monitor and watch.

Barbara swung around wildly, nearly falling down. We couldn't see Grant and company, but apparently she could. She took a few quick steps back. Grant and the officer came into view. They were holding theirs guns in front of them with both hands the way they do on real television. They looked like a pair of bowlegged dowsers trying to find water. Grant's command to "Stop right there!" echoed through the columbarium.

Barbara did not stop right there. But instead of running in the other direction, she darted right past Grant and the other officer. They twirled and pointed their guns. But they did not fire. In a second they, too, were out of the camera's view.

There was a lot of shouting now. And the banging of feet on the marble floor. The officer watching the monitor with us raced out. We all raced after him. And Barbara Wilburger raced right past us. She headed down another long hall of niches. We were all chasing her now. Weedy was clicking pictures like a maniac.

Barbara reached the door at the end of the hall. It was locked. She froze. We formed a half circle around her. Grant was panting like James after his walks. "Bag on the floor," he ordered. "Then you."

Barbara got the instructions wrong. She swung the bag and hit Grant in the head. She tried to plow through us. Gabriella grabbed her around the waist and twisted her to the floor. The two uniformed officers quickly holstered their guns. One pinned Barbara's arms. The other pinned her legs.

Dale Marabout started screaming at Gabriella. "That was not your job! Jesus—I can't believe it! That was not your job!"

Gabriella was rubbing blood off her forehead. She'd landed hard. "Marabout," she said. "Shut the fuck up."

Dale wasn't about to. "You watch. You write. You don't tackle."

Weedy clicked away.

The officers rolled Barbara over. Grant handcuffed her. They stood her up.

Barbara had apparently considered the possibility that she'd be caught. She had a story ready. "My mother killed her," she said. "I knew she put the gun in there. I was just protecting her. Obstructing justice."

Good gravy, she'd even considered what they should charge her with. I knew better, but I couldn't keep my mouth shut. "Oh, come on! Ariel Wilburger-Gowdy a gun owner? That seems a little far-fetched!"

"She's not the Miss Nicey Nice everyone thinks," Barbara snarled back. "She's a witch."

Grant wasn't happy. He recited the Miranda Warning to both of us.

We both ignored him.

"You were having an affair with Phil McPhee," I said. "And so was Violeta Bell. You found out and killed her."

"I'm a tenured professor!"

"The fur balls prove it," I said.

Barbara recalculated. "Phil McPhee killed her. When she found out about me—that Phil and I were in love—she went nuts and threatened to tell his wife."

"And so he had no choice but to kill her?"

"I didn't know until after the fact."

Barbara Wilburger was some piece of work, wasn't she? First she was protecting the mother she hated. Now she was ratting out the man she loved.

The two officers led Barbara out. Grant put his arm around me. Whispered in my ear. "Now, what's all this about fur balls?"

24

Tuesday, September 19

It was only a straw sticking out of a little plastic cup, but from my point-of-view, flat on my back in a hospital bed, still woozy from the anesthetic, it looked like some huge and horrible tool of torture. And Ike, with his big Republican smile, looked for all the world like a sadistic medieval inquisitor. "Have some apple juice," he said.

I'd just had my tonsils out. I didn't want any apple juice or ice cream or vanilla pudding or anything else. I just wanted to go home and hide until the shame wore off.

He aimed the straw at my frown. "Be a good girl."

I shook my head no. A little too hard. My throat started throbbing like I'd just swallowed a cactus.

He wiggled the straw between my lips. I surrendered and took a sip. It did feel good. "See there," he said. "Dr. Ike is going to take good care of you."

"I wish you were a doctor," I squeaked, enduring the pain in order to get my sarcastic remark off. "Then I could fire you and get a new one."

He stuck the straw back in my mouth. "There's no getting a new Ike Breeze."

I changed the subject before things got too gooey. "Paper?"

I hadn't had time to read the paper that morning—I had to be at the hospital at six—so before being carted off to the tonsil-yanking room, I'd asked Ike to make sure I had a paper to read the second I woke up. He held up the front page so I could read it. The headline across the top made my throat feel so much better:

Gun Dealer Identifies Professor

"Glasses, please."

Ike took them out of his shirt pocket and put them on my face with the skill of a blind optometrist. I read Dale Marabout's story:

> HANNAWA—A Chippewa Lake man has identified Professor Barbara Wilburger as the woman who bought a .22 pistol from him during a gun show at the Wayne County Fairgrounds, police said.
>
> Wilburger, 55, who teaches business ethics at Hemphill College, was arrested August 30 at a Bloomfield Township cemetery after she removed a .22 pistol from the burial urn of slain antique dealer Violeta Bell.
>
> "I saw that picture of her being led off in handcuffs and thought, 'Hey, I know that lady,'" said retired county sanitation worker and firearms collector Bruce Bilbowski, in a telephone interview yesterday with *The Herald-Union*.

There were some things in Dale's story that I already knew, of course. That Barbara Wilburger already had been charged with first degree murder. That her request for bail had been denied. That she was rusting away in county jail awaiting the hearing to set her trial date.

Other things I did not know. Things that made her conviction all the more likely.

I did not know, for example, that gun collectors like Mr. Bilbowski do not have to have a license to sell their personally owned firearms at gun shows. And because they are not licensed dealers, they do not have to do a background check. However, they are required to ask their customers for a photo ID. The law-abiding Mr. Bilbowski did just that. Moreover, the serial number on the gun he sold Barbara Wilburger matched the serial number on the gun she fished out of Violeta's ashes.

"I checked the obits for you," Ike joked, forcing me to take another sip of apple juice. "No Dolly Madison Sprowls. So don't let all that good news you're reading make you think you've died and gone to heaven."

I rolled up the paper and swatted him.

Ike got that look in his eye. "I know this was a hard thing for you to do, Maddy. Both James and I appreciate it."

I swatted him again. Getting my tonsils out was a hard thing for me to do. Not only because I was a 69-year-old woman having a child's operation. Not because everyone at the paper was going to tease me. And not because of that propaganda about sleep apnea leading to more serious problems. No, it was a hard thing for me to do because it forced me to admit that I needed both James and Ike in my life. I swatted him a third time for good measure.

Ike leaned back in his chair and let me read. Unfortunately his good behavior only lasted a few minutes. Out of the corner of my eye I caught him pulling the paper top off my little plastic cup of pudding. "That better be for you," I squeaked.

"As a matter of fact it is," he said. He spooned a big lump of it into his mouth. I got his attention. Motioned that I wanted some, too. He guided a spoonful into my mouth.

The pudding was soothing. Seeing Eric Chen standing side-by-side with Gabriella Nash in the doorway was not. I made a painful, pudding-clogged sound that sounded a little like, "No visitors!"

They came in anyway. Eric did not have a Mountain Dew in his hand. But he did have FedEx box. "Package from Canada," he said.

"No doubt a diamond-encrusted tiara from the prince," Gabriella added.

Eric liked that. "Princess Maddy of Tonsilvania."

Ike did not like that. He took the package from Eric hands. "You want me to toss these two troublemakers out?"

I shook my head no. Motioned for Ike to open the package.

Ike sat up straight and slid his legs together. Rested the package across his knees. He reached into his pants pocket and pulled out a penknife.

Yes, Ike is one of those men who always carries a penknife.

He opened the knife and felt the blade with his thumb. Then he slowly cut the clear tape across the top of the package.

If only my surgeon had been that careful.

He rolled the tape into a ball. He looked around for a wastebasket. Eric and Gabriella joined the hunt. They couldn't find one. Ike finally put the ball on my tray. He closed his penknife and put it in his pocket.

Now Ike opened the FedEx box. And froze like Lott's wife as he studied whatever was inside. He finally pulled out a rectangular bundle of bubblewrap.

Bubblewrap held together with lots of tape.

Ike rested the bundle on his knees and fished for his penknife again. He opened the knife and felt the blade with his thumb again. He slowly cut the tape, making sure he didn't puncture a single bubble.

My throat was hurting and I desperately wanted a sip of apple juice. But no way in hell was I going to interrupt Mr. Careful.

Ike rolled that tape into a ball and placed it on the tray. He put the knife back in his pocket. Eric and Gabriella gathered around him for the unveiling.

Ike hooked the edge of the bubble wrap between his thumb and finger and went around and around until it was wound up on his hand. In his other hand was a small wooden box. A beautifully decorated wooden box about the size of a harmonica. The box that Gloria McPhee had placed in Violeta's niche.

Ike handed me the box.

I waited until he slipped his hand out of the bubblewrap.

He put the wrap on the table and leaned toward me.

Eric and Gabriella sat on the edge of my bed. Very close to each other. The thought that those two might be coupling up made me shiver.

Ike was concerned. "You okay, Maddy?"

I nodded. I put my finger on the tiny brass half-circle latch and swung it open. I opened the box. I gasped and swallowed. Moaned in pain. I reached into the box and pulled out a brightly painted lead solider. The little soldier was seated atop a prancing horse. Holding an unfurled Romanian flag.

I flattened out my other hand and stood the little solider and horse on my palm.

"What's that all about?" Ike asked.

Pain or no pain I had to explain. "A Romanian Hussar. A gift from Prince Albert of England to Prince Anton's great-great grandfather."

Ike could see I needed a sip of apple juice. He made sure I didn't take too much.

I motioned for him to take the soldier from my hand. There was a letter in the bottom of the box.

I pulled out the letter and rested the empty box on my belly. The envelope, of course, was sealed, and I had to wait for Ike to hand the soldier to Eric then retrieve his penknife and test the blade with his thumb.

I impatiently wiggled my fingers at him. He handed me the knife. I cut the top of the envelope open. I pulled out the letter inside with my teeth. I read it:

Dearest Maddy,

I spent most of my life looking for these little soldiers. Violeta was looking, too, apparently. And found one.

Anyway, I want you to have it. As fine and rare as it is, you gave me something far more valuable.

Please don't feel guilty about accepting it. I still have a few years left to find the rest of them. (Perhaps when I do, we can get down on the floor together and play with them!)

With deepest respect and, may I say, growing affection,

Anton

PS

Don't worry. I've had it checked by an expert. It is not a fake.

I folded the letter and put it back in the envelope. I put the envelope back in the box. I motioned for Eric to hand me the little soldier. I put that in the box, too. I closed the lid. It was a wonderful gift. From a wonderful man. I reached for Ike's hand. "How long before we can go home, sweetie?"

To receive a free catalog of Poisoned Pen Press titles, please contact us in one of the following ways:

Phone: 1-800-421-3976
Facsimile: 1-480-949-1707
Email: info@poisonedpenpress.com
Website: www.poisonedpenpress.com

Poisoned Pen Press
6962 E. First Ave. Ste. 103
Scottsdale, AZ 85251